THE DOCTOR AND THE DEVIL

VAMPIRES IN VERSAILLES
BOOK THREE

LILY RILEY

PRAISE FOR LILY RILEY

"Scandal, seduction, and supernatural secrets animate Riley's deliciously decadent debut and Les Dames Dangereuses series launch. Riley brings the heat as the erotically charged animosity between Daphne and Étienne...evolves into a genuine connection. This hits all the right notes."

— PUBLISHER'S WEEKLY

"There's a delightful balance between history, romance, and setting. The love scenes are steamy enough to be enjoyable without reaching an erotic level, still, a fan may be needed! The characters vulnerability in going from hunter/hunted to partners and lovers is well done...*The Assassin and the Libertine* is an excellent start to what promises to be an interesting new series!"

— IND'TALE MAGAZINE

"Get ready for historical hotness in a paranormal world that's sure to sweep you away! Lily Riley sizzles with a passionate debut that transports the reader to a version of 18th-century France where vampires roam among the aristocrats, indulging their dalliances and evading those bent on eliminating them...*The Assassin and the Libertine* is a steamy tale sure to stimulate the imagination that will leave you impatiently anticipating Ms. Riley's next installment in this fabulous series."

— KAT TURNER, AUTHOR OF THE COVEN
DAUGHTERS SERIES

"Fast-paced and steamy, *The Doctor and the Devil* is the conclusion to a thrilling historical paranormal romance series that delivers all the heart-stopping action and swoon-worthy romance I could have hoped for!"

— S. C. GRAYSON, AUTHOR OF BLOOD OF
THE SANDS

For everyone who wanted the monster...and also kinda wanted to be one, too.

PROLOGUE
MINA

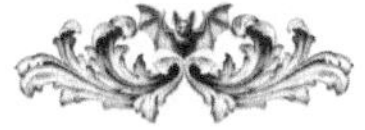

October 25, 1747
Buda, Hungary

Since today is my 17th birthday, I asked the devil for a kiss. He winked at me and asked, "Where?"

"The library will do fine," I said.

He threw his head back and laughed at me, then tugged at my ringlets. Confused and embarrassed, I felt my cheeks burn and stormed up to my room to hide for a bit.

It wasn't until I persuaded the stable boy to explain the jest to me that I understood.

"I am happy to offer you a kiss in his stead," he said with a smirk.

I tried to hide my distaste at the thought of the stable boy's lips pressed against mine. "Thank you," I told him. "But I think I'd rather have a cup of tea and go read a book."

The sound of his laughter followed me out of the stables.

I find the male sex perplexing and annoying. It's a pity the devil is so handsome, since he is such a rogue—or so the housemaids say.

Later in the evening, I was in the library by myself. The cook had given me a spice cake as a treat and I was nibbling it while I read some of Papa's anatomy books, and the devil came in. He sat on the chaise next to me and laughed at my book.

"Shouldn't you be reading something more appropriate for a young lady?"

I didn't understand, so I asked, "What is inappropriate about the vital organs of the human body?"

He looked somewhat stricken, and his eyes took on a strange light that made me feel oddly warm, but he did not answer me. Instead, he tilted his head in that infuriating way that made his dark hair swoop over his eyes and had all the housemaids sighing at him. Since he didn't reply, I assumed our conversation had ended, so I went back to my book and my spice cake. He did not depart, however.

"Didn't we have an appointment?" he asked, after a few quiet moments.

I was certain I looked confused, because he chuckled again. Oh, I didn't want to come off all silly over him, but his laugh makes me think of bitter coffee and too much sherry. It was low and dark and heady and sometimes I thought I could become intoxicated by it. I wished I were more charming or had a lighter temperament to draw it forth more often.

"You asked me for a birthday kiss in the library," he replied, moving closer. I knew I turned bright red at that—I thought he had forgotten my impetuous request.

I tried to calm my pounding heart and will the blush from my cheeks, but I knew it would do no good.

"Did I?" I lied. "I don't remember."

He shifted even closer, plucking the book from one hand and the cake from the other. He set them on a table at our side and licked the sweet crumbs from his fingers. A strange tightness began to build low in my abdomen as I watched him.

I had seen how quickly the devil can move—faster than anything on earth. Yet he drew my hands into his and leaned forward with such slow steadiness, I thought perhaps an hour could have passed. When his lips were but a breath from mine, he paused.

"Would you still like a kiss, little Mina?" he whispered.

I was entranced by his dark eyes. They had always looked black to me, but this close, I could see flecks of chocolate brown and warm copper in them. It made me curiously hungry, but I didn't think it was for food.

"Yes, if you please," I replied, suddenly shy.

He moved a hair's breadth closer.

"Why?"

I blinked, startled by my peculiar feelings.

"I haven't had one before, and I'd like to see what all the fuss is about," I said. It was an awkward, unladylike answer, but it was honest. I expected him to laugh at me again, as he always did, but he didn't.

"Are you ready?" he asked.

I sucked in a breath. "As I'll ever be."

His lovely lips turned up at the corners in a genuine smile and, finally, he pressed them to mine.

It was...odd. It was warm, gentle yet firm, and a little wet, but not in an unpleasant way, and it was over in half a second. I pulled away from him with what I was sure was an unflattering expression, because his brows pinched together in consternation.

"Is that...all?" I asked. I couldn't help it—it just seemed so underwhelming given how everyone spoke of kissing as a riotously pleasurable activity.

He raised one of those devilish black brows at me as if I'd challenged him to another game of chess.

"Spare not my feelings, little Mina." He laughed again. "I'd hate for you to end your birthday on such a disappointing note."

He leaned forward once more and—oh. *Oh.*

Oh.

His mouth sought mine again, and this time he sucked gently at my bottom lip. When I gasped in surprise, his tongue slipped in, slowly caressing mine in the most pleasurable way. Not wanting to waste the opportunity for a lesson, I attempted to mimic some of his movements, licking and sucking in a determined manner, unsure of whether I was performing adequately.

When his hands came up to the back of my neck and threaded through my hair, a deep growl rose from his chest. I pulled away, perplexed. *Was he angry that I was doing it badly?* We both stared at each other for a heartbeat, eyes wide in shock. He opened his mouth to say something, then seemed to think better of it and snapped it shut. He stood abruptly and bowed stiffly.

"I hope you had an enjoyable birthday, Wilhelmina," he said in a clipped manner.

"Did I do something wrong?" I asked, concerned by his sudden change in demeanor. "I am sorry, only...you know I have not tried this before. I apologize for any ineptitude on my part."

Some of his tension abated because that false, teasing devil was back.

"Think nothing of it, little Mina," he grinned, showing off his fangs. "We were all beginners at one time. I can scarcely recall that time myself, but you understand that was long ago."

His response made me churlish, and I frowned at him, hoping to hide the hurt in my expression.

"Thank you for your indulgence," I replied. "It was most instructive."

I picked up the remains of my cake and my book and left the library. When I cast a glance back at him, he was scowling and pouring a hefty glass of something from the crystal decanter on the sideboard. It appeared he was about to enjoy a fine old sulk.

Yes, I *did* find men perplexing and annoying.

CHAPTER ONE
MINA

April 13, 1768
Van Helsing's Clinic, Rue Ordener

THE DEVIL DOES NOT AGE.

The thought struck me like a bolt of lightning as I stared into the onyx eyes I longed to forget but would always remember. I'd just finished locking up my clinic for the evening, intent on getting a much-needed bite of supper and a moment's respite from work, but had tripped over my skirts. I braced myself for the pain the fall would undoubtably bring, but it didn't come. Strong arms righted me, capturing my body in a painfully familiar embrace that afforded me flashes of something much worse than the sting of a scraped palm. With that, two decades of scar tissue ripped open the wounds on my long-broken heart.

"Good evening, Mina."

The words were deep and low, soft and guttural—an elegant growl wrapped in velvet. My heart pounded against my ribs, a mixture of panicked fear and dusty memories of aching pleasure. He looked exactly the same—of course he would. Still beautiful, still magnetic, still powerful, still untouched by time itself.

"Rafael!" His name was a furious whisper on my lips. I felt the blood drain from my face. I recognized the signs of shock accumulating in my body, and I forced myself to inhale slow, deep breaths.

"Mina," he repeated. *Lord, how many nights had I dreamed of that hypnotic voice murmuring my name?* Even though it had been twenty years, I still couldn't comprehend the way it stirred my soul.

No! He made his choices, you silly woman, and they were never for you—or about you. Gather your wits and do not let him in.

It would have been easier if he wasn't holding me upright in the middle of the street. How long had I been clutching at him? Seconds? Minutes? *Oh, Mina!*

I pushed him away, nearly tumbling again. Attempting to recover from the surprise and embarrassment, I brushed off my skirts and fixed my askew spectacles.

"That's Dr. Van Helsing," I snapped.

He arched a brow. I hated that he was as handsome as I remembered. Lean muscle wrapped in moon-pale skin; dark eyes that felt both hot and cold when they raked over me; those high cheekbones and patrician nose that spoke of his family's royal lineage. His full lips parted over those frightening white teeth—two gleaming sets of fangs I'd never seen on another vampire—and he spoke again.

"So, your father finally allowed you to study," he said. It sounded like he was smiling, but his lips were set in a firm line. "I should have expected you'd wear him down eventually. Congratulations on becoming a physician, Mina."

The words stabbed at painful memories, and I flinched. *Is it possible that he doesn't know about Papa?*

"What are you doing here, Rafael?" The shock at seeing this ghost from my past had faded some, and now I found myself looking nervously over my shoulders. People—powerful people—were looking for him and had been unable to find him. *Yet here he is.*

I hadn't seen him in twenty years, except for the brief moments outside Gévaudan when he and Charlotte had come to free Antoine and me from the clutches of the *bêtes de sang*, a dangerous group of vampire soldiers under the command of a corrupt general. He hadn't looked like this, though—dressed in a gently worn black silk coat and leg-hugging black breeches. He'd been in his beast form—a massive creature resembling a wolf, if wolves had crawled their way up to earth from the bowels of Hell.

Is he here for me? Has he come for me? Sadness bloomed in my chest, chasing away the reflexive hope. *Don't be stupid, Mina. It must be some horrifying coincidence. And anyway, you don't want him here.*

"Is that any way to great an old friend?" he purred. "A friend who has very recently saved your life."

He was teasing me, trying to goad me into a spat, but I was too fatigued to play his lofty mind games.

"I haven't seen you in twenty years," I lied. "I don't know what you're talking about. Perhaps you have me confused with someone else."

Breathe, Mina. Air—yes, I need air. And...something else that starts with an A. Ale! Yes, back to what I was doing. Walk away. Get away from him. Calmly. Slowly. Do not run—he would only give chase.

Without waiting for his response, I turned back up the road, desperate to get to the warm, heady din of *Le Raisin Perdu* and to safety—if one could call a shady tavern in the poor end of Paris *safe*. Fortunately, having treated most of the patrons for one thing or another, I could. The tavern would be full, and I longed to have my supper and drown away this unfortunate encounter with several pints of ale. I wanted the company of people, even if I did not partake in the conversation. As a foreigner, it made me feel less alone.

"Oh?" His voice was in my ear as he kept pace with me. "You always were a terrible liar, little Mina."

"Don't call me *little Mina*. Don't call me Mina! I am Dr. Van Helsing! And you...you are...you are *unwelcome!*"

"*Unwelcome?* After all we have been through? After all this time?" He tutted, lips twitching as if he were covering a laugh. "Very well. If you insist on formalities, I will oblige. It has been an age, *Dr. Van Helsing.* How have you been keeping? I'm in town for only a short time—you must come to dine."

'*All this time? Come to dine?*' I stared at him, angry and perplexed. As much as I didn't want to rise to his teasing, my temper flared, and I stopped a few steps away from the tavern door.

"I'm afraid my calendar is quite full," I bit out. "But if you're short on dining companions, I know several people who would dearly love the pleasure of your company. Though, I am not certain you'd enjoy the dinner conversation with The Order."

He stilled, the expression on his face grave.

"Stay away from them, Mina," he warned. "They are not what they seem. And you are not prepared for what is to come."

Unable to control my anger any longer, I exploded.

"You unleashed this plague upon the world, Rafael!" I hissed. "And every day, I try to help hold back the tide of destruction. Do not offer me warnings or advice or inconsequential opinions while I am the one atoning for *your* sins."

Rage and disgust leeched into my words. "I should stake you where you stand."

Betrayal and pain flitted across his face, along with a thousand unsaid words. He looked like he was about to speak, but his gaze snagged on something behind my shoulder. I turned to watch a drunk man stumble out of the tavern, recognizing him as one of the farmers from just outside the city. I'd treated his son for a broken arm last summer, one which I suspected had more to do with a drunken ass of a father and less to do with a tumble from an apple tree.

I scowled. *What a trying day this is turning out to be.* I would simply have to convince Rafael to leave me alone and return to whatever rock—or castle—he'd crawled out from. Steeling myself for another calm, cold tirade, I turned back toward him, only to discover that he'd disappeared. I tried to ignore the throb in my heart that always seemed to accompany his absence—rather, it had...twenty years ago.

Wonderful. Now he would be off lurking in the shadows again, waiting for yet another inopportune moment to risk putting me in danger once more.

Or would he?

It doesn't matter, I thought to myself. *He is here and you've been in danger since he showed up in France.*

I stomped into *Le Raisin Perdu* and sat down at my usual table—tucked into a back corner, cloaked in the gloom of the dingy establishment. As soon as I entered, the warmth of the room fogged my spectacles, and I pulled them off to clean them on my handkerchief. Tonight was busy but strangely subdued, as if the patrons bent their heads and muttered in hushed voices against some unknown, ominous portent.

Now, Mina! You're just being dramatic. Rafael's sudden reappearance has unsettled you. I frowned, lost in memories that I'd been fighting to repress for far too long. Perhaps it was time to simply let them go. *If only I could...*

"*Ça va, Mademoiselle Mina?*"

A plump woman with a halo of wild gray hair approached and handed me a mug of ale. Unlike my French friends, I preferred the bitter, golden liquid to the standard fare of wine —it reminded me of home.

"Yes, Madame Bénard, all is well, thank you," I said, trying for a smile. The sharp innkeeper narrowed her eyes at my feigned positivity and harrumphed.

"You need to eat," she said brusquely. "Our stew tonight is turnip and lentil, but for you, I'll put in some bacon, *d'accord?*"

I opened my mouth to argue—meat was expensive and in short supply—but she waved away my protest and bustled off to shout at a drunken patron. I smiled at her retreating form. Madame Bénard had been one of the first people in the city to show me kindness before she knew of my profession and my skills. I'd been coming to the dank tavern weekly since I'd arrived in the city years ago and now, it felt as much like my home as my small apartment atop my medical clinic. It certainly felt more like home than anywhere else I'd lived, except perhaps...

No! I shook myself from what promised to be some sort of lamentable reverie and took a large swig of ale. I would not allow myself to dwell on Rafael's unwelcome presence, nor the fact that he'd clearly been haunting France for some time now, *nor* the fact that our history was likely to be revealed when The Order finally got their hands on him—which would jeopardize everything I'd worked so hard to leave behind. I massaged the scowl from my brows and tried to lift my spirits with the ambient chatter of the crowd, but their conversations only saddened me further.

"...not enough bread. Never enough food. And with another

babe on the way, why *shouldn't* we get bitten and make the change? Plenty of blood to go around, right?"

"...the blood plague already took my family—all but Jeanette, and she's run off and become a blood whore, now, hasn't she?"

"We can't pay the new tax! Who can? What with the blight wiping out last year's crop and soiling the land, there aren't even enough fields left to plough. Not that *they* care, mind you. Sitting up in that damn palace drinking champagne and eating cake."

"Well, I heard that the Beast of Gévaudan is here now— roaming the streets, feeding on all those pour souls, human and vampire alike. Do you think *The Order* will catch it?"

My ears perked up at the last words, and I swung my head around to find the source. Before I could locate the man, Madame Bénard returned and plonked a heavy bowl of stew on my table.

"Every bite, *d'accord?* You must eat every bite, Doctor. You need your strength, and I can tell when something is vexing you. Besides, you would not want to waste my good bacon!" She set down a thick chunk of dark rye bread and another tankard of ale, then winked at me and hurried off again.

The stew was thick and hearty, and the savory, smoky sweetness did more for my mood than I'd expected. Often when I was working, I would completely forget—or forgo—my afternoon meals. It was hard to think of eating when so many of my patients were starving. Still, Madame Bénard was right. If I wanted to continue my work, I would need my strength.

And if I intend to run and hide from the past that Rafael is here to dredge up.

I pushed the thought aside and swiped a piece of bread through the meaty broth, willing myself calm and praying the ale would soon temper my racing heart. Unfortunately, it wasn't long before my mind returned to Rafael. Why had he come? Where had he been? What was he doing? Why did he still look at me with those same penetrating obsidian eyes—like no time had passed? As if we hadn't been separated by half a lifetime and too many broken promises and too much cruelty.

I downed the last of the ale and stared at the foam swirling around the bottom of my empty tankard. I grimly contemplated alerting The Order.

I knew I should. I knew I wouldn't.

Dieu, Rafael, I hate you.

"Doctor?"

A sallow-skinned man who looked more skeletal than the anatomy etchings in my medical texts stood at my table, clutching a filthy cap in his hands. I recognized him as a young farmer who'd come into the city looking for work after the grain blight decimated his fields last year. He looked like he'd had a much harder winter than the other men here, though that was an unfortunate contest to win.

"Pierre, is it?" I offered a smile.

He nodded. "I'm told you can help...that is, I don't mean to interrupt your dinner, but my wife..." He trailed off, swallowing hard. His eyes flicked to my half-eaten bowl of stew and the bread.

"Won't you join me?" I said, gesturing for him to sit. "Madame Bénard makes lovely food, but I'm afraid it's always too much for me."

He sat but refused to meet my eyes. I pushed the food across the table to him, but he blushed and stammered a half-hearted protest.

"Please," I encouraged. "I was finished anyway, and if I leave anything but an empty bowl, Madame Bénard will gripe at me until the end of days."

Mollified, Pierre grabbed the bowl and began slurping down the delicious stew. Once he'd all but licked the bowl clean, I cleared my throat.

"Your wife?" I asked. "Is she ill?"

"Yes," he said, remembering his purpose. "Well, no—not yet. But..."

At this, he looked around the room nervously and lowered his voice to a conspiratorial whisper.

"She means to make *the change,* and I don't think I can stop her."

"She intends to infect herself with the blood plague?" I asked.

He nodded. "We have struggled, of course, but I am hopeful that my prayers will soon be answered. This season might be better. Jacqueline says she cannot wait and that she will starve before spring's first sprouts. I think she would hold out longer, if she could. I fear her wavering faith in God has already damned her."

I frowned. "What is it you need from me, Pierre?"

"Could you speak with her? Convince her that with all the horrors you've seen, that becoming a vampire is not the answer? If I sent her 'round to your clinic tomorrow, you would see her, wouldn't you?" The pleading in Pierre's tone bothered me, even though it was a story I'd heard a hundred times before.

"If it is her soul you worry after, perhaps it is a priest you should seek counsel from," I replied.

"I've already tried that. She will not go. Please, Doctor," he said.

I sighed. "Why would she listen to me, if not her own husband?"

"You know more about vampires than anyone. You help

people. You're a woman of the church," he urged, leaning forward over the table.

I balked. "A woman of the church?"

"Yes," he said slowly, blinking in confusion. "The acts of charity, the way you help people even when they cannot pay."

"That doesn't make me a woman of the church," I chuckled darkly. "Far from it."

His face fell and he leaned back. Motivated by regret and empathy, I reached for his hand.

"Send your wife," I said softly. "Tomorrow. I will talk to her. But I will only be honest with her, and you must accept that if her mind is set, there won't be anything I can do."

Grateful, he clasped my hands. "Thank you, Doctor Van Helsing. God bless you for trying to save her. There is nothing worse than eternal damnation."

Reflecting on the horrors of my life that had fractured my own relationship with the divine, I frowned.

"Yes," I whispered, more to myself than to him. "There is."

CHAPTER TWO
RAFAEL

April 13, 1768
Van Helsing's Clinic, Rue Ordener

"Do you think anyone in The Order would mind if we just broke in and had a little taste?" asked the first man.

The second man chuckled. "I tell you, with a lady like that, I'd want more than a little taste. That damn doctor is a whole fucking meal."

The first man laughed himself into a coughing fit, then spit a wad of phlegm onto the street.

"Did they tell you what we were watching for? Or are we just supposed to sit here all night freezing our balls off, waiting for some filthy *sanguisuge* to show up and hex her into making the beast with two backs?"

"*Dieu,* I could do with a bit of that kind of magic, eh? Simply knock on that door, call upon the devil, and entice her to lift her skirts for me," the first man continued.

This time, the second man smacked the first upside his head, sending the fool into another coughing fit.

"That's enough, Pascal," the second man said. "*Merde,* anyone would think you'd never bedded a woman before. We're to watch the lady physician and notify The Order if any curious-looking vampires are lurking about. Not those newly turned ones, but one that looks *different,* remember? And if we happen to overhear anything that might be considered *treasonous* to His Majesty or to The Order or to us humans, we're to let them know, as well."

"Right, right. That masked man—Derais—was clear enough on that point. Now, why would he wear a damn mask if he's just going to give us his name? Crazy old sod," the man called Pascal replied. "You know, Hubert, The Order gives me the creeps, and I'm tired and cold. What if we just knock off and get a quick drink? I'd be much more alert with a bit of wine in my blood."

"Focus, man! These bloodsuckers are crafty, and if you're not paying attention, one will slip by you before you can blink," Hubert warned.

The words wrought an ironic laugh from me, but in my current animal form, it came out as a muffled hiss, too soft and small for these mortals to hear. I longed to shift into a more predatory form and rip out their throats for the things they said about Mina—*my Mina*—but that would only alert The Order that I was as predictable as I seemed to have become. I still had much to learn about my foe and killing these men would get me no closer to my end. Besides, Mina disliked when I killed, and if I was to win her back, I would at least *try* to stem my murderous urges. These men, however, were making it a Herculean trial.

Patience, Rafael. Patience! If either of them attempts to harm Mina, I will act. Until then, I must wait and watch.

I yawned and stretched my soft, leathery wings, then folded them back against my body. I twisted around to better see the front door to Mina's clinic, where I'd approached her earlier in the evening. I shouldn't have done it, but I couldn't help myself. The last time I'd seen her—or rather, the last time I'd let her see me—she'd been bound and gagged on the floor of a cave outside Gévaudan. Those abominations of my bloodline, the so-called *beasts of blood,* had abducted her and her human companion. I was forced to reveal myself to her in my wolf form to help my werewolf whelp Charlotte take on the vampire soldiers.

How Mina had looked at me then. Shock, horror, fear, recognition. *Longing,* I dared hope. Still, I would not have chosen that particular moment to confirm what I could assume were her suspicions: I was alive. I was alone. And I was in France.

And so was the blood plague—the curse that could destroy the world.

My family's curse. *My curse.*

These men The Order hired, Pascal and Hubert, stilled as they saw what I'd sensed minutes before—Mina returning from the humble tavern at the end of her street. The closer she drew to her clinic and to my disreputable group's hiding place, the louder my blood sang—calling to her. If I'd been born with a beating heart, it would have pounded in my chest, but as ever, all I felt was a vague sense of need that lessened the nearer she was to me.

She walked with purpose, but she'd always walked that way. Mina had been driven by purpose from the time I'd first met her at the tender age of sixteen, and it was comforting to see that she hadn't lost whatever it was that drove her forward.

"You walk as if your legs can't bear not to run," I used to tease. *"Women are meant to be slow, graceful creatures. Amble a little, for fuck's sake."*

I remembered how her beautiful sapphire eyes would widen when I spoke profanity to her, and it brought forth another chuckle. *How I've missed laughing in amusement.*

A man spilled out of the tavern—not drunk, but tall, thin, and weak—and hailed Mina. As he jogged to catch up to her, instinct propelled my bat wings forward and I fluttered closer, taking up a perch on the underside of a thatch roof nearby. Pascal and Hubert still leaned with forced casualness against the decrepit building at the end of the road, but I could tell they watched Mina intently.

"Please, Pierre," Mina said. "I've already told you. I will do what I can for your wife, but if you truly wish me to impress upon her the danger you believe her immortal soul is in, you will need to find someone else."

"But her soul is in danger," the man insisted.

Mina pinched the bridge of her nose—a gesture I recognized as the summoning of reserves of patience.

"Her life is in danger, Pierre," she said. "The blood plague might not be the most ideal solution to the predicament of hunger, but scores of others have found peace with it."

"Doctor, that's blasphemous," Pierre whispered.

Mina was unmoved. "Your wife's soul is not my concern. But I can tell her about the plague's effect on the body. If that's not the answer you're looking for, then I'm afraid I won't be much help to you."

She turned back to her clinic. The man called Pierre stood in the street for a moment more, then walked back to the tavern muttering to himself. I watched Mina enter and lock the door behind her. She lit a candle and collected several sheaves of paper from the desk, then disappeared into the back to climb the staircase up to her living quarters. Accepting that I would not—at least, for the time being—drain every drop of blood from Pascal and Hubert and leave their withered bodies in the gutter, I abandoned my perch and flew around the back of the building to the narrow alley that ran the length of the block. I'd stashed my clothes in a stack of empty crates before shifting to wait for Mina, but even as I thought about turning back into my human form, I reconsidered.

I needed to talk to her—to convince her to join me...to *help* me. She had been so cross earlier, and as much as I enjoyed riling her and watching the heated blood of frustration pulse through her exquisite body, I didn't think she would take kindly to a second attempt at contact so soon. She needed time, and while I didn't have a lot of time to offer her, I could give her a day to accept that I'd come back.

I am here for you, my Mina.

From my refuse-strewn alley hiding place, I looked up at the glow from her candle moving between rooms. She entered her bedchamber and after a time, the golden halo of light in her rooms went dark.

Did she think of me before she fell asleep? Surely, she would be expecting me to return. Impatience needled me. It was peculiar to have learned so many harsh lessons in the art of patience considering I'd lived longer than most and would remain even after humanity had turned to dust. Mina always brought that out in me. A restlessness that I had once termed ennui, yet she had referred to as stifled passion.

Passion. I wanted it with her. I wanted to once more visit pleasure upon her body and taste the overwhelming lust for life she carried in her blood. It had been so long—too long since I'd had anything that made me feel truly alive. Blood that didn't taste bitter. Sex that didn't fill me with shame, guilt, anger. Conversation that didn't bore me beyond measure. Existence without Mina had been unbearable, but I'd been resigned to it for the last twenty years to protect her...no, that wasn't quite true...to allow her to live, perhaps. I'd wanted to give her a chance to savor the delights of humanity instead of shackling herself to a world of pain and suffering and death. Tenacious as she was, I'd had to be rather *forceful* in severing our attachment and ruining our dream of a future together, so I understood her reasons for loathing me on sight.

Still, my need for her was almost crippling. As I'd never been any good at denying myself the mere morsels of perverse pleasure I could have and too often reveled in my own trappings of sin, I relented.

Just to look—not to touch.

Closing my eyes and letting go of my corporeal form, I turned into mist. Shifting into a formless cloud took a great toll on my energy and would leave me temporarily weakened when I returned to my body—I would need to feed tonight—but I didn't care about that now. The memory of Mina's body in my arms earlier still burned my icy, dead skin. As I floated up to her window, I briefly considered that my actions were invasive, aggressive, and disrespectful...*should I simply turn around and leave her tonight?*

An older memory flashed. She was eighteen. Fresh, young, sweet, determined to change the world. Dark brown curls splayed across the pillow, wide sapphire eyes glazed with sweet contentment, and her ivory skin made rosy by our lovemaking. Her soft, round curves felt so good beneath me, as if her beautiful body was the promise of new life itself. I was cold, deathless, wintry Hades, and she was my Persephone—blooming with pleasure from my touch.

"Come for me, Lady Persephone, and bring spring to my heart," I'd commanded. She'd laughed at me then—laughed at a Prince of Wallachia!—and almost refused to obey. Thankfully, her desire for me had been too great, and she'd come apart around me.

I was so lost in thought I almost missed the soft shuffling

sounds of Pascal and Hubert creeping down the alley toward me. *What are these fools up to?*

"All I'm saying is, how do we know she doesn't have a *sanguisuge* up there with her? I say we just climb up and take a little peek just to make sure." Pascal snickered.

"You are the most disgusting, shameful ass," Hubert hissed. "But I'm not about to let you get an eyeful of that pretty doctor all by yourself."

It appeared that my decision had been made for me. I would not visit Mina tonight. I fantasized about eviscerating the men but forced myself to focus on my plans. Perhaps I could simply lead the men away, giving Mina some peace to rest unbothered for the night.

I swirled down to Pascal and Hubert and called forth one of my other abilities—an ancient form of mesmerism. I *suggested* to both men that they follow a stray dog for a few hours, convincing them that it might be the Beast of Gévaudan. When they caught sight of the animal across the alley, they took off after it with abandon.

Satisfied that Mina was safe from all prying eyes but my own, I allowed myself the small pleasure of drifting up to her bedroom window. Inside, she slept, snoring delicately and murmuring to her dream companions. What I wouldn't give to explore her mind in those moments.

The night air started to warm, and I knew sunrise would soon be upon me. It was time to return home. I shifted into my wolf form, gathered my clothes up in my jaws, and kept to the shadows until I arrived at the edge of the city. Once I found the main road heading north, I took off with supernatural speed. My great claws dug into the damp earth, sending up showers of mud and leaves with every footfall. I inhaled deeply, using my lupine senses to paint a picture of the farmlands around me as they gave way to the towering trees of encroaching forest.

I followed the Seine northwest from Paris, winding through silvery green woods, until I arrived on the outskirts of Rouen. I departed from the main road and climbed to the top of a small hill, on which sat the crumbling ruin of a once-grand feudal castle, *le Château du Diable*. Built during the eleventh century and destroyed during the Hundred Years' War, it had long since gained a reputation as a damned, haunted place, which caused the locals to avoid it entirely.

It was utterly perfect for my needs.

After the assassination of my father, I channeled my grief into the only remaining pursuit—finding my cruelly abandoned true love. *My soulmate, if I'd had a soul.* The moment I received word of Mina settling in Paris, I set my plan to action. My land agent found the property between Rouen and Paris and quietly prepared the castle for future habitation.

The charming ruins were shored up to prevent further decay, but still retained the appearance of an unlivable monument to evil. A crew of loyal workers dug down around the foundations and built an underground abode suited to my uncommon needs. I was glad to have a home here, where I could continue to work on my family's curse and keep a watchful eye on Mina.

I climbed the slick stone walls of the high tower, which would be an impossible feat for any human. The only door into my home was at the very top, disguised beneath a massive granite slab, affording me another layer of protection against any human invaders. Only a very old, very strong vampire would have the strength to move the stone and gain entrance.

I pushed the stone away as if it were a simple wooden door and jumped inside. The six-story drop to the floor was another precaution—I didn't require stairs, and anyone who made their way past the stone door would certainly fall to his death.

The interior of the tower appeared empty and ruined, but

that was just for appearances. The only item inside the round chamber was a rusted wrought-iron brazier that stuck out about a foot from the wall. I pulled on the piece of metal and waited for the muted clanking sound that indicated the hidden passageway was shifting into place. My engineers had been particularly clever in designing the antechambers of my home and the mechanism still delighted me.

A small stone staircase appeared in the floor, which led down to my suite of rooms. Rather than the dark, gothic structure above, my rooms below had an altogether different feeling. I longed to leave behind the miasma of death and decay, so every hallway and room was built with pale, glittering marble floors and white and gold silken wall coverings. The ceilings bore elaborate frescoes of bluebird skies with puffy white clouds, whirling around a painted gilt sun. With the candles and fireplaces lit, I could imagine it was a day out in the sunshine. If this was as close to heaven as I could get, so be it.

As soon as I reached the bottom of the stairs, I shifted into human form. My bare feet padded silently along the plush blue and gold carpets that stretched the entire length of the hallway, winding deeper underground to my bedchamber.

I paused in front of the massive wooden doors carved with scenes from the Hades and Persephone myth, reaching out to stroke one long clawed finger across the smooth face of my Queen of Spring.

Soon, Mina.

Sighing, I pushed the doors open into my grand bedchamber—not filled with dirt, death, and a coffin, as the peasant rumors suggested—but a room dedicated to the beauty and awe of the night. A floor to ceiling mural of the night sky, set with stars and heavenly bodies welcomed me, as did the dark navy blue—nearly black—curtains adorning my massive four poster bed. My dressing room and bathing room led off this main chamber with doors set into the celestial mural disguised as constellations.

I considered ringing for a bath, but given all the transforming I'd done this evening, I needed to feed more than anything. Rather than disturb my manservant, Guillaume, I went to the small armoire near my bed and pulled out one of the crystal bottles filled with blood. This had come from one of my last victims near Gévaudan—a merchant with a penchant for brutality against his wife, mistress, and young daughter. His blood tasted as rotten as he'd been when he was alive, but the memories of his death were that much more satisfying. *God, how he'd screamed!*

I licked the last of the blood from the bottle and set it aside. Exhaustion crept through my veins, and I barely made it to my bed before sleep took me, and as ever, I dreamed of Mina.

CHAPTER THREE
MINA

April 15, 1768
Van Helsing's Clinic, Rue Ordener

THE INSISTENT BANGING AT MY BACK DOOR DISTURBED ME MORE THAN it should have. Since the sun was only just beginning to set, I knew it wouldn't be *him*—or any of my vampire patients—but I'd been on edge for the last two days since he'd shown up.

Heart pounding, I went around back to see who was too wary or nefarious to come in through the front door to my clinic.

"Charlotte!" I exhaled, relief washing over me.

"My darling doctor," she trilled, pushing her way into the back storeroom, arms loaded with baskets of bread, cheese, and vegetables. She set them on my worktable and brushed the crumbs from the mossy green silk of her gown, set off with pink silk rosettes.

"I brought a basket of meat pies, as well—*merde*, where did I put it? I might have left it in my carriage. One short moment and I'll just pop out to check..." the distracted comtesse mumbled as she rifled through her parcels. Before she could leave, an enormous broad-shouldered French officer with striking green eyes and a queue of dark brown hair lumbered into the room, ducking as he filled—and exceeded—my doorway.

"Antoine, *chéri*, did I leave—?"

He looked at her, pushed a linen-covered basket in her hands, and swept her up in a passionate kiss. Once the Comtesse de Brionne was flushed and panting, he tipped his hat to me, winked at his dizzy fiancée, and departed without a word.

Charlotte stared dreamily after the handsome, threatening mountain of a man for long enough that I was forced to clear my throat to regain her attention.

"Sincerest apologies, Mina—you know how it is with sweet Antoine. I would suggest that perhaps my lustful attentions have been exacerbated by my werewolf turning, but frankly, I was always an avid enjoyer of bed sport so that hardly seems like a hypothesis worth investigating. Now, as I said, these baskets have more food this week because we had that horrible late snow and I'm worried about people having enough to eat. I fear the more *les Dames Dangereuses* tries to help, the worse the circumstances seem, don't you? I know you'll ensure this all gets to those who need it most. I don't blame the poor for distrusting us aristocrats, but I daresay it makes it difficult to offer aid when they won't take it," she said, filling the quiet of my clinic with a stream of effusive kindness. Once she had organized the baskets on my table, she finally turned and fixed a penetrating stare on me.

"What?" I chirped, unsettled. "Why do you regard me so?"

She tilted her head at me in a way that reminded me of a curious dog, and I huffed a nervous laugh.

"Have you given any thought to my words the other day?" she asked.

I swallowed. She had come to my clinic earlier this week and revealed she suspected my connection with the Beast of Gévaudan, or "the man in black," as she called him. She hadn't threatened me—rather, she wanted to help me and offered the warning that if she had worked out our historical attachment, The Order would, as well. I hadn't admitted anything to her then, but after Rafael had turned up on my doorstep, I knew it was only a matter of time before she sniffed him out—literally.

I cleared my throat and fiddled with one of the linen cloths covering the basket of meat pies.

"Your suspicions are correct," I said quietly.

Charlotte's lovely face betrayed nothing, but she took my hand and guided me to the chairs that sat in front of the fireplace.

"Tell me," she coaxed.

I sighed. "I haven't seen him in twenty years, Charlotte— not until that evening outside Grandrieu." Emotions tangled in my throat, making it difficult for me to continue.

"Who is he?" she asked.

"What will you tell The Order?" I inquired. "I do not want them to know. Forgive me, *mon amie*, but I do not trust them."

She nodded, sadness blooming on her face. "My loyalty is to you, Wilhelmina. Do not forget, beyond being my very dear friend, you saved my life and the lives of the people I love. As such, I must warn you things within The Order have become very dire indeed. The recent religious fervor led by the bastard Derais has driven the men into a frenzy of hate against the supernatural set. Daphne, Étienne, Antoine, and I are doing what we can to help soothe tempers and keep the peace, but more and more *les Dames Dangereuses* are being edged out of the conversation. Trust between us and The Order has fractured, but no one has yet made the first move. Of course I won't say anything to them. However, I must impress upon you the gravity of their concern. You should know The Order suspects the man in black of a great number of horrific deeds. While I don't trust The Order much these days, I'm still determining the veracity of their suspicions against him. But...if you say you have not seen him for twenty years, I would caution you to seriously consider your loyalty to someone you might not know anymore."

I opened my mouth to say more, but at that moment the bell above my door jangled and a young woman called out for me.

"Dr. Van Helsing?"

I smiled apologetically at Charlotte and hurried into the front room of the clinic. A gaunt young woman stood in the doorway, wringing her hands nervously. She was pretty—or had been, before suffering the starvation that hollowed out her face to a mere skin-covered skull. My heart squeezed at the sight.

"You must be Jacqueline," I began. "Your husband, Pierre, came to talk with me the other night. I expected you yesterday."

"My apologies," she said with a wobbly curtsy. "I was unwell."

I nodded, unsure of what to say that might alleviate some of her anxiety.

"Please, take a seat," I offered, gesturing at a chair along the wall. "I'll be with you in just a moment."

She did as she was instructed, and I went to make my apologies to Charlotte, but when I entered my back room, I discovered that she'd left. On the table with the baskets of food was a small scrap of parchment with a note.

Tell me when you're ready. I'll be here. Be careful.

XO,

Charlotte

P.S. Come to dine this evening! You simply must help me with wedding preparations.

Guilt drifted through me like wisps of smoke from an extinguished candle. I tried to ignore the rueful wash of relief I felt at being able to keep my secrets for a little while longer, even as I sensed the sands of time slipping through the hourglass of my life.

Shaking myself back to my professional demeanor, I stuffed the note in my pocket and smoothed my hands down the soft blue wool of my skirts.

"Jacqueline," I said, returning to the front of the clinic. "Tell me what's been happening at home. How are you faring?"

She smiled at me for a moment, but it slipped from her face with the first tears that spilled from her eyes.

"We cannot endure," she whispered through soft sobs. "Pierre has too little work, and even with me taking in more mending and laundry, it is not enough to put food on the table."

I allowed her some time to cry, awkwardly clutching her hand. When she sniffled a bit and seemed to recover some, I fetched her a glass of water and one of the meat pies Charlotte had brought. Jacqueline's eyes widened at the sight of the food.

"No, Doctor, I cannot—it's too much!"

I tutted and shoved the warm pastry into her hands. "I'll send you with some more for Pierre, as well. You must try to eat something but do so slowly. Small bites, or you will retch. You mustn't overtax your body."

Tentatively, she nibbled a corner of the pie and closed her eyes in bliss. Her tears continued to fall, and I contemplated my next words.

"Pierre told me you were considering infecting yourself with the blood plague," I said. "And he wished for me to talk you out of it because he fears for your immortal soul."

She turned watery eyes on me. "We cannot live on the charity of our neighborhood doctor forever. Blood is plentiful. Bread and money are not."

I'd heard the same story from nearly every poor commoner who'd come through my door over the last few years. The people of France were desperate, and relief was far from their horizons. Some—too many, truly—had made the impossible decision to protect their souls and the possibility of Heaven's mercy rather than agree to turn themselves into vampires. At the beginning of the epidemic, scores had died much faster than the plague could travel. Then, thousands began to face starvation, crippling poverty, and despair and refused to turn the other cheek. They found relatives, friends—even vampires for hire—to infect themselves with the blood plague. I did what I could to stem the tide of confusion, hunger, and misery sweeping across France by educating with as much as I knew, which was paltry. *Insufficient.* For every person I helped, ten more were beyond my help. Too often I felt like Sisyphus, forever rolling the same stone up the same mountain, unable to make any real progress. Or perhaps I was Pandora...doomed to live in a Hell of my own making for succumbing to the sin of curiosity.

For welcoming the devil into my bed...the same devil who would unleash this plague upon the world.

"I am not a priest, Jacqueline," I said with more bitterness than I intended. "I cannot speculate about what happens to our souls when we are infected with the blood plague. I cannot say if it is a punishment from God or a temptation sent to test our faith. What I can say with certainty is that every answer you believe the blood plague offers is equal to yet one more hardship. It is not the flawless solution you wish it to be. You will give up the sunlight. You must subsist on blood, but murder is still a crime, and it takes years of practice to learn how to control yourself when you feed. And what happens if you cannot find someone to feed on? Blood whores are expensive—as is their right—and there are still too few farm animals to subsist on, thanks to the poor crop yields. This is all to say nothing of the fact that King Louis is reluctant to offer any legal or economic protections for vampire-kind, despite the efforts of the vampire emissary and The Order. From a lawful, legal stance, you would be considered less than human and unprotected. Vulnerable."

Defeat leeched into Jacqueline's expression as she took another bite of the meat pie.

"If it is your decision, however, I will not stop you. I am only here to ensure that people make the decisions that they believe are best. I would encourage you to find a supportive maker—one who has at least been a vampire for a few years and can help guide your journey. Someone you trust," I said.

She finished the meat pie and licked the crumbs from her fingers. After taking a large drink of water, she stared hard at the ground between her feet.

"What about..." she paused, embarrassed. "Doctor, can vampires have children?"

Pain—hot and sharp—erupted in my chest. I swallowed the emotions trying to claw their way up my throat. Anxiously, I removed my spectacles and examined them for phantom smudges in a clumsy effort to avoid looking into Jacqueline's expectant eyes.

"Vampires and humans cannot reproduce," I replied, my voice wavering. "But two vampires may have children. It is extremely difficult but not impossible."

Jacqueline sniffed and wiped the lingering tears from her cheeks.

"Pierre would never agree to the change," she said forlornly. "And I desperately want a babe of my own."

"It is worth considering that vampire babes are exceedingly rare and grow up much differently than humans," I admitted.

"Have you met any?" she asked.

I winced seeing the hope on her face. A wave of despair washed over me, threatening to drown me in melancholy.

"Yes," I answered. "I have."

I counseled Jacqueline as best I could for the next half hour but couldn't be sure what she would decide. I hoped Pierre would support her regardless of her decision. After stuffing bread, cheese, and more meat pies into her arms and sending her on her way, I returned to my ever-waiting research in my back room. I'd been trying to understand the plague itself—why it behaved the way that it did, how it existed inside the human body, and if it could be cured. I knew other physicians working for The Order were performing some of the same work, but I had insight they did not.

I knew where it came from and how it all began.

Memories surfaced, unbidden and unwanted. I was sixteen, traveling southeast from Amsterdam through Vienna and onward with my father, the first Dr. Van Helsing—eminent surgeon, anatomist, physician, and scientist. To this day, I didn't know how I was able to convince him to take me along on his travels, lecturing and meeting with royalty and the intellectual elite. Mother had wanted me to stay at home and practice the domestic arts to find a good marriage, but I couldn't bear the thought of being sold off like some prize pig at a market of old, dull, ugly men. After months of begging, my father had relented. Looking back, I think he hadn't wanted me to marry any of the fools my mother favored. He'd convinced her that he might find a suitable match in the wealthy houses he'd frequent upon his travels.

If only they'd known then. If only I had known then.

I'd had an affinity for languages and for science, and becoming an impromptu apprentice to my father's work had been the most wonderful dream. That was what I'd wanted out of life—not to become an idle broodmare spreading my legs at the whims of my future husband's desires.

Things had been ideal until we'd entered the Hungarian city of Buda. After one of Papa's lectures, we'd been approached by a young man working for the illustrious House of Dracul, a royal house from the nearby province of Wallachia. I remembered the invitation all too well.

"Will you come to dine at my master's townhouse here in Buda? He and his family would dearly love to make your acquaintance, Doctor."

"My daughter and I would be honored," Papa had said.

Thus began the most fateful evening of my life.

Deep into my ruminating, I realized I'd been staring at the same page of notes for almost an hour. Night would soon fall, and now that I knew Rafael was somewhere in the area, I was worried about him trying to approach me again and putting both our lives in jeopardy. I enjoyed a fair amount of latitude from the operations of The Order, and I certainly didn't want to test their boundaries—or their patience.

I blew out a breath and rubbed the headache forming between my brows. *Dieu, I am tired.* I knew I had more work to do, but I owed Charlotte a visit to help her prepare for her upcoming wedding. There was also the possibility that I felt a gnawing sense of guilt at keeping secrets from her, considering I counted her as one of my best friends. As a foreigner, friends were hard to come by and even harder to keep.

Would it be so bad if Charlotte and Daphne knew? Would they condemn me for the sins of my past—my weakness of character in the face of the devil himself? Surely, they couldn't fault me for falling in love with the wrong man—not that he was a man.

But he certainly felt like one in my arms.

On the other hand, the blood plague is the thing that Daphne works so hard to rectify in France, and Charlotte was turned without her consent. Rafael is at fault for both.

As am I.

I winced as the realization condensed in my mind, like clouds blotting out the sun, but I was too much of a coward to tell them everything.

I won't risk losing their friendship...yet. Eventually, I will. Eventually, I will have to. Just not tonight.

I put on my second-best gown, an amethyst silk confection embroidered with blue flowers and trailing green vines, and pinned my curls up as best I could without a lady's maid. Charlotte and Daphne never minded my reluctance to abide by the same rules and fashions as the court, but if I didn't at least make an effort, Charlotte would spend half the evening trying to convince me to let her buy me a new wardrobe. Not that she pitied me, exactly, but she insisted the boring parties at Versailles were made more interesting with my attendance, despite my wallflower tendencies and inability to stomach champagne.

I pulled on my thick wool cloak, locked my apartment and my clinic, and made my way to the busy street where I could hire a fiacre to drive me to Charlotte's impressive estate. No sooner had I entered the dim carriage than a pair of fierce hands grabbed me and roughly pushed me back against the seat. Before I could scream, another hand came up to my face, stifling the sound and cutting off air.

Panic raced through me, and I lashed out, kicking at my attacker. I experienced a moment of triumph when I felt my boot connect with soft flesh and bone and heard a gruff curse, but the hand around my face tightened and my victory was short lived. Darkness beyond that of the encroaching night pulled at my senses, and I felt myself slip into the depths of unconsciousness.

CHAPTER FOUR
RAFAEL

April 15, 1768
Rue Ordener

I SENSED TROUBLE BEFORE I WAS FULLY AWAKE, BUT THAT DIDN'T STOP me from launching myself out of bed, shifting into my wolf form, and bolting across the countryside toward her. Even after twenty years, hundreds of miles, and lifetimes separating us, I felt her distress like a spider sensing the vibrations of flies caught in its web. Tremors of panic delicately thrummed along threads of silk that seemed to be affixed directly to my absent heart.

Fear. Anger. Not anger...outrage. Confusion. Disgust.

I struggled to concentrate—to focus on her feelings enough to determine what was happening to her and what shape these dangers would take—but as ever, I couldn't think clearly when it came to Mina. Rage built in me with every strike of my paws upon the earth, and fear for her fragile, mortal body gnawed at me. More memories surfaced as I ran, but this time they carried an ache of a different kind.

Let me make you, Mina, my love. Allow me to turn you so we won't ever be separated by time, I'd begged. Her eyes were a sharp blue that night, like a chunk of sea ice that had been worn by ocean currents into a deadly point.

Not until I know more, she had said. *I love you, Rafael, truly, I do. But I must understand what this curse holds for you. What it could mean for me, too.*

I'd railed at her, then, and stormed from the bedchamber. Ever practical, ever calculating, ever mindful Mina, who would always put knowledge and science and thought ahead of every feeling. Mina, whom I'd said loved reason more than she loved me.

I chuckled to myself now but had been devastated at the time. *What a fool I'd been.* I was so in love with her, I expected her to act as I would have—to throw everything away and dive headfirst into endless nights of ceaseless sexual pleasure and the power of consuming another human's precious life-force. She wouldn't, though. She couldn't. She was Mina, and for me to ask anything else of her...to ask her to be anything other than what she was, was utterly idiotic.

It had taken me years to learn that particular lesson.

No matter. I was back for her now, and it was up to me to convince her that I wasn't the devil she'd left behind. I was an entirely different demon now, and one who would spend however long atoning for all my mistakes.

She must believe me about the blood plague. When I speak with her, she must *believe me.*

Well, I'd have to find her first.

Onward I raced, faster and faster. Paris finally came into view. I reached out with my senses as soon as I drew near, hoping to find her in the jungle of scents and sounds all clamoring for my attention.

My mental connection to Mina flickered, and a spear of icy

fear staked me in place. She wasn't dead—she couldn't be. It would certainly *feel* different. She felt…asleep. Unconscious, perhaps. An involuntary snarl slipped between my bared teeth. If I couldn't find her by sensing her, I would have to use my other skills to locate her.

I shifted to my bat form and flew to Rue Ordener. Her clinic was dark, as was her apartment above. I flew to the back alley, shifted to my human form, and donned the hidden stash of clothing I kept nearby. Nothing grand—simple black breeches, hose, a shirt, waistcoat, and jacket. Shifting was certainly useful, but ungainly when one was transforming in and around crowds of people.

I sniffed around for Pascal and Hubert, but their scents had faded some. Where had they gone? Unease built in me. I walked around to the front of her clinic and caught her scent, along with horse, leather, and wood—a fiacre. Where would she take a hired carriage at this time of night?

Two options came to mind. Either the estate of vampire Duchesse Daphne or the estate of Comtesse Charlotte de Brionne, the werewolf of my somewhat accidental making. Both women worked within The Order, were mated to a vampire and a werewolf (respectively), and had the kind of power that politicians and priests dreamed of. They loved Mina fiercely, which suited me fine, but they were formidable enemies if crossed, and I suspected they had more than one reason to distrust me.

I'd need to be on my guard and tread carefully.

Still, perhaps I could find Mina before she arrived at either *château*—if she arrived. The thought sent another spike of heated anger through me, and when I loosened my clenched fist, rivulets of blood dripped from the indentations my claws had made. I took a deep breath and forced myself calm as the tiny wounds healed.

I reached out again with my senses, detecting Mina's fading scent. Within moments, I was able to pinpoint its direction, and I took off at a rapid clip. After an hour of winding through the streets of Paris, I finally sensed I was nearing my destination.

At the end of a small lane, I spotted the dilapidated fiacre. Behind the small carriage sprawled a grim-looking cemetery, complete with overgrown graves and crumbling tombs. It was obvious the dead here didn't have many mourners to honor their memory.

As I approached the fiacre, I heard the labored grunting of two men wrestling with a weight between them. Willing myself calm again, I approached, only to see my old friends Pascal and Hubert struggling to lift an unconscious Mina down from the door of the carriage. I scanned the area again, trying to determine where they would take her in such a forgotten place. If they were trying to violate her—my claws lengthened at the thought—it seemed rather out of the way for them when they could have had her in the fiacre. *Unless they already have...*

"Gentlemen," I said smoothly. "It appears you need some help."

"Fuck off," Hubert grumbled. "This doesn't concern you."

"Be on your way, Monsieur. We don't need your help," Pascal huffed.

I chuckled—the deep, monstrous sound echoing in the night.

"You misunderstand me," I rumbled, fangs and claws lengthening. "It appears you *will need* some help."

I launched myself at Hubert, the closest man. Before his shock could register, I sank my claws into his neck and twisted his head from his shoulders. His body fell to the ground with a soft thump, and the wet sounds of blood leeching from his decapitated head. The elegant scent of copper and salt drifted up from the pile of human at my feet, making me nearly feral with hunger and violence.

An ear-piercing shriek split the night, and Pascal dropped Mina and stumbled backward. He recovered and bolted toward one of the old mausoleums, which struck me as odd until I saw the faint flicker of candlelight glowing from the cracks in the door. *A hideout of some sort?*

I caught up to him easily and lifted him by the throat. He whimpered and kicked, and I felt the frenzied beat of his pulse beneath my fingertips.

"Tell me," I soothed, compelling the truth from his lips and ignoring the siren song of fresh blood. "You watched Mina for The Order. What were you doing with her this evening?"

"They wanted her," he choked out.

"Yes," I grinned, displaying my infamous dual sets of fangs. "Don't we all?"

His eyes widened in fear and surprise. "It's...it's you! The Beast! The Master of all Vampires! The devil himself!"

"Enchanté," I said, inclining my head slightly. "Do call me Rafael." I allowed my human face to transform into a demonic shape, sprouting horns, a forked tongue, and wholly black eyes with red pinprick pupils.

Pascal squeezed his eyes shut and pissed himself.

"Why did The Order want Mina?" I repeated, in a deep voice that sounded like a legion of angry demons.

"They're looking for you," he whispered. "They think she knows more than she's telling. They wanted her in for questioning. Please don't kill me!"

"Questioning?" I echoed, concern knitting my brows. "What kind of questioning?"

Pascal pressed his lips together, but I couldn't tell if it was from fear of me or fear of The Order.

"What kind of questioning?" I boomed, infusing the command with more compulsion.

His eyes snapped to mine, and I let my demon visage melt away until I looked human again.

"They plan to question her as a witch," he finally said.

A witch. Mina was no more a witch than I was a demon. The Order would torture and murder her to get to me. Either they had become more desperate and dangerous than I'd realized, or their fear of the blood plague had introduced madness into their ranks. I'd known about The Order for years but had let them operate as they willed, especially after the Duchesse de Duras had joined and been turned. She and her mate, the recently made Duc Étienne de Noailles—who was, himself, a vampire and the vampire emissary to King Louis XV—had been fighting what I knew could only be a losing battle. Rights for vampire-kind. Peaceful coexistence between the vampire poor and the human aristocracy. *Absolutely ridiculous.*

Clearly, The Order had moved faster into cowardice, suspicion, and panic than I had anticipated. I knew what would come next. The systematic removal of every vampire they could get their hands on, along with their allies.

Pascal flailed limply, reminding me that I still held him by the throat. I quirked a brow at him.

"Were they all agreed on this course of action?"

"All but *les DD*. They could not be told," he said.

"Ah yes, *les Dames Dangereuses*. How could they not know? Don't their numbers outweigh the men of The Order by now?"

I'd asked the question rhetorically more than anything, but the look of confusion on Pascal's face told me he wouldn't be much more help.

"Well," I said brightly. "Pascal, I'm delighted to offer you two options this evening. I can either drain your entire body of blood and leave your withered corpse under a tree for the crows, *or* I can turn you and offer you the gift of immortality for the price of entering my service."

Tears slipped down Pascal's cheeks. "You know what The Order has planned for *les sanguisuges*," he whispered. "I am damned either way."

I tutted. "*Tsk,* Pascal, *mon ami*, we are all damned. Some of us simply face judgment day a bit later than others. Which will it be?"

A strangled sob rose from his throat. "I will not risk my immortal soul to delay the death of my body."

"So be it," I replied, sinking my fangs into his throat. The need for blood surpassed all other thoughts and emotions—it had been too long since I'd fed. Unlike many of the newer vampires, I could survive on smaller amounts of blood, but when I used my abilities more frequently, I required more. Changing shape, in particular, was quite draining. Already, I felt strength and power returning to me, drugging me in the way it always had and always would. If only humans understood how precious blood truly was—this sticky, honeyed liquid that animated bones and flesh—they might not consider the blood plague as the shameful alternative to starvation. It was worth more than ten thousand loaves and fish.

Foolish humans.

I drank until I felt Pascal's life-force ebb away, then collected his and Hubert's bodies. I felt a pang of something... disgust? No. Pity, perhaps, at adding yet more lives to my tally of sins. Or perhaps it was regret for Pascal's misplaced loyalty and misguided piety. Either way, instead of tossing the bodies into the undergrowth for the animals to find, I located a rusted shovel leaning against one of the tombstones and dug makeshift, shallow graves for both men. It was too bad The Order had involved these poor human fools, and it was too bad they had come for my Mina.

I heard the faint rustling of silk fabric and soft moans emanating from near the fiacre, and I rushed over to find Mina coming to. She was murmuring something insensible, but I didn't see evidence of a head wound. I picked her up and carried her back inside the fiacre, and her head lolled limply against my shoulder, her glasses dangling haphazardly from one ear. Intrigued and somewhat concerned, I inhaled at the crook of her neck and detected a faint bitter scent carried along in her blood—laudanum.

Pascal and Hubert had evidently needed to drug her to ensure she was compliant and cooperative for The Order's brutal questioning. The knowledge reawakened the rage in me, and I fought to tamp it back down.

From my experiences with forms of opium, I knew she would need a safe place to sleep off the soporific effects of the drug. I was reluctant to return her to her home since The Order would likely send more thugs 'round to kidnap her again once they learned of Pascal and Hubert's fates.

I could attempt to take her to Charlotte's home, or Daphne's, but I was uncertain about how they would receive me. Additionally, I wasn't certain about their level of involvement with The Order's new and dangerous tactic. I believed what Pascal had told me, but I found it hard to believe that both women had been completely unaware of such an evil plot brewing from within their midst.

That left me with one option. I could bring her to my home, *le Château du Diable*, to recover. She would be furious upon waking, which could put my greater plans in jeopardy, but since I didn't trust The Order to leave her home in peace and I didn't trust *les DD* because they operated within The Order, I didn't have much of a choice.

Merde.

I found a stale-smelling blanket beneath the seat of the

fiacre and tucked her in as best I could. Then I climbed out onto the seat of the small carriage and picked up the reins. It would have been faster for me to turn into my wolf form and carry her across the countryside, but I didn't want to risk being seen and I wasn't certain I'd be able to hold onto her very well when she was in this drug-induced stupor. The threat of sunrise loomed.

I was grateful for the cloak I'd stolen from Hubert's body, since it allowed me to hide the blood smeared across my face, neck, and hands. I should have washed after burying the men, but I hadn't thought I would have time. Hopefully, I could clean up when I arrived home...before Mina truly awoke.

I urged the horse faster across the countryside, racing against the dawn. By the time my château came into view, the sky was already a worrying shade of lilac. I pulled up short, jumped from the driver's seat, and pulled Mina from the fiacre. With a growl and the tearing of fabric, I shifted into an enormous bat creature, stretched my massive leathery wings, and gingerly lifted her into the air. It was during times like these I found my secret front entrance a troublesome feature, but having the door hidden at the top of the highest tower was the best form of security.

Only slightly more inconvenient was the fact that it was at this moment Mina regained consciousness.

CHAPTER FIVE
MINA

April 16, 1768
Château du Diable

SOMETHING IS WRONG.

My stomach lurched with the movement of my body, but I felt as if I were underwater, moving slowly through icy currents. My mind was at odds with the rest of me, utterly blissful in a sleepy stupor I couldn't seem to climb my way out of.

What is happening to me?

I felt a strange pressure around my chest, as if my stays had grown too small. Had I laced them too tight when I dressed for my evening? Was I at Charlotte's château? Where was she? Where was I?

Confusion clouded my mind, but instead of panicking, I grasped for it like a thick blanket and wrapped it tighter around myself. Everything felt off-kilter, but so delicious.

I heard the rush of wind in my ears and a lilting giggle, which I realized had slipped from my lips.

Why am I laughing?

I cracked one eye open, expecting to find myself at home in bed, rousing from some curious late-night dream. Or perhaps I was at Charlotte's home, tucked into one of her guest room beds after having one too many glasses of champagne with dinner.

No, that's not right. I hate champagne.

Still, nothing could have prepared me for the sight I beheld.

I stared up at an enormous creature—so massive and terrifying, it looked like Hell had spat it out for being too much a horror. Half bat, half demon, it held me in its huge claws, carrying me through the air on tattered, leathery wings. Fear unlike anything I'd experienced seized me, and I opened my mouth to scream. Oddly, a hysterical laugh pierced the night instead of a shriek, and the hell-beast looked down at me. *Is that blood on its face? Is it going to eat me?*

The idea seemed so preposterous. *Have I survived all that I have to be eaten by a giant devil bat?* What a bizarre end for a doctor trying to unlock the secrets of the blood plague. Instead of feeling what would be a normal surge of terror, I could only feel...relief. *At last, the weight of obligation, responsibility, and guilt will be lifted. It is only too bad that I am here alone, and no one will know my fate.*

More laughter bubbled up from within me, until tears streamed down my cheeks, and I gasped for air. Suddenly, I found it very hard to breathe, as if my lungs would not obey the needs of my body.

The monster holding me swooped downward, and we entered a dark, crumbling stone tower at the top of a forlorn and forgotten castle. The pressure on my chest eased some, and I found myself in a heap of confused limbs on a cold stone floor. Darkness pressed in, making it impossible for me to see. From my left, I heard an ominous and nauseating popping, squelching noise—much like the sound of bones breaking beneath flesh—but it stopped almost as soon as it had started.

Silence descended, which felt infinitely more terrifying.

"Mina," came a voice. I knew it, as if from a dream.

I scrambled to my feet but was too unsteady. I pitched forward but found myself encased in arms like bands of iron, which lifted me from the ground and carried me from the darkness of the cold tower.

My stomach rolled with the movement, and I squeezed my eyes shut to steady my equilibrium. I heard us move softly down a long hallway, entering door after door until we reached some place warm and quiet.

I heard the soft crackle of a fire in a hearth as cold but gentle hands unpinned my gown and loosened my stays. When I was down to my chemise and stockings, I felt myself being lifted again and tucked into a soft bed layered with fur and velvet blankets. Warmth seeped into my limbs and tugged at my senses, pulling me back toward the abyss of sleep.

Curiosity had me opening my eyes to look for the hell-beast from my nightmares, but in the barest glow of firelight, I only saw a man standing before me.

He was terrifying and beautiful, with long black hair, the chiseled cheekbones and patrician nose of royalty, and obsidian eyes that made me think of forbidding caves at the bottom of the deep ocean. Cold, fathomless, incomprehensible —but not empty. Filled with horrors and mysteries. His features were neutral—his expression impassive, and I realized that his entire mouth and face was covered with blood and filth. Something distant in my mind suggested that it probably wasn't his own.

Everything about the man was familiar and yet alien to me. Even as my body responded and my arms reached for him, my heart pounded a warning in my chest. I was prey to this predator, but that didn't dampen the echo of my body's need for him.

Rafael.

Sleep and the drug that whispered through my veins wrapped me tighter and I slumped back onto the pillows, but I kept my gaze on the dark man standing there, staring at me in the flickering golden glow spilling from the hearth. I wanted to ask him questions, but when I opened my mouth through the syrup of fatigue, only one phrase oozed forth.

"You came back for me."

He did not react, and it occurred to me that I might not have spoken at all. It was then that sleep finally claimed me, and I remembered no more.

FEVERED VISIONS HAUNTED MY SLEEP. SOME FELT LIKE MEMORIES. Some felt like nightmares, and I mourned my ability to distinguish between the two. One image surfaced again and again—Rafael covered in blood.

Queasiness swirled through my stomach, and I moaned through parched lips. I kicked the damp, sweat-soaked sheets off and blinked in the near darkness. I was in the same room as before, but this time I was alone. A small table next to the bed held my spectacles and a porcelain ewer of water, an empty goblet, and a shallow bowl of some thin, savory broth.

I sat up against the pillows, put on my spectacles, and poured myself some water. *Where am I? Where is Rafael? I didn't dream of him again, did I? How long have I been here? What happened?*

The more I came into consciousness, the faster the questions raced through my mind. Panic started to build in my chest, and it took a great feat of strength to prevent it from taking control of me. I sipped the cool water and inhaled slowly to calm myself.

Before I could dwell too much on my troubling circumstances, there was a soft knock on the bedchamber door.

"Yes," I rasped, my voice hoarse from thirst and disuse.

I'd expected a servant to enter, but Rafael stepped into the room. My heart seized in my chest and my breath caught, as it did every time I looked at him. Rather than his customary all-black suit, he was clad in a loose, white linen shirt, soft leather breeches, and a floor-length red silk dressing gown, open and trailing behind him like a royal robe. The gold embroidered dragons of his family crest glittered in the low firelight, making them look almost alive.

He padded into the room on bare feet and came to sit at the foot of the bed. I shifted slightly, pulling away from the all-too-intimate move.

He noted my discomfort and smiled.

"I'm glad to find you awake, little Mina," he soothed in his deep baritone. Seeing the obvious wariness on my face, he continued. "You have nothing to fear from me."

I sipped at my water and narrowed my eyes.

"That remains to be seen, Rafael."

He tutted and leaned down onto his side, propped up on one elbow.

"It's twice now that I've saved your life. Still, you recoil from me. Is it from our past, I wonder? Or something else?" He grinned at me, the scant light glinting off his lethal fangs. Beneath his teasing, I sensed something sad in his words, but my mind felt too fuzzy for me to explore it properly.

I gripped the water goblet tighter in my hands. I knew he could sense my emotions—not that it would take a vampire's keen senses to perceive my distress—and I didn't want to give him any more of an edge than he already possessed.

"What happened?" I asked tightly. "How did I come to be here—wherever *here* is?"

I wasn't sure what I expected, certainly not a straight answer or the bold truth of what happened. Rafael had been a spoiled young man and had enjoyed teasing me too much when we were younger. He loved playing mind games and speaking in riddles, and he had the patience of eternity to frustrate anyone unlucky enough to get drawn into a verbal battle. Sitting across from him now, I felt like a mouse staring down a rather large, rather hungry alley cat.

"Mina," he purred. "You are still overcoming the effects of the drug you were given. You're weak...tired...cold."

On the last word, his gaze dropped from my face to my nipples visible from beneath my worn cotton chemise. Despite the dim light in the bedchamber and the blackness of his eyes, I recognized the shimmer of lust. Self-conscious, I tugged the thick coverlet up to my neck.

"Yes," I lied, not chilled in the slightest. "It's frigid in here."

He quirked one sharp black brow at me, then waved his hand at the waning embers in the fireplace. With a soft word in an unrecognizable language, the flames roared to life.

My eyes widened. "Not a side effect of the blood plague?" I questioned. "Is this from the curse? Or have you been studying witchcraft?"

"Perhaps I made a deal with the devil, and he took whatever was left of my pitiful soul after all," he quipped drily. "In exchange for a wealth of varied dark powers."

I glared.

He laughed again and rose from the bed, his lean muscles flexing like a lithe jungle cat.

"Later, Mina. For now, you need rest and food and drink.

Restore your body and then I will give you the answers that will satisfy your mind." The low timbre of his voice and the heat in his eyes set my skin aflame.

I sipped at the water again to try to cool my temperament.

"Whose blood was it?" I asked suddenly.

He was quiet for a moment. Then, "Why?"

I was glad that he didn't pretend to misunderstand.

"I want to know," I answered. "Are they still alive?"

He tilted his head at me in a curious way, as if observing a specimen in a bell jar.

"Not on this plane of existence, no. Why do you want to know?"

I narrowed my eyes. "I don't want to be responsible for any more deaths."

"You are not."

"Let me judge that for myself," I replied. "Whose blood was it?"

"Are you so bored and righteous that you must assume the guilt for things which you do not control? I am flattered by your self-flagellation for my sins, Mina—it shows you still care." He chuckled.

I couldn't be sure if he was teasing to get a rise out of me or if it was because he didn't want to tell me. Twenty years ago, back at the very beginning, I would have taken the bait— blushing and stammering and protesting that I didn't care for him. *I don't care about you*, I would have said. *You're nothing more than a scientific curiosity to me and a patient of my father. You aren't even human.*

How cold I'd been then.

And you're so much warmer now, came the sarcastic answering thought. And yet, I wouldn't admit to him that I still cared.

"The blood plague leeches across the continent because of

your family's curse," I said coolly. "Your father tasked my father with finding the solution. He failed...*we* failed. So yes, as much as it is your fault that the plague escaped the confines of your ancestral home, it is equally my family's fault that it has not been stopped. *My fault*, Rafael. Every vampire and every death can be laid at my feet because of what my father and I could not do. Tell me whose blood it was."

I folded my arms across my chest, waiting for him to answer me. Our eyes locked across the bed in a stalemate of iron wills. A lesser person would see Rafael's stoic expression as halcyon as a marble bust, but I recognized the subtle changes that I'd long ago memorized. The dilation of his pupils, the slight flare of a nostril, the barest twitch of his lips...*frustration*. Exasperation. Annoyance. Hunger.

"Two men," he finally said. "Shall I tell you about their deaths, sweet Mina, so that you can comfort yourself while you pray for our forgiveness?"

Two men.

"Oh no," I whispered, realization dawning. I should have expected this outcome. *What a fool I'd been!* "Not Pascal and Hubert?"

Rafael's eyes widened almost imperceptibly, and he sat back on the bed.

"You knew them?" he asked, somewhat accusatory. "You knew these men were the ones watching you, salivating over you and your body...slaves of The Order." His last words came out with remarkable venom.

It offended me that he thought I was so clumsy and weak as to not notice two such stooges haunting my clinic and my apartment for weeks.

"Of course I knew them," I bit back. "Not only do I have eyes of my own, but I'm the only doctor around for this world of monsters you created. Every vampire who came in through my clinic told me the clods were skulking around, reeking of sweat and drink and The Order's dusty robes."

I swallowed my satisfaction when I caught a glint of sheepishness in Rafael's eyes. It was not enough to keep my anger at bay.

"You don't know what you've done," I muttered.

"I saved your life," he said sharply. "Those *clods* kidnapped you, drugged you with a truly inappropriate amount of laudanum, and had every intention of delivering you to The Order for questioning."

That caught my attention. "Questioning?"

"For witchcraft," he said, leveling me with an intense gaze. "Because they would use you to get to me."

"You lie! That cannot be true," I argued. "I've been an ally for The Order. Yes, I knew they wanted to watch me to see if you'd come around, but they wouldn't..."

"Wouldn't they?" Rafael snapped as he surged to his feet. "How much do you know about The Order, Mina? How much have your friends Charlotte and Daphne told you? How much do *they* know? It wasn't too long ago that The Order was aiding the church in its hunt for witches. They're still bribing, murdering, exploiting, punishing, and torturing people."

I stared at him quizzically. "And what has your family been doing for eons?"

The specter of rage flitted across his face but was gone quickly.

"That was a long time ago," he gritted out.

"Yes, well, it was long ago that The Order hunted witches," I replied, getting out of bed to pace the room in agitation. "What do you care about The Order when you can easily hide from them—outrun them—outmatch them in every way? And why did you come here if you knew they would hunt you? Is it for sport? Is it because you're bored with your life in Wallachia and your treasure trove of women and your damn castle? Is it because you're punishing me by spreading the blood plague—infecting everyone in the country that I've come to love and call my home?"

I flung each question at him like a weapon, becoming angrier by the second. He stood by the fireplace, arm braced above the mantle, staring into the flames but tensing with every barb I hurled. Other than that, he did not react.

"Damn it, Rafael, why did you really kill Pascal and Hubert?"

Finally, his composure cracked, and he moved to me in a blur of brilliant supernatural speed. He grabbed me by the shoulders and pushed me harshly against the wall next to the bed. His grip was firm, but not tight enough to be painful. A startled gasp parted my lips, and his dark gaze snagged on the movement. His eyes turned solid black with pupils of red, like rubies set in onyx pools.

"Because," he growled. "They came for you. They dared to lay their hands on you. They hurt you to get to me. I should have made them suffer, Mina. God, I wanted to. I wanted to invade their minds and spear them with a thousand unique agonies until they begged me for the release of death. I should have broken a bone for every impure thought they had about you. I should have ripped out an organ for every vile word they said against you. I could have given them so much pain, Mina —you'll never know how much."

Horror—and shamefully, excitement—rendered me speechless. A tear slipped down my cheek, catching on the glass of my spectacle. I released a silent, shaky breath, then opened my mouth hesitantly, unsure of what to say.

"I killed them because they came for you, Mina," Rafael repeated, his demonic eyes never straying from my lips as he bent to kiss me. "And you are *mine*."

His mouth descended to mine, and the moment our lips met, twenty years of betrayal, pain, loneliness, regret, and longing surged forth. Before I could access the logical part of my brain and know enough to stop this foolishness, I clung to him, sliding my hands to the nape of his neck to pull him closer.

When we'd been young together—or *younger*—our kisses had been tentative, exploratory, sweet. He always touched me as if he was afraid to break me, despite having the years of practice learning the value of his own supernatural strength.

That innocent hesitation was gone now. In its place was sheer power, monstrous hunger, and desperate need. His soft lips moved over mine while his tongue sought entry—plundering as if he wanted to consume my very soul. When I sucked at his roving tongue, I felt his deep growl of pleasure more than I heard it, vibrating from his chest as he pressed his body into mine. His arousal hardened against my stomach, unleashing a storm of desire.

I wanted him. I needed him.

I hated him.

CHAPTER SIX
RAFAEL

April 16, 1768
Château du Diable

GODS ABOVE AND DEMONS BELOW, SHE TASTED PERFECT. SHE WAS every ray of sunshine I'd missed in my life of darkness. She was everything I loved about humans—promise and curiosity and hope. If I'd been born with a heart, it would have beaten only for her. She was my world, my past, my future...*my redemption.*

I pushed her harder into the wall, loving the way her body felt beneath mine. Her thin chemise was so threadbare it might not have existed as a layer between us, and the thought drove me almost feral with lust, so great was my need to claim her.

Mina. My Mina.

Her tongue swept mine, lightly grazing my fangs. The feeling was like a bolt of lightning, making my hard cock ache. The pain of my need was almost too much to bear, but I would take this torture over anything—everything—in the world.

My hands moved of their own will, sliding down her shoulders to caress her breasts through the soft fabric of the chemise. When my thumb found the peaked, pebbled nipple of her left breast, she whimpered, and the delicate sound of pleasure nearly unmanned me.

She arched against me like a bow being pulled taut. My hand drifted down, seeking the hem of her chemise. When I lifted it to slide one cool palm up the heated skin of her thigh and round hip, her eyes flew open. Despite the lust in her gaze and the scent of her arousal, I sensed her sudden shock and regret.

The ache of my unspent desire was chased by the acute agony of shame, remorse, and despair that for her, this was a mistake. It was not surprising then, when she put her hands to my chest and pushed me away—gently but firmly.

"No, Rafael," she huffed, but I was already across the room. "We cannot do this. I will not do this. I am not yours—not anymore."

Anger flared, white hot. *You will always be mine,* I wanted to say. Instead, I bowed my head.

"As you wish, Doctor. Forgive me for...taking liberties. I will not touch you again until you ask."

"I shall not ask," she grumbled, allowing the last of her lust to dissipate like fog chased by the sunlight of her anger. "I'm not here to be some kind of royal consort while you wreak havoc on all of Europe, only to go back to your throne and sire some selfish, monstrous heir."

Sadness bloomed in my chest, but I deserved her anger.

"I will send a maid in shortly," I said, barely keeping the bitterness from my tone. "She will help you bathe and dress and break your fast. You are still recovering from the drug, but unfortunately, The Order's actions have forced my timeline and we have much to discuss."

Her eyebrows arched.

"I can take care of myself," she protested. "I know how to

manage the sickness from opium. I do not need you, or your maid, or your hospitality. I should like to return home."

I sighed in irritation. "While you are not a prisoner here, you would require my help to leave this fortress and daylight is upon us. I must rest. After that, I will say my peace and then the decision will be yours."

"Decision?" she echoed, her curiosity piqued.

"For now, we are safe here," I said, ignoring her question. "My servants are at your disposal. They will attend to your needs if you simply name them."

Something like guilt flashed across her face.

"Rafael, I..." she swallowed. "I'm sorry for..." she gestured vaguely toward the wall. "—for *participating*."

I smirked. "Do not apologize to the devil for indulging in sin."

She bit her bottom lip, chagrined. I tried to ignore the desire to bite her bottom lip for her. I inclined my head once more and headed for the door, ringing for the maid as I left.

I could not look back.

I had stationed Mina in a guest bedchamber, but every room beneath the castle was fully equipped to address any manner of need. Just now, I wanted distance from her—from the desire I still fought and the petty hurts her words had inflicted. At least now I had a more accurate idea of what she thought of me after twenty years.

I knew she would be wounded given how we'd left things —how I'd left things. As easy as it was for me to forgive her anger, it gutted me that she believed what everyone else seemed to believe—that I was the one to let loose the blood plague and inflict my family's curse upon the world.

It was so easy for everyone to believe the worst of me, the selfish second son of Wallachia's royal family. The wastrel, the rogue, the spare. *The devil.* Only lately had I stopped believing those things of myself, so I supposed it would take Mina and the rest of the world time to catch up.

Unfortunately, it was time I didn't have.

Yet, I could wait an afternoon. The events of the previous few evenings hadn't left me much time to sleep, and after using my powers gratuitously, I needed time to restore my energy. Having drained Pascal, I didn't yet require more blood, but I didn't want the hunger to strike and shorten my temper any further with Mina. What I was about to do required great patience. As a preventative measure, I entered my library and went to the sideboard with several crystal decanters of blood and spirits. Longing for warmth in the absence of Mina's body, I mixed myself a drink of blood and *țuică*, the potent alcohol from my homeland. The older I got, the harder it was for me to become intoxicated, but it certainly wasn't for lack of trying. Regenerative abilities had disadvantages, but most newly turned vampires wouldn't know that until a few decades into their eternities.

The heady mix of blood and alcohol burned as it went down, settling like brimstone in my gut. Rather than returning to one of the bedrooms to lie down for a spell, I sat in the plush velvet armchair that faced the polished stone fireplace. With a thought and a word, the waiting logs began to burn, and I settled back into the chair, willing dreamless sleep to come.

When I woke, I was sure I'd only dozed for a few moments, but the carriage clock on the mantle indicated otherwise. It had been several hours, and the sun would soon be setting. I hoped Mina had also rested and eaten, but I wondered if that was likely given her stubborn streak. She *would* refuse any comforts I offered out of a misplaced sense of petulant independence. I knew she could take care of herself—she obviously had for the past twenty years—but as my guest, it was my job to take care of her.

As your guest and your future wife, came the whisper of hope from the space where my heart should have been. *Hmm. Perhaps. Perhaps not,* came the answer from my logical mind.

I roused myself and washed, then changed into a fresh shirt, breeches, and banyan. Rather than the red and gold of my family's house, I opted for a deep sapphire velvet, partly because I wished for something warm and comforting, and partly because the blue reminded me of Mina's eyes. I strolled down the hall in mink-lined slippers and paused outside her door. I'd long ago sworn not to use my abilities to spy on her or invade her privacy, which included compelling her, reading her thoughts, or using my supernatural senses to pry into her solitude, but the conversation between Mina and my servant carried loudly enough that I didn't need to betray that promise.

"He's owned it for ten years, mademoiselle, but hasn't been living here all that time," the servant said.

"Ten years! He's been in France that whole time?" Mina exclaimed.

The servant sounded anxious. "As I said, he hasn't spent all his time here. He travels extensively. He's only been in residence primarily for the last year or so, I think. Truly, it's hard to know. We don't always see him when he is here. We simply do our day-to-day duties on the off chance that he'll arrive."

I could practically hear the wheels turning in Mina's head.

"That must frustrate you," she replied.

"On the contrary, mademoiselle, he is a most generous employer. Ever thoughtful, never abusive. I don't believe a word of the stories the other villagers say," the servant replied earnestly.

Satisfaction shined through me, if only for a moment. I'd plucked this young girl from a particularly vile marquis's household, along with her two younger brothers. I paid my servants handsomely and treated them better than I would have treated my own family, knowing what it was for them to serve a monster. At times, when melancholy seized me, I often wondered if my servants would be the closest I would ever get to a family of my own.

Chasing the ensuing storm from my mind, I squared my shoulders and knocked. The servant rushed to open it, and I entered to find Mina bathed and dressed in the gown of pale lemon silk I'd secured for her. With her beauty and the bright blue of her eyes, she looked like the sun. My chest tightened at the sight.

"You look exquisite," I murmured. "I hope you were able to eat and rest in my absence."

"Yes, thank you," she replied politely, if a little cold. "The gown is very fine."

The servant girl smiled, curtsied, and left us to our simmering tension.

Mina wrung her hands together and paced next to the bed. Twice she tugged her spectacles from her face and cleaned them, then replaced them atop her pert nose. Despite her anxiety, I was pleased to see she had recovered much from the near overdose of laudanum and our...*encounter*.

"I don't often wear light colors," she said nervously. "I like them, but they're so impractical for me as a physician—especially for vampires. The stains are terrible, you see, when one's life is ruled by blood."

I raised a brow, my nervousness melting with her amusing observation.

"Yes," I said with a grin. "I know."

She blushed when she realized what she'd said and who she'd said it to.

"I'm sorry, I didn't mean..."

I tilted my head as she swore under her breath and forced a brittle smile.

"Mina," I began, coming slowly to stand next to her. "Be easy, please. Too many people in this world fear and despise me, and it would be a tragedy if you became one of them. I'm sorry for earlier and I meant what I said. There are a great many things I need to tell you and after that, it will be your decision to determine your fate—and mine."

Her lovely eyes widened, and she blew out a breath, steeling herself for something unpleasant.

"Very well," she said. "I am ready."

I chuckled. "Not here. I have something else I'd like to show you, and it will make the telling somewhat more bearable."

I held out my arm for her, and she hesitated.

"Please, Mina," I implored. "Just trust me a little longer."

Nodding, she wrapped her hand around my arm, and warmth bloomed beneath her touch. I smiled gratefully and led her back down the hallway.

As we passed room after room, her little gasps of delight at my home pleased me. We paused quietly so she could admire the palatial library, the frescoed ballroom, and the Roman-styled baths—the gallery of my favorite paintings and sculptures accumulated throughout my travels. She stared in confusion and envy at my laboratory, filled with state-of-the art equipment and volumes of scientific literature from cultures around the world.

I urged her on until we arrived at my chosen destination, my favorite room in the castle apart from the library. We descended two flights of marble steps into a candlelit alcove facing two massive oak doors carved with reliefs of Persephone in the Underworld.

Releasing her hand, I opened the doors and ushered her in. The first thing one sensed when entering this part of the castle was the warm air, thick with humidity. The second thing was the peculiar fragrance—warring scents of damp earth, a thousand varieties of perfumed flowers, rot and decay of old vegetation, and everywhere *life*. Then, as one's eyes adjusted to the low golden glow of the candlelit space, one could truly appreciate the wonder.

Mina stepped forward and turned in a slow circle.

"Rafael," she whispered. "It's like stepping into a jungle from a storybook! How is this possible?"

"Welcome to my sunken greenhouse," I said, pleased that she appreciated my favorite marvel. "The glass windows above us are hidden in the grounds around the estate and difficult for those above to see, but they let in enough light during the daytime for the plants to grow. I've collected most of these as seeds or cuttings from my travels and have longed for a place to nurture them. Plants, you see, when tended properly, can thrive for almost as long as I can. It's harder to keep and care for pets when their lifespans are but the blink of an eye for me."

She faced me, something like pity on her face. Ignoring it and the twinge of emotion it elicited in me, I continued.

"The ponds on either side contain several varieties of fish and frogs, and insects do much of the pollination. Those over there are the largest lily pads in the world," I explained, pointing to the massive leaves floating atop shallow black water.

Mina strolled along the marble paths, smiling in wonder. The tropical air condensed in small droplets on her glasses, and she took them off absently to clean them. "It's extraordinary," she whispered. "How does it stay so warm in here? I don't see any fireplaces."

"They are below us," I replied. "Stacks of bricks and tiles are heated much like they were in Roman bathhouses. The tiles beneath us bring the heat up, and it spreads out through the marble and rises upward. The sunlight during the daytime helps to heat the space, but of course, I only come here at night. My staff light the candelabras along the walls in the evening for me."

We walked beneath delicate trailing vines, hanging mosses, and fragrant tropical flowers until we reached a small grotto with a waterfall set back against the wall. A small table and two chairs sat in the middle of the grotto and spread before us was a sumptuous picnic.

Mina sat dutifully and waited as I poured her a cup of herbal tea—her preference from years ago. I poured some for myself and offered her a plate of sandwiches and almond cakes, as well as a crystal bowl of vibrant tropical fruits.

"Astonishing," she murmured, selecting a sliced mango.

Overhead, something flitted close to her hair, and she startled.

"Apologies for the behavior of my bats," I chuckled. "They can be rather greedy, but you needn't worry. These fellows only eat fruit."

I tossed a banana off to the side to entertain them and turned back to Mina, who was eyeing me with what I assumed were a million questions in her mind.

"Ask away," I said.

She scrunched up her face, pointedly searching for a place to begin.

"Botany, Rafael? Truly?"

"Mina, of all the things you could ask, you cast doubt upon my secret hobby?" Amusement sparkled in my tone, like bubbles in champagne.

She sipped her tea. "Never in my life would I have thought that you would find fascination in one of the sciences."

"You wound me, my dear. I am not the same vampire I was

all those years ago, hiding from my tutors and cheating my way through exams. Besides, it was your father who sparked my interest in the subject," I said.

"Papa?" she asked, eyebrows lifting. "How?"

I sighed. "Mina, here is as good as place as any to tell you what I must."

Sensing my trepidation, she placed a hand on my arm. "Despite our past, Rafael, I am here to listen."

I took a deep breath and began.

CHAPTER SEVEN
RAFAEL

April 16, 1768
Château du Diable

"When you and your father came to our townhome in Buda that evening, neither of you could know what kind of an effect it would have on our family. My father had heard of your father's reputation—and now, the great Doctor Van Helsing was in our part of the world? If anyone could have found an end to our ancient curse, it would have been him. What my father didn't count on, however, was you," I said.

"Me?" Mina echoed, her brows knitting together.

I nodded. "When it was agreed that you and your father would come to our ancestral home in Wallachia to help find a cure, we all believed it would only be a matter of time before the good doctor found what we needed and the both of you would be on your way. You were just a girl, then—a young, annoying, impetuous sixteen. No one paid much attention to you, Mina."

She snorted. "And these are the words of a gentleman."

I grinned in response. "I never claimed to be a gentleman, and I was always a terrible prince."

"Pray, continue delighting me with these flattering memories," she quipped.

"For the two and a half years that you stayed with us, my father grew to suspect my *attachment* to you. At the time, it meant little because Laszlo was set to replace my father as heir to the throne of Wallachia, and I was free to be the spoiled monster I was, indulging every whim of sin and vice. My father frowned upon my flirtation with you but knew that stopping it would only increase my ardor," I explained. "But then the unthinkable happened."

Mina placed her teacup onto the table with shaking hands.

"We fell in love," she murmured.

I nodded once, swallowing around the lump of emotion in my throat.

"You were eighteen then. Your father—while making great strides in understanding the blood plague—was no closer to finding a cure than any of the others had come. He discovered so much about it, but when he couldn't explain to my father *why* only my family would be born with the curse and every other sufferer simply had to be bitten, my father lost faith."

"Yes," Mina nodded, shuddering with the awful memories. "I remember the argument they had. I half expected your father to impale mine and leave him to rot on that horrible castle's battlements."

I frowned. "I won't pretend that didn't cross his mind."

Squeezing her eyes shut, Mina blew out a breath laced with disappointment.

"My father accomplished a great many things in his life," she said. "But on his deathbed, the unanswered riddle of the blood plague was all he spoke of."

I froze. "His deathbed? Mina, when...?"

She waved away my concern. "Long ago, Rafael."

I swallowed. "I'm so sorry. I didn't know."

She lifted a shoulder in forced casualness, but I sensed the air between us thickening with grief.

"It was a natural death," she said. "Given the horrors we've seen in this world, I think that's something we can at least take comfort in."

Realization dawned. "That is why you were able to study," I said. "He didn't want you to when he was alive, but with his death, you must have found a way."

"My mother's passing preceded his by a few short months. I think his broken heart played a factor in his decline, as was his desire to be with my mother in Heaven. I was lucky to grow up without much family. My parents left me with their modest estate and a comfortable annuity. That, along with my father's reputation, was nearly enough to earn my place at the university in Padua," she said quietly.

I couldn't contain my shock. "They allowed a woman to study?"

She turned a disapproving gaze on me. "Don't be ridiculous. I bound my breasts and attended as a man. Wilhelmina is very close to Wilhelm, you see, and rather easy to forge on the necessary documents. By the time I earned my degree and made my way to Paris, most people who truly needed my services were willing to overlook the inconvenience of my gender."

I barked a laugh and sat back, enjoying the swell of pride and admiration I felt for her.

She misinterpreted my laughter and sniffed in affront.

"I would never allow my sex to get in the way of a first-rate medical education," she said haughtily.

"I cannot, for one moment, believe how stupid and blind

the other students and faculty must have been to not recognize your feminine charms," I said.

She smiled at that, warming me more than the thick tropical air of the greenhouse.

"Rafael, while I appreciate all that you're telling me, not much of it is new information. I knew your father disliked and distrusted me; I knew you were a spoiled wastrel who I fell in love with, anyway; I knew your father and mine had a falling out. What you haven't told me, however, is what happened the night we were supposed to elope," she remarked. Then, there was a delicate tightening of her jaw and her eyes narrowed. "And why you betrayed me."

"Yes, my dear, I'm coming to that. When I proposed to you that night, I couldn't believe that you would dare to say yes. Knowing what it meant for you…knowing what it meant for me…what it would mean for us. When I planned our elopement, I thought I'd accounted for every eventuality, except, of course, for my brother Laszlo's disappearance."

Shock startled a gasp from Mina. "Wait, he disappeared the same night? I didn't hear of his absence until the following year. Why didn't you tell me?"

I shook my head. "I didn't have time, Mina. I was in the stables, preparing for our departure when I found out. The stable master told me he'd caught Laszlo saddling our fastest horse the evening before. He gave me the letter Laszlo had left for our father."

"What did it say?" Mina asked.

"Laszlo had fallen in love," I answered. "The girl was one of my mother's French maids."

Mina's brow furrowed. "French maids…not Marguerite?"

I nodded. "The very same."

"She was very beautiful," Mina remembered. "But Laszlo

was always so serious. I can't believe he was ruled by his passion enough to run away with a maid."

"We all underestimated him," I admitted. "But as it is said, *'Smooth runs the water where the brook is deep.'* Nevertheless, he alone noticed me making plans for us and beat me to it. His letter to my father said as much. He and Marguerite were leaving to start a life together, and it was useless for my father to pursue them. He had no interest in the throne and felt that I deserved a share of the responsibility of our family's weighty history."

Mina plucked another slice of mango from the fruit bowl, and I watched her take a bite and lick the juice from her fingers. My cock hardened immediately, and I gripped my chair, struggling to keep my thoughts on my confession.

"I took the letter to my father immediately," I choked out, nearly drowning in my desire. "And what a fool I was to do so. Upon reading it, he flew into a rage, sending men after Laszlo and demanding to know about the elopement Laszlo had mentioned. *Our* elopement, Mina. He told me he was disowning and disinheriting Laszlo and that I would be taking his place. If I refused—if I went ahead with our elopement—he would hunt us down and kill you."

Mina froze at that, dropping the fruit onto her plate.

"He wouldn't," she breathed, incredulous. "I know your father never cared for me, but he wouldn't resort to murder."

I laughed. "My father was almost four-hundred years old by then. He had been on and off the throne of Wallachia several times—each time seized through war and violent bargains. He alone started the false rumors that my brother had the penchant for impaling people, all to spread the fear that would help our family maintain control of Wallachia. It was my father who enjoyed torturing prisoners. Vlad—*Laszlo,* as he always was to me—never tortured or killed anyone unjustly off the field of battle."

"Why didn't you tell me any of this before?" Mina asked, astonished.

"Because most of that happened before I was born. I was a late addition to my father's house. I wasn't born until 1701, long after my father had given up the hope of a second son. He and Laszlo came from a different time—one where brutality and fierce religious devotion reigned. I was more *Age of Enlightenment* than they were, much to my father's disappointment."

"You told me it was rude to ask a vampire his age," Mina said. "But you never told me you were that much younger than your father and brother."

"My point in telling you all of this is not to trouble you with my family's wretched history. The only reason I did not meet you the night we were meant to elope was because I believed my father's vow. If I didn't step in and take Laszlo's place, he would kill you and, I suspect, your father. I couldn't let that happen. I planned to bide my time and wait for things to settle, then hunt down Laszlo and force him to come back and make peace with Father," I continued, rubbing at the ache building in my chest. The pain of revisiting those memories warred with the impulse to lay everything bare before her.

Mina stood abruptly, tears gathering in her eyes.

"I waited that night," she exclaimed, her voice echoing off the glass and stone walls. "I waited for you to come and take me away. I waited for us to start a life together, Rafael. I would have walked through Hell for you. Why couldn't you simply tell me?"

"Don't you understand? I didn't want you to walk through Hell for me. I wanted you to have sunlight and flowers and *life*. Even if that meant life without me," I said quietly. "I knew you would take on the world to be with me, so I did the only thing I could think to do."

"You slept with another woman," she said bitterly.

"No!" I grabbed her arm and pulled her to me, holding her fiercely against my chest. "No, I didn't. I told the stable boy to *tell* you he'd caught me with another woman. I wouldn't touch another woman for years after that."

Mina was as still as a statue in my arms.

"I went back to Amsterdam the very next day, forced to endure my mother trotting suitor after suitor in front of me in a desperate attempt to marry me off and put an end to my incessant wheedling to attend university," Mina said. "Father continued to travel more and more after that. He still sought answers for the blood plague, and so he kept watch for news of your family."

"I'm sorry," I confessed, knowing the words meant little in the face of her pain.

"It is done," she acknowledged, the hurt still evident in her voice. "I am glad you told me."

The soft trickle of the waterfall was the only sound for several minutes as I gathered the courage to finish.

"I did as my father asked. I stayed to learn how to rule. His rage at Laszlo never cooled, and for a long time, I didn't hear anything that would give me a clue as to my brother's whereabouts." My words became a whisper of lingering grief and emotion strangled my voice. "I was left alone with my father, without Laszlo to buffer our fractured relationship. My father hated me and resented that I was the one left to carry his legacy. Our remaining years together were..." I faltered. *Brutal. Unkind.* "...difficult."

Before she could say or do anything that would diminish my resolve, I carried on.

"And then while I was away, traveling back from the

Ottoman Empire, I received the news that my father was assassinated. He died as cruelly as he lived, and I barely escaped the ensuing political chaos. I went into hiding for a time, traveling under different identities. Soon, I had word of a mysterious disease—the blood plague—cropping up in the eastern part of France. I suspected Laszlo had something to do with it, or the men my father had sent after him who'd never returned. I set out after him. More and more cases were popping up, and it wasn't long after that the rumors took on a life of their own. Unfortunately, I still seem to be at the heart of them, even though I've been trying to stop the spread of the plague."

Mina's jaw dropped. "What? You have? How?"

"Your father inspired my interest in botany. I've been using his notes to try and find a cure myself. I enjoy the study of plants, but I wouldn't have come to it if I hadn't been seeking a cure for the destruction my family's curse has caused," I admitted.

Appearing bewildered and overwhelmed, Mina sat back down, rubbing at the spot between her brows.

"Why does The Order believe you are to blame?" she asked. "Why are they hunting you, Rafael?"

"Truthfully, I do not know. I can only guess Laszlo's disappearance and my father's death have left me the sole heir to that particular mantle," I said. "And there is some truth to that. If I'd sought my brother sooner, perhaps this would have been in my power to prevent. Besides, my reputation for being a young rogue that led to the moniker "Devil" surely helped the rumors spread. Only now, I'm far worse than a wastrel and a cad—they all see me as Lucifer himself."

We were silent for a time, listening to the fluttering of the bats and the steady symphony of frogs and insects heralding a new day.

"Sunrise is upon us," I said, surprised that I'd lost track of time.

"So," Mina began slowly. "Your father is gone. Your throne is gone. You've been here hunting Laszlo and trying to stop the blood plague, all while The Order nips at your heels. Where do I fit in?"

I stared at her, perplexed.

"Where do you fit in? Mina, yes, I am here to right my family's wrongs, but I am also here for you. I've never stopped loving you, my brilliant doctor, and it's the promise of a future with you that has inspired me to do better for this world. I hoped to have more time...to be further along in my search for the truth and the cure, but The Order's actions have forced me to show my hand sooner than I wished."

I reached for her, but she pulled away, rising to her feet.

"And with all of this—with twenty years of absence between us—I'm simply supposed to take you at your word? To trust you? We don't even know each other anymore, Rafael. I didn't know any of this! You had no idea my father had passed. You don't know what I've been through over the last two decades! You think that coming here, weaving this tale of woe—true or not—and remembering my favorite tea blend is enough to wash away the grief, the betrayal, the time?" Mina whirled around the grotto, tears shining in her eyes.

"I have nothing *but* time. My love for you has not changed. Twenty years is nothing to me," I insisted.

"It is to me!" she shouted. "You could have written, you could have sent for me, you could have shared some of this precious knowledge. We could have spent some of those years working together, looking for Laszlo, trying to find a cure. But instead, you selfishly sat in waiting, allowing me to think the worst of you because—why? You weren't ready? Your greenhouse was still being built? You didn't yet possess the answers that would make it impossible for me to refuse you?"

She shook her head in disbelief.

"All this time I've been atoning for what I thought were your sins, and now you tell me they are Laszlo's? What am I to do with this information, Rafael? I forced my heart to heal from you long ago, secure in the knowledge that you didn't care. You were happy with your father's legacy and a family curse that leeched from the confines of your horrible castle."

Stunned into silence, I could only watch as the tempest of her righteous anger dashed any hopes of our future together.

"I spent twenty years believing it was my fault. *I* wasn't enough for you. You allegedly fell into the arms of another woman because I wasn't enough...I wasn't a princess, I wasn't immortal, I wasn't a vampire, I wasn't worldly enough, I wasn't wealthy or charming or glamorous. I was the simple human daughter of a human scientist—the scientist who had failed you. That's why I believed it."

She shook her head again, and the motion gutted me to my rotten, black core.

"It wasn't that I thought the worst of you all these years, Rafael. It's that I thought the worst of *me*."

CHAPTER EIGHT
MINA

April 17, 1768
Château du Diable

My words were like cannon fire in the softness of Rafael's underground jungle. Suddenly, the warm, damp closeness of this tropical atmosphere felt all too suffocating, and I was desperate for fresh, cool air. Rafael had gone still and silent, and part of me wondered if he'd heard my words at all. I turned from him, hurrying toward the massive oak doors that would lead me away from here. *Away from him.*

I climbed the stairs and strode down the main hallway, my mind a tangle of conflicting emotions. I wanted to be outside in the cold sunshine, or back in my clinic, or sitting in Charlotte's parlor at *Château de Ruisseau Magdelaine*, laughing at scandalous stories of her love life before Antoine. I wanted to be anywhere but here, where I felt the walls pressing in on me and the weight of expectation like a millstone around my neck. Aimlessly, I drifted down the hallway until I found myself standing in the doorway of Rafael's laboratory.

I stepped inside, my curiosity overpowering my need for mindless escape. Floor to ceiling bookshelves lined one wall, while the other held countless glass specimen jars filled with all manner of flora and fauna. A great table stood in the middle of the room, covered with scientific equipment—some of which I'd never seen before. My gaze snagged on a beautiful brass compound microscope at the center of the table. Next to it lay an open book—Rafael's observations.

Without thinking, I bent over the book and read some of his tightly scrawled notes. It seemed he'd been experimenting with the effects of garlic and wolfsbane on two types of vampire blood, his own and a turned vampire. I shifted my attention to the microscope.

Dieu, but I wanted one. They were incredible instruments that many of the brightest minds were using and improving upon, but they were too expensive for me to purchase. I leaned forward to peer into the eyepiece.

I gasped. Based on the appearance of the specimen, I wagered it was a blood sample, but I'd never seen blood like this before. The power of magnification made the cells enormous to my eyes.

"It is a new model," came a deep voice at the door. I froze, embarrassed about being caught but too entranced by what I was seeing. "The magnification is one hundred times what the human eye can perceive."

"It is truly remarkable," I murmured, afraid to meet his gaze.

"What do you think of my observations?" he asked, leafing through the pages in his notebook.

Is that…nervousness in his voice?

Finally, I looked up. I did not possess the ability to lie easily.

"The experiments with garlic and wolfsbane have been

done," I said. "They are nothing more than folk cures. They do not affect the disease."

"Yes," he nodded, looking oddly chagrined. "Yes, I'd read that."

"Why did you try to replicate the experiment?"

Rafael shifted, avoiding my eyes. "I thought, perhaps, if I tried with different types of blood, it might yield different results."

I nodded, impressed. "That is a sound hypothesis. What did you discover?"

"The results were the same," he answered in a deflated tone.

"Ah, but you learned something in the process, didn't you?" I encouraged. "And your manner of testing is smart. Why should we expect that the results of different treatments should be the same on your blood over the blood of a turned vampire? Much differentiates your abilities from theirs. It would make sense that you would react to stimuli in different ways."

Pride flashed in Rafael's face but evaporated quickly. In its place settled his mask of cool indifference.

I chewed at my bottom lip, embarrassed by my earlier outburst and rejection of his hopes. I didn't want to be at odds with him, and I didn't wish for us to go back to the way we'd been—separated by so many things. I wanted him near. I wanted to believe what he'd told me. But I needed time to reconcile twenty years of disbeliefs. How could I make him understand? How could I ask him for patience when he'd waited so long already? What could I say to ease my own anxiety?

"You have a very fine laboratory," I offered stupidly.

"Thank you, Doctor."

Ah, so we're back to Doctor. I cringed.

"Rafael, I am sorry for my outburst. My anger tells me that the wounds I claimed to have healed long ago were not so smartly healed. I reacted...badly," I apologized.

He tilted his head to study me, but the mask did not waver.

"You must be wanting to return home," he said distantly. "I'm certain your friends will be worried."

His manner sickened my heart—it seemed he was not the only one with the capacity to cause pain.

"No, but...well, yes, I'm sure they are. Do you think they are safe?" I wondered.

He lifted one shoulder in nonchalance. "If you trust them, then I do."

"That's a non-answer," I shot back.

He pursed his lips, and I found myself staring at his perfectly formed mouth.

"Mina, if you do not wish for me to pursue you, I will keep my affections to myself. But I'm afraid I must ask you for help. I need to find Laszlo, and I want to help end this blood plague. I have failed on both accounts thus far. As you said, The Order is closing in on me and I don't have people I can trust. I need your keen mind and the skills of your friends."

His tone was pleading, but his handsome face betrayed none of the emotion contained within him.

I sighed. "Well, if it was The Order who tried to take me, I suppose I'm already in danger."

Rafael grabbed my hand in one of his supernaturally quick moves. His eyes bored into mine with the intensity that frightened and excited the primal parts of me.

"Mina," he rumbled, his low voice barely more than a growl. "I won't let anything happen to you. I would ruin this world without a thought to keep you safe—even if you do not wish to be mine."

Yes, yes! My body arched toward him, spurred by its

magnetic attraction to the man I'd long considered my mate. My traitorous mind halted the move but couldn't stop me from closing my eyes and tilting my lips up to his for the kiss I knew would come.

The kiss I'd told him I didn't want. *Mina, you wretched liar.*

I felt the air between us change as he leaned forward, but the kiss never arrived. In an instant, he was across the room at the doorway again.

"Follow me," he said, turning away. "I'll ensure you're safely returned to Charlotte's home."

Every silent step he took down the hall was another crack in my already bleeding heart.

"YOU'LL FORGIVE ME IF I DON'T COME WITH YOU," RAFAEL said stiffly. It was well after sunrise, but it was impossible to tell given the depth of his underground abode.

Guilt and frustration gnawed at me as he led me through the labyrinth of hallways and tunnels on our way back to the empty, crumbling tower.

"Rafael," I started, unsure of what I was planning to say. "I'm sorry for earlier. Truly."

He did not stop or look back. "Yes. So you've said."

"You must understand," I tried again, reaching for his arm. "I need time to think about everything you said to me. There were a great many revelations in your words—twenty years of my belief in untruths and half-truths that I will have to come to terms with. I am sorry for what you endured in that time— for your father, for the loss of your home, for the arduous road ahead of you. I am sorry for our miserable separation and two decades of heart-wrenching loneliness. I felt those things too. I do not pretend that my life has been easy in the wake of your abandonment, but I have crafted it into something of my own."

Finally, he paused. We reached the threshold of the tower, some sixty feet below the hidden entrance to his castle. He turned to face me, his expression dark and forbidding.

I forced myself to continue. "When I thought that you were responsible for the blood plague—the only disease my father truly failed to understand—I thought it was my calling. My punishment for falling short of expectations, my family's expectations, your father's expectations, your expectations. I threw myself into this work because I felt like I owed it to everyone. Finding out so much of that is wrong has left me...*unmoored,* in a way. I care for you, Rafael. I always have. I always will. But I have been alone so long, you must at least give me leave to find my own way through this."

He raised his hand to caress my cheek but did not touch me. His fingertips hovered for a moment, and his lips parted on a breath.

"Mina..." he whispered.

I moved to lean into the touch, but he pulled his hand away, jaw flexing tightly. Whatever he'd been about to say died in the space between us. He reached for a wrought-iron candelabra sticking out of the wall and wrenched it back. There was a series of loud groans and clicks and a small stone staircase unfolded out of the wall, winding its way up the tower to a small round door hidden in the ceiling.

Rafael stepped back, letting his hand fall to his side.

"There is a windlass at the top of this tower that will help you descend. My coachman is waiting to assist you, and then he will take you on to Charlotte's. I will await your decision about Laszlo and my work on the plague, but please make haste. I fear for the safety of France, as well as for you. Trust me when I say The Order is a powerful and unfortunate enemy," he said, his words clipped.

I wanted to say goodbye. I wanted to say countless things. But before my thoughts could take form, Rafael inclined his head in a tense bow and strode back down the hallway from whence we'd come.

Feeling chastised and raw with emotion, I blew out a shuddering breath and began the long climb up the stairs. The farther away I moved, the worse I felt. I regretted some of my words, but not all of them, and Rafael's reaction shamed me and made me feel the worst kind of guilt at hurting him. Then, thoughts of anger would surface at my shame—could he really expect me to fall into his arms after twenty years and countless lies between us? Never mind the fact that we'd shared that kiss...*Mon Dieu, that kiss.*

I licked my lips at the memory.

He'd tasted so much better than I remembered. I couldn't count the number of times I'd dreamed of such kisses. And the way he looked at me as if I were the only woman in the world, like Eve stepping in the garden to meet Adam. No, not Adam... Someone more primal. One of the old gods.

Hades.

Memories came hard and fast then, and my knees nearly buckled with the remembered pleasure of making love. Rafael had thought himself Hades ...dark, forbidding, cold, and immortal. He'd called me his Persephone and told me I'd bloomed at his touch. I was so young, so naive, so much like spring to his hellish winter.

How much I loved him. *How angry I am at him.* What kind of life was he imagining for us? We would be parted by time or some unnatural death. I would age, gathering wrinkles and aches, and he would simply *be.* Trapped like an insect in amber.

I wouldn't pretend the idea of the transformation hadn't crossed my mind. In all my work and research, I'd considered making the change. But each time, I would think of the warmth of the summer sun and the vibrance of a rainbow after a thunderstorm and reject the idea of living without those wonders. Certainly, the night held its charms, but I wanted it all. Sun, moon, stars. Day and night. Spring and winter.

Myself...and Rafael.

I'd reached the top of the staircase and cast one long, dizzying look back down. Then, steeling my courage for what I knew lay ahead, I pushed open the trap door and stepped into the chilly April morning.

AFTER THE SOMEWHAT AWKWARD DESCENT WITH THE WINDLASS AND no small amount of complaining on my part, I found myself facing Rafael's impressive carriage. Four sleek, black horses, so perfectly matched they could have been two sets of twins, stamped impatiently in front of the large black conveyance. A footman helped me inside, and I frowned at the beautiful interior. Deep, plush seats covered in red velvet and satin cushions spoke to Rafael's early years as a tempting rake. I didn't want to consider how many women he'd had in this carriage.

Thick fur blankets and a small basket of almond cakes sat on the empty seat, needling me with even more guilt. He'd obviously ensured I would have every comfort, even if I treated him abominably. As much as I felt like I didn't deserve such kindness, I wouldn't want to snub him any more than I already had, so I sat back, wrapped myself in the cozy blankets, and nibbled at the sweet pastries.

The carriage lurched forward, and I leaned back against the cushions. My mind swirled with the chaos of the previous evenings, making it hard for me to focus long enough to examine my feelings. Emotions clashed and my heart pounded, but I suspected some of that had to do with what I knew would come when I showed up at Charlotte's château. I was certain Charlotte and Daphne hadn't been involved in my kidnapping, but I was even more worried The Order had managed to plot and carry out a mission without their knowledge. That meant there was a chance *les DD* had underestimated the old fools.

I took a deep breath and closed my eyes. There was nothing I could do until I arrived, and though I had no idea what I would say to her, I trusted she would at least hear me out when I explained everything. At least, I hoped.

The gentle rocking of the carriage soothed me, as did the small charcoal heater tucked beneath the cushions, and it wasn't long before I drifted off. I awoke sometime later with the sensation of the carriage slowing and noticed that the light filtering in through the curtains had brightened to a silvery cold afternoon. When we finally stopped, the driver climbed down and opened the door for me.

I wondered what Rafael's servants thought of him, and of me—if they'd heard us arguing and thought badly of me for it. I started to say something to the driver but thought better of it. It was just as well, as I was knocked off my feet by the most horrific-looking wolf creature that anyone could imagine. It was as if a normal wolf had mated with a demon, with long gangly limbs, massive jaws, enormous claws, and murderous red eyes. I would have screamed if I didn't already know this particular beast.

"Comtesse," I huffed. "Forgive me for my impertinence, but

in this form, you are rather weighty. Would you be so kind as to get off me?"

The terrifying beast whined and licked my face, upsetting my spectacles. Then, with a horrendous bark, she sat back on her haunches. I got up and brushed myself off, frowning at the huge tears her claws had made down the front of my lovely lemon-yellow gown.

"*Merde*," I swore. "This was a new gown, Charlotte, and I rather liked it."

She whined at me again, then trotted off toward the front of her ostentatious, yet stunning, estate. Once we entered the grand foyer, she shifted shape—a gruesome process that I was completely entranced by. Her lupine snarls of pain became human bellows as she turned back into the beautiful chestnut-haired comtesse I knew and loved.

Once in human form, she ran to me and threw her arms around my neck, holding me in an impossibly tight embrace.

"Oh, Mina!" she cried, tears spilling down her cheeks. "We were so worried! We've all been out searching for you! We knew something was wrong, but we couldn't figure out what happened or where you went! Where have you been, my friend? What has happened? Are you well?"

"Yes, Charlotte, I'm well. I will tell you everything, *chérie,* but...don't you think it might be easier to have this conversation with a few more..." I waved vaguely at her nudity. "...layers?"

She sniffled and wiped her tears, then giggled.

"Of course, Mina! Our attitudes toward clothing in my household have become rather lax since Antoine and I have grown accustomed to shifting. Don't worry—I did speak with the household staff about it at length." At that moment, a young maid rushed forward with an exquisite dressing gown of shimmering pink satin. Charlotte donned the gown and led me upstairs.

"Daphne and Étienne will be along later this evening. We organized search parties, you see. Antoine and I took the day shifts, and Daphne and Étienne took the night shifts. We were able to follow part of your trail, but…" she grew quiet, then offered me an anxious smile. "Well, we can all discuss things when everyone arrives. Let's get changed, and I'll have lunch laid out in the dining room. I've had some gowns tailored for you—don't look at me like that, Mina, this is as much for my benefit as it is yours—and they're in the lilac guest room down the hall, where you usually stay. I've taken the liberty of having some of your things brought here. Nothing special, just some of your books, notebooks, toiletries, and your doctor's valise. Anything to make you more comfortable here, *chérie*. Daphne left a notice on your clinic door and informed your neighbors that you would be taking a short holiday away to visit family in the country. Hopefully, we can get to the bottom of things soon and you won't have to take too much time away from your patients. Mina, darling, is this all too overwhelming? I'm *so* sorry—listen to me, prattling on when you've been through God-knows-what trauma. Are you simply exhausted? Do you need to rest first?"

Charlotte capped this loving tirade with another fierce hug and a soft kiss on my cheek.

"Thank you, Charlotte," I replied. "No, I am well. I wouldn't say no to lunch and a clean dress, but I'm ready to tell you everything."

CHAPTER NINE
MINA

April 17, 1768
Château de Ruisseau Magdelaine

CHARLOTTE WAS EAGER TO HEAR MY STORY BUT INSISTED I TAKE SOME time to rest, bathe, and put on one of the new gowns she'd had made for me. Even though I avoided spirits most of the time, she persuaded me to take a snifter of brandy into the large copper bathtub the servants had set in front of the fireplace in my guest room.

"It's the best way to warm up," she'd said with a wink. "Now, off you go, and take your time. It's hours still before Daphne and Étienne will awake. I'm sure Antoine will return any moment now, and you can tell us all you need to."

I swirled my fingers lazily through the steamy lavender-scented water, sipping at the brandy. Charlotte had been right. Warmth settled in the pit of my stomach and stretched through my limbs as I sat thinking.

Had I been unfair to Rafael? Had he been unfair to me? Most

likely we'd both been a bit unfair to each other. I didn't know what I wanted to say to Charlotte about him—about my feelings for him now...after everything. I didn't think I knew the truth of my feelings myself. *Dieu, I am sounding more and more like some overly romantic French woman. Pull yourself together, Mina!*

The cognac started to sour in my stomach, and I remembered I'd only eaten a few almond cakes, some of Rafael's exotic fruit, and thin broth over the last couple of days. Delicious smells wafted up from the kitchens—baking bread, freshly brewing coffee, and roasting meat. Though Charlotte and her fiancé were werewolves and could subsist entirely on raw meat, they'd both had rather epicurean tastes in their human lives and continued to eat their favorite dishes with gusto. They employed a larger kitchen staff than almost any other household outside of Versailles.

Stepping out of the bath, I picked up the lovely garments that had been laid out. Rather than the formal court dress that Charlotte often preferred for herself, she'd selected a more modest design without the wide *panniers* that were fashionable evening wear. I pulled on the clean chemise and soft woolen stockings, then layered the quilted stays and fine linen petticoats. The bodice and skirts of the outer gown were a shimmering lilac velvet with silver flowers embroidered throughout. It was beautiful—certainly finer than anything I had in my closet. *Almost* as fine as the lemon silk gown now lying ruined upon the floor.

I dressed myself without the help of a lady's maid, and I was eminently more grateful that Charlotte had taken my status and profession into consideration when ordering the gowns. I pinned up my long, dark hair, replaced my spectacles, and made my way downstairs—only slightly unsteady from the heady warmth of the cognac.

I found Charlotte in the dining hall, dressed in a stunning gown of rose-colored silk with ivory bows.

"Mina, you look absolutely lovely. Do you feel a touch restored?" she asked, gesturing to the seat across from her.

"Yes, Charlotte, thank you. Has Antoine returned?" I replied, taking my seat.

She nodded. "He arrived home not too long ago," she said. "He is resting for now. It's been a long few days for all of us."

I frowned. "I'm sorry my absence has been so troublesome for so many of my friends."

"Hush, Mina, don't be ridiculous! We're *family*. We'd all go to the ends of the earth for you, *chérie*. Now, are you hungry? You must be. Me, I am simply famished! I had the chef prepare enough food to satisfy an army."

With a wave of her hand, her servants brought forth silver platter after silver platter covered in delights to tempt even my humble palate. I tucked in to cuts of ham, savory pies, roasted fowl and fish, poached eggs, bread, pastries, cheeses, and two decanters of wine. Charlotte was satisfied that I had an appetite—she watched me like a hawk.

After we both finished platefuls of food, she led me to the front parlor and sat me in front of the fireplace in the most comfortable chair. We took a moment to settle in as the coffee and sherry was poured, and then she looked at me with the intensity of a cat eyeing a canary.

"Now," she urged. "Start wherever it pleases you."

I swallowed, suddenly nervous.

"It is difficult for me to know where to begin," I said. "So I think I will start with the events of the other night, when I was supposed to come here."

Charlotte refilled my coffee cup and hers, and I continued.

"Did you know The Order sent men to watch me?" I asked.

Shock flashed in her eyes, followed by instant anger.

"What? No! They wouldn't...how could they...without Daphne's and my permission! They know you are protected!" Her claws grew, lethal and sharp, until she took a breath to calm herself. "I'm so sorry, Mina! Daphne and I should have expected them to do something reprehensible. These men watching you—what happened with them?"

"After weeks of watching and following me, something changed. The night I was meant to come see you, they kidnapped me, drugged me with *far* too much laudanum, and shoved me in a carriage. They were taking me to the cemetery, Charlotte—the secret entrance to The Order."

Charlotte's eyes widened, and she pursed her lips.

"Monsters!" she spat. "We will make sure they pay. How did you escape?"

"Certainly not under my power," I said.

Charlotte understood immediately.

"The man in black?" she asked.

I nodded. "Rafael. Former—rightful—Prince of Wallachia."

"A prince!" Charlotte exclaimed. "Well done, Mina."

Ignoring her teasing grin, I continued.

"Rafael followed us and killed both men," I said bluntly. I didn't want to think about it too much, or the guilt would wash over me in a tidal wave. "He took me to his castle outside Rouen so I could recover from the laudanum. He said I would not be safe back at my clinic. According to one of the men, Pascal, The Order sent for me so they might question me about Rafael's whereabouts." My anger and betrayal laced the words with venom.

"Question you?" Charlotte's brows narrowed.

"As a witch," I said coldly.

"No," she breathed. "They wouldn't! Torturing witches has been banned for years! Even with the men in The Order becoming more polarized against the supernatural cause, such measures would mean they'd been hiding more from *les DD* than Daphne and I realized." She paled at the thought. "Could Rafael be mistaken?"

I shook my head. "One of his unique powers is the ability to...*compel* the truth from people. It would have been impossible for Pascal to lie."

Her eyes snapped to mine. "Do you trust him?"

"In this, I think so. I don't know what other motivation he would have to lie to me about it. You told me yourself The Order has been moving farther away from Daphne and Étienne's influence. They have been holding back the tide of brutality against vampires, but we all knew it was only a matter of time before their strength would be overwhelmed by the power of hate."

Charlotte stood and paced in front of the fireplace, anger rippling over her skin and making her eyes flash lupine gold and red.

"Even knowing that, it appears The Order has made the first move," she murmured, oddly calm. Without warning, she picked up a small vase from the mantle, studied it for a moment, and then heaved it against the wall with a fierce roar. The vase exploded into a cloud of porcelain dust.

"*Chérie,*" she said, kneeling at my feet. "I'm so deeply sorry. I should have prevented this. I'm overwhelmed by my rage and regret. I swear to you, dear one, their transgressions will not go unpunished."

"Do not berate yourself for the sins of others," I said, grasping her hands in mine. "That is a lesson I'm working to unlearn myself."

She smiled, wiped a tear from her cheek, and sat back down on the chaise across from me.

"There's more," I said, sipping my coffee to gather courage. "It is about the blood plague."

At that moment, Antoine stepped into the room with a soft knock on the doorframe. He looked more at ease than the last time I'd seen him. He was dressed in a loose cotton shirt and soft buckskin breeches, and his wavy brown hair hung loosely about his shoulders. With the moon-shaped scar across his temple and his slightly crooked nose, he reminded me of Ares, the god of war, but his temperament was infinitely more patient.

His eyes flickered over the smashed vase and then back to Charlotte, who shrugged by way of apology. He dropped a soft kiss on her forehead before bowing low to me.

"Doctor," he rumbled. "I'm most relieved to find you well."

"And you," I said. "You have my thanks and my apologies for suffering my misadventures."

"Darling, did you eat? There's plenty of food in the dining room if you'd like," Charlotte offered. Her tone was melancholy and distracted, and my gut twisted at the thought that she was blaming herself for what The Order had done.

Antoine inclined his head, studying me with his emerald eyes.

"It can wait, *l'amour*. I have a feeling the good doctor is about to tell us something rather important."

They both fixed me with a stare that made me want to squirm.

"You make me nervous—both of you! Stop looking at me like I'm a specimen to be studied. I said I would tell you, and I shall," I snapped.

They waited.

"The blood plague originated from Rafael's family," I said. "It began as an ancient curse upon his household and his family line. *Cursed to walk the earth forever for one's sins, drinking the blood of the damned,* that sort of thing. No one remembers much about the exact beginning or circumstances, which have been lost to time. What has lingered—up until quite recently—was the responsibility of the family to contain the curse. They did not turn others outside their family—it is forbidden and taboo. They are permitted to turn their mate during their wedding so they can continue their lineage. The offspring of those unions, while extremely rare, are born vampires. So far, they have been the only vampires *born* and not *made*. They're unlike any turned vampires you'll meet, possessing unique abilities beyond heightened senses and strength. They grow ever more powerful as they age, but the mantle of madness waits for the ones who live too long."

Antoine sat on a chaise opposite me, which looked amusingly small beneath his large frame. Charlotte sat next to him, clasping his hand.

"My father and I were brought to Wallachia to help find a cure for the family—the House of Dracul. There were two sons, Laszlo and Rafael. Laszlo was heir to the throne, but he fled to be with the woman he loved—a maid from their household. His father disinherited him and forced Rafael to take his place. It was around this time that the blood plague first escaped the confines of their castle."

"It was not Rafael's doing?" Charlotte asked, unable to hide her surprise and disbelief.

"Not according to him," I replied. "No, that is unfair of me... I do not believe he lies about this. He does not know exactly who is responsible, but he has come to France to find his brother and determine if he is the source. He wishes to help."

Antoine's brows shot up. "Help? How?"

Strangely, revealing Rafael's secret passion for botany felt like revealing something too intimate.

"Rafael has been searching for his brother and for a cure, just as I have. He knows The Order hunts him. He knew The Order had men watching me. He loathes The Order and does not trust them, and after the events of the other night, I'm not ashamed to say I trust them even less than I did before."

I looked pointedly at Charlotte.

"Daphne and I have been cautious about how much we revealed to The Order of *les DD's* activities. I regret the amount of time and energy I've given to them thus far, but trust that from now on, everything changes. As soon as Daphne and Étienne arrive, we'll figure out what our next move shall be," she insisted.

Antoine's face darkened. "Whatever we do next, we must proceed with caution. The Order still has the ear of the king, which makes defying them akin to treason."

Charlotte nodded. "This betrayal truly is horrible news. Both the vampires and the human peasants are already at their breaking point. If tensions increase, I fear an outright war. If only we knew more about what The Order knows and plans... It seems *les DD* will be embarking on our most dangerous missions yet."

Worry swirled in my stomach. For so long, I'd refused to join my friends in their secret organization because I thought myself separate, somehow. Neutral. It seemed I would be taking a stand after all.

"Mina," Charlotte said lightly. "Is there anything else?"

She pinned me to my chair with a knowing look. I swallowed, the lump in my throat full of emotion.

"Ah, I do believe I'll have some lunch after all," Antoine offered awkwardly. He tipped Charlotte's face up to his and kissed her softly on the lips. Her cheeks flushed pink.

"Go easy on her," he murmured as he left the room.

His departure made me feel uncomfortably exposed, and I folded my arms across my chest.

"Long ago, Rafael and I were in love," I finally admitted.

"We had plans to elope, but the night we were meant to leave, Laszlo's absence was discovered."

Charlotte sat forward on the edge of her seat, eyes wide in surprise.

"At the time, I wasn't aware of Laszlo's disappearance. That night, I was told that Rafael had been found in bed with another woman. I was devastated and angry, and because of his reputation, I believed it—too readily, perhaps. When I told my father, he was furious. He packed me up and sent me back to Amsterdam the very next day. My mother considered that the end of my ambitions for becoming a physician and tried for ages after that to marry me off. It was fortunate that she gave up after a while." Memories tightened my chest and tears threatened.

"After she and my father died, I had the time and freedom to pursue my career. I would hear occasional things about Rafael's family, but nothing substantial. I nursed a broken heart for a long time—years. Then news of the blood plague reached me, and I knew something had gone wrong in the House of Dracul."

"Oh, Mina," Charlotte breathed. "I'm so sorry. I could *kill* him for what he did to you!"

I shook my head, and the tears started to spill. I dashed them away with the back of my hand, but they would not stop flowing.

"I knew it was him in the cave outside Gévaudan, Charlotte —I realized he'd been the one to turn you. I'm so sorry, my friend. I have failed you!"

Charlotte rushed over and threw her arms around me.

"Hush, Mina! You have *not* failed me. I might not have chosen this fate, but it is mine alone. And without this curse, I would not have the gifts that allowed me to save Antoine. It is not your fault!"

Her kindness only made me cry harder. "Yes, it's my fault. My father and I should have found a way to cure the plague before it could spread. I should have gone after Rafael when I first heard about the blood plague outside Wallachia, but I didn't. And I should have told you about him sooner."

She wiped my tears on her handkerchief and clasped my hands.

"You're telling me now, Mina. These things are hard things to bear alone, and it grieves me that you have had to hold them within yourself for all this time. Rafael is certainly a villain for his behavior and what he put you through. To say nothing of turning me into some sort of hellish wolf monster with a taste for flesh," she added wryly.

"He came for me the other night," I said. "And again when The Order tried to take me. The things he told me, Charlotte...I don't know what to believe anymore. I don't know what to think."

"What do you mean?"

"He said he has returned for me. He's loved me all this time. He revealed that the night we were meant to elope, his father found out about Laszlo and forced Rafael to stay...that if Rafael tried to run away with me, his father would come after us and kill me," I blubbered. "Rafael says that in order to protect me, he had the servants lie about him sleeping with another woman—that he wasn't untrue to me that night."

"Oh, what rot," Charlotte scoffed. "That's it, Mina—I am going to cut off his head."

"He has been in France for almost ten years—just outside of Rouen. He has been looking for Laszlo and trying to find a cure for the plague on his own, and..." I swallowed nervously. "Waiting for the right time to make himself known to me in the hopes that we could finally be together."

Embarrassed with the display of far more emotions than I

normally allowed, I buried my face in my hands and waited for my dear friend to pass judgment. The only sounds in the room were the soft crackle of the fire in the hearth and the steady tick of the clock on the mantle. After what felt like an eternity, I peeked at Charlotte through my fingers. Her face was a curious mixture of anger, confusion, and sympathy.

"Charlotte?"

"I can't decide if I want to cut off his head or bring him here and watch him grovel until you two can run off and rut like wild animals. Possibly both, but not in that order," she grumbled.

I couldn't help but laugh, the relief feeling like sunlight after a storm. I should have known that she would stand by my side.

"I feel the same way," I said with a watery smile. "But it doesn't matter now, because I rebuffed his advances and yelled at him for making me believe the worst over the last twenty years."

"Rightly so," Charlotte chirped. "What did he expect after so long with no word? That you'd simply open your legs and let him in?"

"You mean, *open my arms*?"

"Oh no, darling," she said. "I definitely meant *legs*."

I felt my face turn as red as a beetroot.

"What happened then?" she prompted.

"Well, he went cold on me. I fear I've really hurt him," I answered.

"*Good.* He can have a taste of his own medicine," she sniffed. "Was that the end of your time together?"

I sighed. "He asked me to help him find Laszlo and to continue looking for a cure for the plague. He seemed concerned that The Order is now after him so aggressively that it puts me in danger."

"Yes, that *is* a problem," Charlotte replied, her brows knitting in the familiar way that meant she was working out a particularly difficult challenge. Then, noting the anxious look on my face, she patted my knee.

"Don't worry, Mina. We're not going to let anything happen to you. We *might* let something happen to Rafael for this mess, but it wouldn't be death or anything so permanent—just possible maiming."

I chuckled. "He is powerful, Charlotte, but maiming would be as permanent for him as it would be for any vampire or human."

"Would it? Pity. And I suppose if you two reconciled, you'd want the use of all his appendages," she nodded. "Well, thank you for telling me all of this, Mina. I know it wasn't easy. But please believe me when I say that you won't have to bear these burdens alone anymore. When Daphne arrives this evening, we'll figure out a solution and damn *anyone* who gets in our way."

CHAPTER TEN
RAFAEL

April 21, 1768
Dunkirk

I waited in the gloomy corner of *La Sirène*, drumming my fingers in annoyance on the filthy wooden table. In the twenty years between my failed elopement with Mina and now, I'd courted patience and had worked to curb the brash appetites that earned me the nickname "Devil" in my younger days, but in the last few weeks, I found patience eluding me once again.

I had all the time in the world, but the people around me did not. Time had become one more enemy for me to plot against

I was here because of a rumor and a begrudging lead—compelled through force from my last feed. The drunk fool had been harassing a blood whore down by the docks, and I was happy to remove him from her presence. Under the influence of my will, he told me to come here and wait for the ancient captain of a Hell-borne nightmare ship, the *Blood Bane*. According to a few sailors and soldiers, rumor had it the ship was crewed entirely by vampires—a fanciful notion, considering none of them could be on deck during the day, but I wasn't here to test the veracity of their legends. As the tales went, in their lifetimes, they'd been corsairs for King Louis XIV's vendetta against the English and the Dutch, but had turned pirate after the disappointing Treaty of Utrecht. When the blood plague arrived in France in 1748, those remaining leapt at the chance to pillage with near invincibility for the rest of their days. The hard, grizzled crew reconvened under the brutal captain, Lucien the Bloodless—so called because of his cold demeanor, supernatural condition, voracious appetite, and unwillingness to waste a drop of the life-giving liquid. They say he never let a single captive live.

One wonders how the tales were told.

After gathering up the shattered remains of my absent heart left in Mina's wake, I went back to work—playing out one of my recent leads in the hopes that it would bring me to Laszlo. If it was true that Lucien was the first vampire turned here twenty years ago, I had a lot of questions for him regarding his maker.

The tavern was cold, damp, and sparsely populated, mostly with men whose true loyalty was to the drink and none other. The very atmosphere of the place felt like purgatory—one had the sense of being enshrined in a fog of stillness and despair. It was nearly midnight when the bell above the door jingled—not a welcoming sound, but simply the herald of something else foreboding. The man who entered could have been a beggar by the looks of him, but I knew he was the one I'd come for.

Long, gray hair clung to his scalp and fell in greasy braids down his back. His pale beard matched, except for the rust-colored mustache that could have been the filth of old blood. It was possible that his stained, tattered clothes were more grime than fabric. His keen and all-seeing eyes, however, were the lightest shade of blue—so bright they almost looked white. It was somewhat unnerving being pinned by his icy gaze, and I wondered if that was the main reason for his nickname.

It was no surprise to me when he came to my table instead of approaching the bar.

"I heard you were looking for me," he said in a rough voice that sounded like low waves on a gravel beach.

"Captain," I greeted, smiling enough to show him my dual sets of fangs. "I'm honored to make your acquaintance. Won't you join me for a drink?"

The lines on the old man's face spoke of a hard and dangerous life, but his expression betrayed nothing as he sat across from me. I gestured for the barkeep to bring us a round of whatever they served around these parts.

"You aren't the first to come for me," he said, shrewd eyes assessing me. "But I expect you might be the only one who lives through the experience. *Might.*"

I ignored the threat and inclined my head. "If you can call this life," I retorted.

A glint of surprise flashed in his eyes. "What else would you call it?"

"Where I am from, we call it a curse."

"Only the self-righteous would call immortality a curse," he snarled. "For those of us who lived human lives scraping barely enough existence from the boots of everyone above us, immortality is yet another means to an end."

"What end is that?" I asked.

He shrugged. "Survival."

Two tankards of foul-smelling ale landed in front of us, practically thrown by a nervous tavern maid. I saw a hint of sadness tug at my companion's features and laughed.

"So, you have been a vampire long enough to understand

one of the varied costs of *survival*—the inability to drown one's loneliness and sorrows in spirits." I raised my mug to him. "To you, Captain, and your health."

He nodded at me, downed the entire tankard at once, and grimaced.

"You're not here on behalf of the English, the Dutch, or the French," he rumbled. "So, you're not here to try and hang us for piracy. It's been some time since we've been out to sea—long enough that our ship is probably more barnacle than timber, which makes me think this ain't some ill-advised revenge scheme. And I'm sure you aren't foolhardy enough to set out just to test the legend of the 'damned and damning Lucien the Bloodless.' Why are you here, then, old master?"

"I'm looking for someone," I answered.

"I thought you were looking for me," he said wryly.

"I'm here for your maker," I replied. "Perhaps you might point me to the vampire who turned you."

A condescending laugh scraped up through his chest and spilled forth from his lips.

"That *would* be telling," he said. "I'm no rat. A man's maker is his own business."

"Normally, I would agree with you," I said, leaning back in my chair. "And truly, I'm loath to pry into any man's personal affairs. But I'm afraid it's rather important."

"As is my honor," he replied.

"Come now," I soothed. "Honor is a luxury men like us cannot afford."

"Perhaps our honor is all we have," he argued.

I tilted my head. Without looking, I sensed that the remaining tavern patrons had left their seats and were shuffling toward the door. Four more grizzled, grim sailors stepped into the room, forming a barricade against the front door. The tavern maid and the barkeep scurried away into a back room, keenly aware of impending trouble.

I swirled the ale in the bottom of my tankard as two more men filed in, blocking off the back door that led to the adjacent docks.

"You say honor is all you have, and yet you think to ambush me with ten men?" I tutted.

"T'ain't an ambush, old master," the captain replied. "Just a precaution. We don't like strangers coming around here asking questions they ought not be asking."

"Captain." I sighed. "I have enjoyed our small chat, and I have afforded you the respect I think a man like you deserves. My patience, however, has its limits, so I'll ask you politely once more. Will you tell me who your maker was?"

The old man grinned at me, his yellowed fangs lengthening with the challenge.

"I will not."

His men stepped forward on hesitant, yet loyal, feet.

"Alas, I'd hoped to keep this friendly," I said, downing the rest of the bitter ale. "It's too bad. I rather liked the idea of a crew of vampire pirates marauding around the sea, plundering unsuspecting ships in the middle of the night. I'll try to spare some of you."

The two sailors on my right and left sides lunged at once, seizing both of my arms. They hauled me up while another vampire smashed one of the chairs, plucked one of the sharp legs from the pile of splintered wood, and drove it into my chest. I grunted with the force of it, and it hurt like the devil, but it was almost worth the pain to watch their faces fall when the realization dawned that I wasn't expiring like some commonly turned vampire. In shock, the men at my sides loosened their grip, and I shoved them back.

With a deep growl, I pulled the stake from my chest and

the wound began to knit together almost immediately. Captain Lucien gaped at me, confusion and fear playing at the lines on his weathered face.

"You see, Captain, for a vampire to die by wooden stake, he must be stabbed through the heart, a condition which affects turned vampires. Those of us who were born with this affliction never had hearts to begin with. All you've really done here is annoy me and ruin a perfectly good shirt," I said, exploding into my monstrous wolf form. I grabbed the nearest vampire and ripped his body in half, then tossed the pieces across the room. I snagged the other at my left, closed my jaws around his neck and wrenched his head from his shoulders, spitting it at Captain Lucien's feet. The other vampires fled through the front door, screaming all the way.

I pinned the captain with a steely gaze and shifted back into my human form. My clothes hung in tatters about me, and the black, viscous blood from his dead men dripped from my hands and face. Captain Lucien stared at me for a beat, then reached for the sword at his hip. Before he could draw, however, I forced him back into his chair with the sheer force of my will and compelled him to answer my questions.

"Who was your maker?" I snarled, power thrumming through my words. I wasn't surprised to feel resistance from him—he struck me as a man with a strong will.

"I don't know," he spit through clenched teeth.

Hm. Something between a lie and the truth. I had one more way of finding the information I'd come for, but it was a last resort.

Again, I compelled him, infusing my words with as much power as I could.

"Who was your maker?" I shouted.

His face twisted in rage as his lips formed the words.

"A girl," he choked out. "That's all I know."

A girl. Could he mean Marguerite? There was only one way for me to be certain, and it was something I dreaded. Keeping Lucien immobile with my will, I sank my fangs into his neck and drank.

Drinking from other vampires was taboo for a reason—it was damn near poison and would make one horribly ill. I'd even seen young, newly turned vampires die from it when the bloodlust seized them in a feeding frenzy. As an older, naturally born vampire, it would weaken me temporarily but not enough to stop me. The benefit of taking such a risk was that I would be able to taste for the captain's bloodline and determine if it was indeed Laszlo who turned him.

Beneath the warm, coppery tang of blood was something vaguely familiar...not my bloodline, but perhaps a degree or two removed...possibly someone Laszlo had turned. It could have been Marguerite. *Interesting.* I spit the rest of the foul liquid onto the floor and pushed Lucien back down into his chair. Dazed, he clutched at the wound on his neck that oozed thick, black blood.

"Not to worry, Captain," I said. "I didn't take enough to end your interesting, immortal life. As I said, I rather enjoy the idea of a roving crew of vampire pirates. It feels like something my father would have approved of, and I'm nothing if not sentimental. Now, if you'd be so kind, I'll relieve you of your greatcoat. I don't want to scandalize that fetching tavern maid."

Trance-like, he shucked his filthy coat and handed it to me with a glazed look in his eyes and a slack expression. I pulled it on and released my hold on him. He shook his head to clear it and regarded me with murder in his odd, pale eyes. I waited a moment to see if he would try for his sword once more, but when he did not, I inclined my head and wrapped the coat tightly around my bloodied, naked body.

"It's been a pleasure, Captain Lucien," I muttered to him as I strode out the front door.

Once outside, I walked down the docks to the end of the pier, trying to collect my thoughts and calm my predatory instincts. I inhaled the cold, salty air, heavy with the brine of the ocean and the smoke from nearby fires. The gentle lapping of the water on the timber piles and the soft rush of the waves crashing on the nearby rocks helped to soothe me and temper my anger.

The dark part of me wanted to kill the old captain and his crew for daring to challenge me, but that would likely attract attention and wouldn't serve any purpose other than soothing my frustrations. If I was honest with myself, the only way I wanted to vent those emotions was to chase Mina down, tear her clothes from her lush curves and bury myself inside her—reminding her of all the ways I could bring her pleasure and all the reasons we belonged together. Unfortunately, I'd rushed into telling her everything, and I'd consider myself lucky if I hadn't lost her for good.

Hell, what a mess. I wasn't any closer to finding Laszlo, I'd scared Mina off, and with every move, I sensed The Order closing in. I knew they'd hear of what transpired with Captain Lucien—the bastards had ears everywhere—but it was a risk I'd had to take. Moving in the shadows the last few years hadn't worked, so perhaps it was time to take some bigger chances.

As you did with Mina? The cruel thought snaked through my mind. I didn't regret telling her everything, but I berated myself for pushing her and forcing her to accept it before she had time to think on things. I would give her that time. I wouldn't—*couldn't*—risk losing her again. I needed to be patient—the one thing I struggled with when it came to Mina. *No matter.* I'd waited years to reunite with her and had a lifetime of loneliness before that. She was worth the time and my patience. She was worth everything.

And in the meantime, I would find Laszlo. My traitorous brother had a lot to answer for. Pulling the collar of the great-coat up to hide some of the blood smeared across my face, I ducked my head down and made my way back through the darkened streets of the port city.

As I wound between the narrow alleys, I heard a scuffle that gave me pause. Outside a tavern, a couple was cloaked in darkness—a young woman's tearful pleading and the older man's rough words informed me that the tryst had less to do with pleasure than power. The thought sickened me, and my fangs lengthened reflexively.

Ah, well. I need to feed this evening, anyway.

I approached the couple quietly, scenting fear and panic on the wind. It stirred my hunger and my bloodlust.

"Good evening," I murmured.

"Fuck off," the man grunted, not bothering to face me in lieu of caging the woman against a slimy, moss-covered wall.

Suddenly, the frustration, tension, anger, and passion for vengeance collided in me. I seized the man by his collar and whirled him around.

"I've never understood the type of man who can so easily torment another human for pleasure," I said. "But I think I will enjoy tormenting you." Then, to the woman, I said: "Take your leave, Mademoiselle."

She ran without a second glance.

"Who the fuck do you think you are?" the man growled. "You'll pay for that."

His fist flew clumsily, but because of our intimate proximity, it managed to connect with my cheek. The brief flash of pain excited me, and I grinned at him.

"Remove your clothing," I instructed, forcing him with my

will. Alarm lit in the man's eyes, but he did as I commanded. When he was naked and shivering from the frigid sea air, I released my hold on him.

"How does it feel to be so vulnerable?" I asked, pushing him back against the cold brick wall. "To be in the thrall of another being so much more powerful than you?"

"What the fuck are you?" he hissed, and I recognized the acrid scent of urine. The bastard had pissed himself. "Are you the devil?"

"Yes," I rumbled, infusing my answer with the terror of Hell's legions. I felt the man's heartbeat stutter beneath my fingers, and I wasted no more time. I sank my fangs into his neck and drank deeply. The smooth, salty, coppery liquid ignited in my mouth, and I felt strength and energy returning to me. When I sensed his body dying and his soul departing, I dropped his lifeless form onto the ground. I cast Captain Lucien's coat over the dead man, then donned my prey's clothes. They were too large for my lean form, but they would be good enough for now. Hoisting the man easily over my shoulder, I hurried back to the docks and threw him in the black water. His blood had restored me, and his flesh would nourish the creatures in Poseidon's realm.

"You walked a dark path in life," I said. "May your death serve a greater purpose."

"A fine sentiment from a creature born upon a dark path," came a soft voice behind me.

I whirled around, poised to strike at whoever had managed to sneak up on me. I couldn't remember a time when that had happened before—always hearing, smelling, sensing better than others. My shock intensified, however, when I stared into a pair of dark brown eyes that I knew all too well.

"Ah, so here you are. Hello, Marguerite," I murmured.

CHAPTER ELEVEN
MINA

April 23, 1768
Cimetière des Innocents

"I DO NOT THINK THIS IS A GOOD IDEA," I SAID TO DAPHNE AS SHE adjusted her black domino mask over her face.

The beautiful blonde duchesse peered at me with her piercing violet eyes and offered a sympathetic smile. Her vampire fangs glinted in the spare light of the moon peeking through the carriage windows.

"I know, *chérie*, but it cannot be helped. We must know what The Order knows. So far, they think Charlotte and I are ignorant about their activities regarding your abduction, and we must keep it that way to protect you. Would you feel comforted if we went over our plan once more?" she asked, placing her hands in mine.

"No," I muttered grimly. "But we should go over the plan again, anyway."

Charlotte fidgeted with the clasp on her jewel-encrusted *chatelaine*—a lovely broach she wore at her waist that featured several secret compartments. Hiding places, I knew, where she kept tools of her trade: a garrote, capsules of poisons and drugs, various keys, and God knew what else. She struggled to pin it to her bodice, and Daphne leaned forward to help.

"Daphne and I will attend the meeting in a few minutes," Charlotte offered. "So that we may learn what they know and keep up the appearance of our ignorance. Antoine and Étienne, who don't often attend the meetings, will wait here in the carriage to ensure your safety. The Order would hardly expect you to be right outside! We'll insist we don't know where you are and haven't heard from you, of course. We'll discuss our current missions in the hope that we can figure out more of what The Order plans to do about you and Rafael. After the meeting, we'll go back to my *château*, have several large glasses of wine and some excellent food, and formulate a plan of attack for *les DD*."

"You just want to skip to the wine part," Daphne teased, finally fastening the *chatelaine* to the bright blue silk of Charlotte's skirts.

"How dare you!" Charlotte responded with mock affront. "I'll have you know I would prefer to skip to the food, too. I'm positively ravenous. Let's hope these pompous windbags don't drone on for too long. I may just shift and eat some of them."

I smiled at the cousins' lighthearted attempts to cheer me, but reality settled back in too quickly. Before I could say anything more, Antoine and Étienne knocked softly on the carriage door and tugged it open.

"Our patrol of the area turned up nothing. No villains or beasties anywhere near," Antoine rumbled, rocking the carriage slightly as he lifted his massive form in to sit next to Charlotte.

"Well, except for those inside this carriage," Étienne said

with a grin. "Daphne, *mon amour*. You look radiant. Must you waste such a lovely gown on those dusty old prats?"

She dropped a chaste kiss on the vampire rake's knuckles.

"Yes, *chéri*, but you're welcome to help me out of it when we return home," she said with a wink.

Charlotte groaned and rolled her eyes, while I averted my gaze. I could hear Étienne's seductive chuckle and was unprepared for the wave of guilt and jealousy that washed over me. How many times had I dreamt of Rafael and I teasing each other in the same way? Had I ruined my chances for any romantic future with him?

What future? My thoughts demanded insistently. *The future where you cannot be together because of who he is—what he is—and who you are? Not only does a lowly physician have no place with a prince, but a human has no fate with a vampire who will walk the earth for eternity.*

The reflections soured my stomach, adding to the anxiety I already felt about Daphne and Charlotte meeting with The Order and pretending like nothing was different. It was dark enough in the carriage that I had to strain my eyes to see them, but I could make out their silhouettes by the light of the moon. They were checking their weaponry—daggers sheathed in leather garters, pistols stuffed in the pockets of their *panniers*, garrotes disguised as bracelets, and stiletto knives hidden in their elaborate coiffures. Despite my concern and love for my friends, I knew they were more than capable of taking care of themselves.

Once they were satisfied with their armaments, they kissed their mates goodbye and squeezed my hands in comfort.

"All will be well, Mina," Charlotte said as they alit from the carriage. "You'll see."

"We promise nothing bad will happen to you," Daphne insisted. "And nothing bad will happen to us, either."

"Absolutely," Charlotte agreed. Then, throwing a mischievous grin over her shoulder, she added, "But if anything does, rest assured Daphne and I will disembowel the lot of them and feast on their entrails."

"Hush, my love—I'm already hungry," Antoine growled. "Be safe."

"We will," Charlotte replied. She fixed Antoine with an intense stare. "Protect her, darling. At all costs."

He nodded firmly, eyes fierce.

With that, they left, trudging through the mud from the late-April rain. I watched as they wound their way through the long-forgotten graves until they reached a mausoleum at the back of the cemetery. Daphne pulled on the heavy door, and flickering golden candlelight spilled across the ground for an instant as they entered The Order's secret entrance. Darkness quickly followed as they disappeared into the tomb and closed the door behind them.

"I hope they will be well," I whispered.

"Don't worry, Doctor," Antoine said, his deep voice vibrating throughout the carriage interior. "Charlotte is my maker. I'll be able to sense if she's in trouble. Besides, The Order has no reason to suspect they know about your attempted kidnapping."

"Antoine is right, *mon amie*. I would wager The Order will imply you were abducted by Rafael and use that to try and force *les DD* to bolster their efforts in hunting him down. Without the tortured testimony of Pascal, there's nothing that would connect those two men to The Order," Étienne added.

"At this point, do you believe they would listen to reason?" I asked. "Perhaps it would be in everyone's best interest if Rafael and I were to come before them and explain the situation."

Antoine scoffed and Étienne tutted gently.

"No, Doctor. I don't know that truth has much to do with anything at this point. Trust me as one who has been hunted —and nearly murdered—by The Order before. When this man, Derais, started spouting his poison about vampires being the spawn of Hell and threatening the law and order of France, the wealthy, fearful fools heeded his words. We all see the tension building between the classes. If the aristocrats have an enemy to turn their ire against, they'll do so to gain support and keep the out-of-balance status quo. When it comes to these men, I'm afraid to say if their minds are determined by fear, and I believe they are, their course has already been set," Étienne replied.

I knew he was right, but I was still disappointed by the truth of his words. I tried to distract myself from the chaos of my mind, but my thoughts continued to return to Rafael, The Order, and the past twenty years. I chewed at my bottom lip. I needed to focus on a problem. Whenever I became sad or distracted at home, I typically turned to my work.

"Antoine," I said suddenly, shattering the silence that had descended inside the carriage. "What did you mean about your connection to your maker?"

"Just that," he replied. "Despite my love for Charlotte, this connection between us only grew after she turned me. No matter where she is, I can sense strong emotions from her. Anger, frustration, fear, joy. I feel it almost as if it were my own."

"And you, Étienne? Do you share the same connection with Daphne?" I wondered.

"Not nearly as strong, but yes. I believe most vampires feel such a tie to those who drink of their blood. A way to keep track of one's blood offspring, I suppose."

I heard the rustle of fabric in the darkness and suspected he'd shrugged.

"How interesting," I said absently. My mind immediately returned to Rafael, and I wondered what it would be like to feel so connected to him. What it would have been like for him to sense my emotions for the past twenty years—all the loneliness, hurt, emptiness, fear, frustration, and tender joys I'd collected in my life. He might have sensed them from his hidden world, perhaps while he slept and dreamed during the day. Would it have made a difference? Would he have come for me? Part of me was seized with a powerful melancholy, despondent at the thought that he'd been so close and still hadn't sent word of his presence or motives, and the other part of me felt a pervasive sadness that he, too, had been alone in that time, unable to reach out.

"I can practically hear your mind racing, Doctor," Antoine said. "What do you wish to know?"

"How long does such a connection last, I wonder? Does it lessen or intensify over time?"

"I was only recently turned," he answered. "But I don't feel much of a change in it now than I did before. I am getting better at managing the entirety of another person's emotions, but I suppose I feel them the same way."

"The same for me," Étienne said.

"Forgive me for my bluntness, but how many people have you turned?" I asked the vampire.

"Only Daphne," he replied. "Before her, I couldn't fathom spending eternity with another person. In a momentary lapse of judgment brought on by the loneliness of my early vampire days, I offered to turn my half-sisters—they were wee things when I was a new vampire—but they refused."

"Your Rafael," Antoine inquired, shifting to better face me. "Has he turned many?"

Shame, guilt, and anxiety rose in my chest. How much could I tell these men? Certainly, I trusted them, but how could they understand my complicated history with the man everyone believed would be the downfall of humanity?

"Truthfully, I do not know," I answered honestly. "But when we—Papa and I—were at their home, it was forbidden for them to turn anyone outside of their family. Only the partners who married into the family would be turned. It was their great penance, they told us, to live for eternity with this curse and to remain isolated from the world and the people they wanted and needed."

"Honor can only take you so far," Étienne said. "The preceding generations must have been driven mad with such cruel fates."

"As I understand it, many were," I said.

"Poor devils," Antoine muttered. "That is great penance indeed."

"Many believe their crimes warranted such measures. And after knowing the head of that house, I think I can understand why," I said quietly.

Antoine froze then, stilling the carriage with his movements. Before I could ask, he and Étienne were on alert, charging the air with tension like the lightning that precedes the heavy thunder of violence.

"Something is wrong," he growled. "Panic, fear—I can practically taste it."

"Should we intervene?" I asked, fear lacing through my body.

"No," Étienne practically shouted. "We must trust them. We promised to stay here with you and keep you safe. I'll stay here with Mina, Antoine. If you shift and move around to those trees behind the mausoleum, you might be able to hear what's going on underground."

Antoine was already shucking his heavy coat and pulling

off his boots. I was grateful for the darkness, but I slammed my eyes shut for good measure. Étienne chuckled.

"Are you not a doctor? I'm certain you've seen him in the flesh," he teased, but there was an undercurrent of unease in his voice that I did not care for.

"I am!" I insisted. "But I am not examining him right now, and I don't fancy peeking at my best friend's fiancé."

The carriage lurched as Antoine exited, and I heard the nauseating sounds of bones breaking beneath flesh and tortured groans that morphed into lupine whimpers. He'd transformed into his wolf form.

"I think your modesty is safe," Étienne murmured. "He's gone."

I opened my eyes again but needn't have bothered. The moon had moved behind a copse of trees, blacking out everything I'd scarcely been able to see before. It should have felt unnerving to be in utter darkness across from such a lethal predator, but I felt a strange comfort with these men. I'd saved both of their lives before, and I knew they were men of honor—they would lay down their lives to ensure my safety.

For a few moments, the only sounds I heard were the rustle of the bitter wind through the trees and the occasional hoot of an owl. The silence only served to exacerbate my anxiety.

"Some people say owls are ill omens," I whispered nervously. "But I've never found that. I think they're wonderful creatures, cloaked in night and keeping vermin in check. They aren't harming anyone, and yet superstitious fools will kill them because they think that will keep death at bay."

"People will do anything to keep death at bay," Étienne said distantly.

I cringed. He might've been thinking of his turning or of the lives he'd ended in order to feed himself. I hadn't meant to offend him.

"I'm sorry," I said. "I didn't mean…"

"Worry not, dear doctor," he interrupted. "It only piques my curiosity that you speak of owls in the way that I wish people spoke of vampires. Cloaked in night, keeping vermin in check."

"Humans are *not* vermin," I insisted. "And many of you do harm people, whether intentionally or not. The blood plague turns you into parasites who must absorb the blood of another, and too often your kind kills the providing host."

"Yes," he agreed. "That is unfortunate. Not all makers are equipped with the knowledge to help their whelps understand when to stop drinking. And certainly, there must be consent between both parties. Daphne and I have been trying to build a program of education from Versailles, but our efforts are failing. It seems the king is more interested in eradication than education."

His last words were sharp with frustration, and I wasn't certain if it was because of his fear for Daphne and Charlotte or if it was because his work as an emissary was proving to be nearly impossible. Likely both.

Antoine suddenly crashed through the carriage door, back in his human form and entirely naked. I shut my eyes again.

"They're coming," he huffed, tugging his pants on. "Charlotte and Daphne are coming back. They're unharmed but upset. Worried. Something has gone wrong."

No sooner had he pulled his shirt over his broad, muscular chest than the comtesse and duchesse stumbled into the carriage. The moon had moved from behind the trees, caressing their faces with a pale, pearl-like glow. There was fear in their eyes.

"Home," Charlotte shouted at her driver. "Immediately."

Daphne wedged herself next to Étienne, then leaned forward and grasped my hands.

"There is a problem," she said.

Dread pooled in my gut, swirling furiously like Charybdis before Odysseus.

"What?" I asked on a breath.

Charlotte perched on the edge of the seat next to me and put her arm around my shoulders.

"The Order has Rafael's brother."

CHAPTER TWELVE
RAFAEL

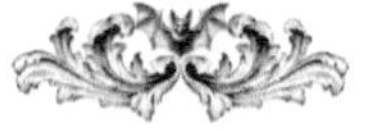

April 23, 1768
Dunkirk

"Perhaps I believe you. Then again, you haven't given me much reason to," I growled at the woman sitting across from me. She tilted her head, her shrewd eyes assessing.

"Why should I lie? I had no reason to approach you. I could have stayed in hiding, watching you flail and falter as you hunted us." She sneered, her shapely cherubic lips tilting up at the corners. It was an unfortunate characteristic of Marguerite's exceptional beauty that disdain and sarcasm intensified her attractiveness. When she'd been a maid in my father's household, I'd wondered if she exacerbated every ill temperament to show her face in its most attractive light.

"Hunting isn't quite what I was doing," I replied. "And I was close enough before you revealed yourself to me. It would have been a matter of time before I discovered you and Laszlo's whereabouts."

Her brown eyes twinkled beneath long sweeps of dark

lashes, and she lifted one pale shoulder in an artful shrug. Everything about her felt predatory and calculating, like a viper waiting to strike.

"Perhaps," she murmured, echoing my earlier word. We stared at each other for a long while, her slender fingers drumming lightly on the lacquered table in their townhouse.

When she had approached me at the docks, she'd been dressed in a silk gown of deep sea green—beautiful and lavish, certainly, but some years out of fashion. She persuaded me to accompany her to their townhouse, which was in a nicer part of town overlooking the ocean but protected from the chilly storms that raged in the winter. Not that either of them would be bothered by the cold or damp.

The townhouse was well appointed, and I suspected Laszlo had brought enough money with him when they eloped to keep Marguerite in style, but given that our father had disinherited him, I wondered how long that money had lasted. Was that Marguerite's game? The money had run out, and so she'd tired of her immortal companion.

"Why would The Order come for him? They seem to want *me* in connection with the arrival of the blood plague," I asked. "And how did they find you here when I only just discovered you myself?"

"Maybe you're not as clever as you think." She smiled. "And I suspect they're after your entire line—everyone in the Dracul family is at fault for the blood plague."

I narrowed my eyes. "It's Laszlo who ran from his responsibilities and let loose the curse upon the world. I've been trying to fix things for the past twenty years—at *great* personal cost."

"What do you know of responsibility?" she hissed. "You forget, I worked in your house long enough to see you squander money and title and kinship on satisfying your pleasure. Long before that *girl* came along. You encouraged your wanton reputation and strained the ties between your family, pushing Laszlo away and saddling him with the entirety of a kingdom he never wanted to begin with."

"He wanted it before *you* came along! And you turned his head, feeding him God knows what lies, all so he would whisk you away from your life in service." I snarled. "You were greedy and manipulative then, and you're just as bad now. If he is with The Order, it's probably because you betrayed him so you wouldn't be tied to the penniless, nameless, first-born son of a disgraced family."

Cold anger rolled off her in waves, giving her the appearance of a vengeful Amphitrite.

"Believe me or don't," she bit out. "But I'm telling you he was taken by men four days ago. I know they worked for The Order because I overheard them as they carted him away."

"How did you overhear them? How did they manage to take him? He would have been able to break any bonds and escape. Why didn't he?"

"I was coming home from my modiste when I saw them. I hid, naturally. They drugged him with an injection of quicksilver," she answered.

My lip curled in disgust. "You hid while your maker—the purported love of your life—was taken away, likely to be tortured or murdered."

"If they'd taken me, too, I wouldn't have been able to solicit your help in getting him back," she said grimly. "As much as it pains me to admit, I need your assistance, Rafael."

"You didn't seek me out, Marguerite. You waited until I was practically at your doorstep. What have you been doing since he was taken? Awaiting final measurements for your new gowns?" I shot back.

"I knew you were in France," she said coolly. "I was making

preparations to find you, but instead, you turned up here asking after that fool pirate."

"You lie too easily," I hissed. This woman had seduced my only brother and taken him from me—ruining more than our lives. It was because of her I'd had to abandon Mina to stay and take Laszlo's place. It was her actions that set this whole course in motion, and I suspected she'd schemed all of it from the very beginning. I couldn't understand or believe that Laszlo loved her truly and madly, as I loved Mina. Marguerite was beautiful, but cold, distant, and dangerous.

"Dismiss me if you must, but you know something is wrong. If you'd been a better brother and had maintained your connection to him, you would have sensed it already," she sneered.

Her words cut straight to my heart—to the guilt that lingered there over the fracturing of my family. Over the past twenty years of tense silence between us and the unspoken understanding that neither had the temerity to seek the other out.

"Besides." She arched her brow. "He is obviously not here. Do you believe I have him bound and gagged somewhere? The most powerful vampire in a thousand years—restrained by his newly turned wife?"

Wife. *Wife.* So, they had married in secret after all. I didn't know why it bothered me so much. It made sense that they would marry—he was too proud to keep her as some false consort. She would have demanded it. Still, the word needled me for everything it meant. Laszlo and Marguerite had had their twenty years of love while I'd had to give up everything —*everything*—to take his place under Father's cruel eye.

I glared at Marguerite, suddenly feeling drained from the long, frustrating evening. Dawn wasn't far off, and both of us would need to rest. I blew out a breath.

"Very well, Marguerite. I'll play along. The Order has Laszlo. What do you want to do about it?" I rubbed at my temples. It couldn't be true, could it? It must be another of her lies.

She looked at me like I was an imbecile.

"I want you to go get him. Return him to me, obviously," she spat. "I want you to stop cowering in the shadows—the both of you—and seize the power that lay carelessly at your fingertips. Go to The Order, wherever those bastards are hiding out, break down that door, and drain every single one of those old fools for daring to challenge your mighty legacy. You have the strength, the power, the wisdom, and cunning to do it, Rafael, so stop bleating like some wounded animal and remember who you are." She stepped forward, grabbing me by the shoulders and shaking me with each word. "Remember *what* you are. You are a Dracul! You are a Hell-cursed monster who has walked more nights than most men could dream."

I was stunned into silence, my eyebrows lifting at her sudden passion.

She gestured wildly around her. "You possess abilities that Lucifer himself would envy and would have used to lay waste to Heaven's self-righteous legions. If you won't be responsible for your kingdom or your failings, be responsible for your brother," she pleaded, collapsing into a chair under the weight of exhaustion, or perhaps defeat. Her steely eyes met mine, imploring and shimmering with unshed tears. "Go, Rafael, and bring him back to me."

I stared, angry but oddly inspired by Marguerite's tirade. What could she want from this endeavor? Could she really love him? Was this how she won him over—by charming him and flattering him and making him feel like he was so much more than a pawn in my father's political games? Was he really in the hands of The Order? If so, how could that have happened?

Sudden anxiety gnawed at me—was it possible she was telling the truth?

She shook her head, sighing heavily, and rose to her feet. When she spoke, I could hear the fatigue and exasperation in her tone.

"Sunrise approaches. There is a guest room downstairs. The servants have all been dismissed, but I'm sure it will still be comfortable, even if it's a bit dusty and stale. Rest here today, if you wish." She inclined her head in a curt nod and left the room in a swirl of deep sea green silk.

Weariness dragged at my limbs as I found my way downstairs, shuffling toward the small guest room. Marguerite had been right—the room hadn't been aired out in years and the dust and cobwebs were thick throughout. I didn't particularly care, except that it made me wonder how long ago it truly was that the money had run out. Perhaps longer than I'd originally thought.

I shook the dusty blankets out and climbed into the soft bed. *Laszlo, Laszlo. Why her? Why at that moment?*

And then, as exhaustion pulled me into sleep, I thought of Mina.

I AWOKE HOURS LATER, JUST AS THE SUN WAS SETTING. I TRUDGED back upstairs, hoping to borrow some of Laszlo's clothes to replace the ill-fitting ones I'd stolen from last night's meal. I didn't see or hear anything from Marguerite, but it was possible she was still sleeping. I decided to wait and amused myself by perusing their home.

They hadn't bothered to keep a kitchen but had instead

turned the space into a small painting studio and gallery. Oil paints and watercolors littered the rough wooden table in the middle of the room, along with brushes and sheaves of paper with painting studies and sketches. Someone was a talented artist, and it grieved me immeasurably to not know whether it was Marguerite or Laszlo.

I continued my tour, rifling through an office—nothing out of the ordinary, except that it seemed Laszlo had made some rather poor investments. I sneered. *Was Marguerite lying? Had Laszlo simply left here and ventured across the sea to escape her disdain?*

Something about that didn't feel quite right, though, and I pushed the thought aside. I was driving myself mad with the possibilities of my brother's fate. It would be best if I could simply find him and ask him about the past twenty years. *Would he even tell me the truth?*

Having finished my explorations, I realized it had been nearly an hour since I'd risen, and night had fallen. I didn't know Marguerite's habits, but I decided if I were to play her knight in shining armor and rescue my brother from his captors in this farcical tale, I could at least demand the use of some of his clothes so I could travel home comfortably.

I crept upstairs to their bedroom and found myself facing a single locked door at the top of the landing. I knocked and waited, but no sounds spilled forth. *That's interesting.*

After another minute, my anxiety flared, and I kicked the door in, tensing as it shattered into an explosion of sticks and splinters. The room was empty, the bed undisturbed. It was tidy, as if it had been used recently, but obviously not last night. Where had she gone? Had she slipped out to hunt while I slept?

Unease threaded through me as I scanned the room,

looking for signs of anyone—anything. When had she left? And why?

"Marguerite?" I called out. I listened for the creak of floorboards, the rustle of fabric, the rattle of the cold sea breeze through an open window but heard nothing. The silence blanketing the townhouse felt unnervingly lifeless.

Despite my dislike of my brother's *wife*—even the thought made me growl—I worried that something had happened to her in the daytime while I'd slept downstairs. I had no firm evidence or reason to believe foul play, except decades of intuition and the knowledge that if it was indeed The Order playing these games, they would stop at nothing and had every resource at their disposal.

Above all, I needed to return to Paris. I found Laszlo's wardrobe and pulled out a smart black waistcoat and breeches, along with a worn linen shirt and a fine wool overcoat. The garments fit me better than my dinner's, but still not as well as my own. It didn't matter. I only needed them to wear until I reached the outskirts of the city, and then I could shift into my wolf form and run the rest of the way.

I left the townhouse, still scanning for any sign of Marguerite. Not even her scent lingered here, which confused me more than anything. It was almost as if I'd been with a ghost, and no trace of her remained after our encounter. While I didn't believe that, there was a part of me that clung to my earlier unease.

I walked casually through the city, trying to avoid notice and pacing myself to reach the outskirts in good time. Fortunately, no one paid attention to me. In this frustrated, heightened state, death would surely meet anyone who attempted to delay me. But finally, mercifully, I crossed the road at the bottom of a hill, and the farmlands gave way to green fields and budding forests. The winter had delayed the onset of spring, but I marveled at how nature demanded new life.

The roads were empty, but to be safe, I hiked a bit to a small glade of trees to shift into my wolf form. Picking up Laszlo's borrowed clothes in my lupine jaws, I took off heading south, hoping to reach Paris in two days' time. At a full run, if I only stopped for sunrise and didn't pause to feed, I could just make it, but I would be weak when I arrived. It was a chance I would have to take.

My paws dug into the wet earth, flinging mud around me as I ran through the trees. At this speed, it would be difficult for humans to see me, and I could only hope my luck would hold.

Onward I raced, not daring to stop until the sky began to lighten and the stars faded from view. I bolted for a cave in a nearby hill where I could rest for the day, and then as soon as the sun set, I was off again. Perhaps it was my exhaustion and hunger that drove me so quickly, or perhaps it was my worry for Mina, or the whispering doubts I had about Laszlo and Marguerite's fates—either way, I reached the countryside outside of Paris just before the sun started to rise on the second morning. During the entire journey, I'd wondered about my next steps...where I would go, what I would do, how I would verify Marguerite's story, and I'd come to one dreaded but somehow inevitable conclusion.

My paws crunched along the gravel drive up to the grand entrance of the stately château, and before I could shift and knock, the massive door flew open. I faced a bristling, irate brunette with flashing, red-gold lupine eyes.

"Well!" The Comtesse de Brionne huffed. "It's about time you arrived."

CHAPTER THIRTEEN
MINA

April 26, 1768
Château de Ruisseau Magdelaine

From my guest room in Charlotte's château, I heard a commotion in the front hall, which I expected to be news from the remaining agents in *les DD*. After we'd returned from Daphne and Charlotte's meeting with The Order, they'd spent the following nights planning and sending messages to their agents, desperate to gather word of anything that could help us determine our next move.

The Order had abducted Laszlo. They were keeping him in a locked room underground, drugged with quicksilver and nearly feral from hunger. Daphne and Charlotte both reported a peculiar sensation when they entered the mausoleum, something they'd never felt before. They asked me if I knew of any supernatural repellants other than the false folk cures, garlic and wolfsbane, but I knew of none. They described a feeling of illness and terror but could not explain its origin. I had no doubt The Order had something nefarious up their sleeves if they'd been able to keep a powerful old vampire like Laszlo incapacitated.

Laszlo. I knew they would not feed him, and it was possible —difficult, yes, but possible—for a vampire to starve to death. The Order was holding him for questioning, likely torturing him for information on the whereabouts of Rafael, unaware or uncaring that Rafael was innocent of their accusations. Perhaps Laszlo was responsible for the blood plague, but I couldn't find it in my heart to believe that was true. The Order would execute him, Daphne had said, if he couldn't prove useful.

One fewer vampire, they'd said, clearly drawing a line in the sand. It was a wonder Daphne and Charlotte had made it out of the meeting alive. Well, undead.

My thoughts turned to Rafael. Where was he? Where had he gone? Was he safe? Did he know about his brother?

And then, my traitorous heart thudded in my chest. *Does he still want me after I turned him away?*

I tugged the wool wrap around my shoulders, cold despite the slow warming of the April days. Winter had clung too long to France, but finally we'd had a couple of scant sunny days that felt like spring forcing its way through.

Another servant hurried down the hall and knocked at my door.

"Doctor," she whispered. "I think you'll want to come see this."

Usually, when people said that it meant a visceral appointment for me. Collecting my medical bag, I frowned down at my spring-inspired gown of cream decorated with a riot of tiny flowers. Charlotte had picked the fabric for me, and while I'd balked at the impracticality of it for my line of work, I couldn't help but feel delightful cheer when I put the gown on.

"Do I have time to change beforehand?" I asked the young housemaid.

"No, mademoiselle. But I don't think you'll want to, anyway," she added cryptically.

I furrowed my brow.

"Why?"

She beckoned me into the hallway and nearly pushed me toward the main staircase. When I peered down into the grand foyer, I understood the commotion.

Rafael stood in the middle of the marble floor, completely naked aside from the mud and traces of dried blood around his mouth. Charlotte stood in front him, chattering animatedly, oblivious to his unclothed state. Two servants waited patiently at the edge of the hall, poised to offer whatever their mistress required. At present, I thought that should be clothes, but that seemed to be the least of anyone else's worries. I fought to stem the annoyance I felt at everyone else having a full view of Rafael's *endowments*.

I couldn't help but allow myself a thorough look. If only for scientific purposes, I told myself. How had the vampire changed since I'd last let my eyes rove over his beautiful body —twenty years ago and yet yesterday?

He hadn't.

His lean muscles—honed through years of a soldier's training and a predator's hunting practice—flexed beneath moon-pale skin. A dusting of soft, dark hair sprayed across his chest and tapered down his abdomen. I blushed when I looked lower, embarrassed to be staring at a man I no longer claimed. Lifting my gaze back up, I noticed the tension in his shoulders as he crossed his arms over his chest and the hard lines of his jaw. His eyes were locked on Charlotte's, and they flashed with restrained anger and powerful promises. He wasn't threatening her, but he wasn't pleased with what she was telling him. A loose lock of his black hair fell forward across his brow, and as he pushed it away, his arm drew back from his chest enough that I saw what made my heart nearly stop beating.

A recent wound of fresh pink skin, directly over his absent heart. It was a rough wound that was still healing, which meant not only had someone staked him, but the fight had been a struggle for him, as well. *He is not dead,* my mind cried. *But he could be dead.* That was the hardest part about immortal beings —the fact that you could rely on their immortality...until you couldn't. The fear that followed stopped me in my tracks. Panic clawed at me, hot and sharp, until the room started to spin, and air became thick. From below, Rafael's gaze flew to mine.

In less than an instant, he was at my side.

"Mina," he murmured, smooth and low, like a bow being pulled across a cello. The comfort of my name on his lips pulled me from the brink of fainting.

"What are you doing here?" I asked, my voice hoarser than I wanted it to be.

His eyes narrowed.

"You are pale...and weak," he said, by way of an answer. "You have not been eating. Or sleeping."

"I have been busy," I huffed, pushing him away from me. "I don't need a nursemaid, Rafael. Especially one who has his own troubles." I gestured to the healing wound on his chest. It looked much worse up close—the skin around it puckering and raw.

He did not smile. "Busy? Too busy to take care of yourself?"

By that point, Charlotte had climbed the stairs and regarded us with a mixture of annoyance and excitement. She practically vibrated with her struggle to keep both contained.

"She has been refusing almost every tempting morsel I've sent up to her," she chastised. "Including almond cakes!"

Rafael's eyes widened, and he turned an accusatory gaze back to me.

"And all day long I hear her pacing about in the house, stomping from room to room. She says she's busy with her work on the blood plague and our plans, but if you ask me, it's but one thing," Charlotte continued, apparently set on revealing every ounce of my emotional distress over the last few days.

"Traitor," I muttered.

"One thing?" Rafael echoed.

"Yes, I think she's lovesick," Charlotte stated matter-of-factly. I'd never thought ill of my friend, even before I knew her so well, but in that moment, I wished for the world's strongest muzzle. I groaned inwardly. Attempting to change the subject to anything that wasn't an exercise in torturous mortification, I coughed.

"Charlotte, have you been formally introduced?"

She tilted her head at me and stifled a giggle.

"No, but we're very well acquainted. We are connected by blood, after all."

"I didn't mean..." I blushed again, embarrassed. "I know *that.* I just meant, have you had a proper introduction? You've been calling him *the man in black* since you met."

She laughed. "Please, Doctor, do introduce me to your —*ahem*—dear friend. Prince Rafael, is it? How would you prefer to be addressed, Your Highness?"

Rafael tried valiantly to cover his smirk, and I wished the ground would open and swallow me whole.

"Prince to a seized principality, Comtesse, and traveling discreetly. Rafael is fine," he said.

"Oh, certainly he is," Charlotte teased, winking at me. I scowled at Rafael's throaty chuckle and snatched the velvet dressing gown that she'd been carrying, thrusting it into Rafael's arms.

"Here," I hissed. "Charlotte, do you have a room for him?"

Her eyes glittered with mischief. "Why, the Rose room—right next to yours, of course."

A garbled noise between a squeak and a curse slipped from my lips. Charlotte finally took pity on me as she turned to Rafael and curtsied politely.

"Rafael, I bid you welcome. As morning is nearly upon us, I'm sure you'd like to bathe, feed, and rest before we discuss our plans. I'll send a bath up for you at once, and in your room, you'll find a sideboard with spirits and fresh blood. Please don't hesitate to ring for anything at all, and I shall see you in the evening. Mina, *chérie.*" She smiled at me as she turned down the hallway. "Do be careful."

Rafael shrugged on the banyan and opened the door to the large guest room. The windows had been blacked out and long, dawn pink curtains hung in front of them, giving the room a fresh yet cozy feeling. The spring evening had become chilly, and a small fire crackled in the white marble hearth. Rafael strode in and surveyed the room, nodding appreciatively.

"It's not as grand as you're used to," I said anxiously, strangely defensive despite Charlotte's palatial château. "It's not a castle. But Charlotte keeps a warm and welcoming home."

"I've spent far more days in far worse places than châteaus and castles," he said softly, exhaling a little and rolling his shoulders. Weariness flowed off him like water. "This is the warmest welcome I've had in a long time, and one I deserve far less."

Anyone else would be surprised by Charlotte's willingness to overlook some of Rafael's faults, especially considering he had turned her into a werewolf without her consent. I hadn't had the chance to ask him if it had been intentional or an accident.

The atmosphere seemed to thicken with the tension of the last few days, and our stilted goodbye before that. I'd spent countless hours thinking about him—his words and his kiss. It had driven me to distraction and frustrated me beyond measure. I'd thought I'd moved on from him after twenty years of separation, but the last two weeks had proven me wrong. With a grudging acceptance, I was forced to acknowledge my feelings were as strong as ever for the vampire who'd long ago shattered my heart.

Not that it would—or could—change anything.

I watched him silently, running his long, pale fingers over the heavy brocade curtains. His demeanor was diminished, so unlike the bold, brash vampire I knew years ago and even unlike the passionate, dangerous man who'd showed up at the threshold of my clinic. Something had happened in the last few days.

"How—how are you?" I tried. It was a stupid question, but my anxiety had the better of me and I'd never been eloquent enough to drip honeyed words like a courtier.

He turned to me, dark eyes filled with emotion, on the precipice of saying something when one of Charlotte's housemaids interrupted us, bringing in the large copper bathtub. In the ensuing parade of servants who came through to fill the tub with piping hot water, I slipped out and stepped back into my bedchamber.

Rafael would want privacy, but I was far too restless to sleep. I undressed down to my chemise and unpinned my long, brown locks, running a fine bone comb through them. I should try to return to the library to do some more research, but the thought of Rafael being under the same roof was almost too much to bear. As much as I knew how sleep would elude me, focusing on research would be even more futile.

My reflection in the mirror stared back at me, looking pale and drawn. I frowned, rubbing at the wrinkle between my eyebrows. Perhaps Charlotte and Rafael were right, and I needed some food and rest. I pulled on my dressing gown to head to the kitchens for something to eat when there was a firm knock on my door.

I might have pretended it was Charlotte or one of the maids, but inside, I knew who it was. There was only one person it *could* be.

"Rafael," I whispered, opening my door.

He stood clad in the same deep red banyan as before, cinched tightly at his waist. The thin triangle of pale skin below his throat showed he wasn't wearing anything underneath. I swallowed—my mouth suddenly dry.

He looked somewhat restored, and I suspected he'd fed as well as bathed. His damp hair hung just above his shoulders, loose and wild, making him look every inch the foreign prince he truly was.

"We were interrupted earlier," he said. "My apologies."

I nodded, unsure of what to say.

"I'm glad to find you here," he said after a few moments. "Safe with your friends."

"You found your way here too," I said quietly. "Though I suspect you realize the circumstances are rather unfortunate."

"Laszlo," he acknowledged.

"I'm so sorry, Rafael."

He stepped into the room, closing the door behind him.

"I don't want to talk about Laszlo, Mina." His gaze was like fire, blistering in its intensity.

"What do you want to talk about?" I asked automatically, suddenly breathless. I took a step back, and he followed me into the room, tracking me like a predator. My heart pounded in excitement, and heat dropped low from my stomach, as if I'd swallowed a hot coal.

"Why aren't you eating? Or sleeping?" he asked.

I paused. "I told you."

"No," he said, taking another step toward me. "You lied to me."

"I have been busy," I insisted.

One more step forward—a hair's breadth away.

"Do you know what I think, Mina?"

He raised a hand to my cheek but stopped just shy of touching me.

"I think you were distracted. Perhaps you were thinking of me as much as I was thinking of you."

I closed my eyes, somehow both ready—and not—for the kiss that I prayed would come. Seconds ticked by on the mantel clock and the fire crackled in the hearth—the only sounds other than our breathing. When I opened my eyes, Rafael was looking down at me with a thousand unknowable thoughts flashing in his gaze. He stood there, frozen like a marble statue.

"Mina," he whispered. "I promised you before. I will not touch you until you ask."

I closed my eyes, knowing I would regret everything. Fearing even more that I would regret nothing. *Damn us both.*

"Rafael," I begged, more breath than sound. "Kiss me."

Instantly, his lips were on mine. His kiss was soft at first—restrained. Tentative. The gentleness of it brought tears to my eyes, and I felt them spill over as he sucked at my bottom lip, wordlessly seeking entry. I opened my mouth to plunder his, sweeping across his tongue in lush strokes, goading him into *more.* More passion, more fire, more heat. More Rafael. I sighed in contentment at the familiar taste of him—the bite of some sweet spirit, the faint savory tang of blood, and the delectable warmth that was all Rafael.

My hands came up to tangle in his hair, and he growled appreciatively, guiding me back toward the bed. Without thinking, I slipped my hands down his face, his neck, and across his shoulders, pushing his dressing gown down and letting it slide to the floor. His lean muscles flexed beneath his pearl white skin, and light blue veins traced paths across his arms, shoulders, chest, and abdomen. He looked exactly as he had twenty years ago, when I was so in love with him I was prepared to throw everything away so we might be together. That included my family, my future, and even my mortality—a secret I hadn't shared with him back then.

"Mina," he said, low and lush. "May I undress you?"

His eyes had melted into solid pools of black, and his pupils flashed red. He was keeping an iron grip on his control, even more so than when we'd been young and every intimacy had been full of hesitation and care. Despite his devilish reputation, he'd treated me then like something precious and breakable. Now, however, it stirred a thread of ire in me.

"That was the point of all this," I huffed, trying to untie my dressing gown in haste. His cool hands stilled on top of mine.

"You wanted me to stop before," he pointed out.

"Yes, but not *forever*." I yanked at the knot, tightening it in my frustrated attempt to loosen it. "I was angry with you, Rafael. I am *still* angry with you. Frankly, I am angry with me too."

"If you are so angry, why do you want this? Why do you want this if you are not mine? If I am not yours?"

"Because, you fool, I will always want you. I will want you when I hate you, I will want you when I am angry with you, I will want you even if I married another man tomorrow and gave him six children," I snapped. I abandoned the knotted tie of my dressing gown, close to tears, and dangerously close to destroying my ardor.

Rafael seized my robe and pulled me tightly to him, challenge flashing in his black and red eyes.

"Do not speak of other men to me, Mina," he snarled. "Even hypothetical ones."

I snapped my mouth shut, feeling guilty for goading him, but the deep, dark, wicked part of me thrilled at the primal side of him. Excitement skittered across my skin, tightening my nipples and igniting the inferno in my blood. He traced his hand down the swell of my hip and slipped his finger beneath the belt of my robe.

"Allow me," he rumbled, slicing the knot with one sharp nail. The robe fell open, and he dropped to his knees. Catching my eye with a heated glance, he arched a brow.

"I kneel to no one but you," he said.

He lifted my chemise with one hand, the other tracing a feather-light patch up my leg, from my ankle, to my calf, to my thigh, and finally to the dark thatch of hair between my legs. He leaned forward, his warm breath tickling the sensitive skin of my groin and paused for a moment.

"Tell me again that you want this," he said, the rough edge to his voice the only sign that his cool temperament was wavering.

"Please, Rafael," I whispered, abandoning every logical thought in my head. "Tonight, I am yours."

CHAPTER FOURTEEN
MINA

April 26, 1768
Château de Ruisseau Magdelaine

HE LINGERED A MOMENT, EXHALED SOFTLY, THEN LEANED FORWARD TO drop kisses up the insides of my thighs. I squirmed in anticipation, twining my fingers in his lush, dark waves, gently urging him higher. I might as well have tried to move a mountain for all the good it did me.

Sensing my frustration, Rafael chuckled, then dragged one finger along the seam of my sex, pressing gently at the apex of my pleasure. My knees almost gave out from the shock of the sensation. He let go of the hem of my chemise, and I tugged it up over my head, not wanting anything else between us. Just as he was about to set his mouth to my sex, he sat back on his heels and stared up at me.

"My Mina," he whispered reverently, running his hands through his hair. "Even with eternity, I could never get used to the sight of you. My goddess of spring, Persephone—you are the most beautiful creature I've ever seen."

A blush bloomed across my cheeks and chest at his worship, but I didn't have time to reply. With vampire speed, he rushed forward and wrapped his hands around my ass, pulling my sex to his lips. Devouring me with lips and teeth and tongue, he left no part of me untasted or unloved. His fangs grazed the peak of my pleasure, sending a jolt of prickling pleasure through my entire body. Faster and faster he licked, working me into a panting puddle of sexual need. When I was nearing the crest of that impending *petite mort,* Rafael slipped his finger inside me, being careful to retract his claws. I desperately ached for release, but as I was about to come apart, he withdrew and sat back on his heels.

I growled a string of curses I'd never used before and gripped his hair by the roots while he chuckled mischievously.

"I will not leave you wanting, Mina. This helps your pleasure to build. I've waited twenty years for this—I'm going to make up for every night we spent apart." His voice vibrated over my skin and sparked lust along every nerve.

He stood and hoisted me up, carrying me over to the bed. Even with the coolness of his skin, I felt fire pulsing through him and sensed the wildness he fought to contain. God, how I wanted him to let it loose.

After laying me gently on the bed, his hands mapped my body with maddeningly delicate touches. When his fingertips ghosted my full, aching breasts, his fangs lengthened with desirous reflex. In the dim light of the fire, his black and red eyes glittered hungrily, but it wasn't for blood.

He crawled up my body, lightly scoring his fangs across my overheated skin—not enough to draw blood, but enough to coax torturous sensations in my most intimate places. Desire pooled between my legs and my core clenched in anticipation.

"Rafael," I gasped, feeling his claw circle the bud of my pleasure once more. It was a lit match in a keg of black powder, bringing me closer to the edge than I'd been before. I squeezed my eyes shut, arching my hips and grinding against his fingers.

"Open your eyes," he demanded, his voice scraping out around his fangs. It was rough—bordering on violent. His control started to fray as he palmed my breast with one hand, never relenting the maddening slow circles his fingers traced on my sex. When I didn't immediately acquiesce, he growled, pinching my nipple and slipping two fingers inside me.

"Look at me, Mina," he snarled. "I will see you come with your eyes open. I will know every flicker of passion in your gaze —will swallow every sigh when you fall to pieces at my touch." His voice was deep and captivating, making it impossible to disobey. I beheld him playing my body like some beautiful instrument, the sight both exquisite and damning. *I was lost for him.* Heat built like an inferno, and again I chased it, begging him with moans and sighs to end my agony.

Again, he pulled back. This time, my frustration summoned tears. As I opened my mouth to shout at him and curse him back to Hell, he placed a gentle but firm hand at my neck and laid his body atop mine. His erection pressed hard against my sex—the friction against my clit making me feral.

His deep, sensual laughter sounded through me.

"Yes, my goddess. Finally, you are as wild for me as I am for you." His demonic eyes shone with possessive heat, and I saw flames reflected in them. "I see how you look at me when I fight back the demons beneath my skin. I smell your excitement—hear your racing heart when I growl and bite and give chase. I'm going to make you scream, Mina, and remind you of just what a beast I am."

His lips descended to mine again but gone was every pretense of hesitation and sweetness. He nipped at my lips and thrust his tongue into my mouth with another chest-deep growl. Finally, his knee came up between my legs and nudged them apart, and with one swift, satisfying thrust, his slid into my slick, desperate channel. For one precious heartbeat, we stared at each other, frozen in time, understanding that this had been inevitable, and there was no going back from it. My wanton body demanded the release he'd joyfully denied me, and I wrapped my hands around his ass to pull him deeper still.

"More, Rafael," I pleaded. "Give me what you promised." I arched my back, seeking the delicious friction between our bodies.

Finally, blessedly, he began to move, starting slowly and building in speed and ferocity.

"Everything," he grunted, matching his thrusts with the timing of his words. "You have everything of mine, my goddess. You are everything. I will give everything and anything to please you. I will destroy everything that would keep you from me. I will give you pleasure and pain if you wish it and take only what you offer. You are mine, Mina. *Mine. Mine. Mine.*"

The darkness and dangerous threats in his words sent such passion through me, I was afraid to examine it closely. Lightning arced across every fiber of my body, drawing me forward to heights of pleasure I'd never known before—even with Rafael. Heat built to a firestorm—like a slumbering giant of a volcano awakening after millennia of being forgotten. Flames devoured me to the brink of combustion, and just when I felt like I'd burn down everything around me, pleasure seized me. My orgasm erupted with a shuddering scream and distant ringing in my ears. Rafael followed me over the edge, letting out a savage roar and sinking his fangs into the tender flesh of my breast. The sudden jolt of pain sent a second orgasm rocketing through me, and I clung to him, riding out the waves of alien contentment as my body reveled in the feeling of being joined to him—with him.

We laid there—time forgotten—as we came back to ourselves. Rafael propped himself up and looked down at me, marble-like biceps flexing.

"Are you well, Goddess?" he asked, black eyes intense. *Searching for regret.*

I smiled and reached up to tuck one wavy black lock behind his ear.

"I am, *Devil*, though I'm certain we've woken the entire household, and I don't know if I'll ever be able to face them again. Are you well?" I whispered.

He flopped down next to me and pulled me into his arms, tucking my head against his chest. With a kiss on my forehead, he swaddled our entwined bodies in the soft blankets we'd discarded in our lovemaking.

"You are my waking dream, Mina, and here you are in my arms. Of course I'm well."

Thoughts began to circle as sleep pulled at me. *What will happen next? Where has Rafael been? What does this mean for us? What does it mean for me? What do I want it to mean?*

Rafael pressed a finger into the furrow of my brow.

"I can practically hear you panicking in here," he said with a wry smile. "What's the trouble?"

"I'm not panicking," I protested. "I'm worrying. There's a difference."

He chuckled. "I don't suppose I could convince you to leave the worrying until we wake later tonight."

"If only it were that easy," I sighed. "The real world outside beckons, Rafael, despite my desire to keep it at bay."

One cool hand slipped down to caress my hip and give my ass a firm squeeze. Heat sparked in my belly again, a soft breath on passion's waning embers.

"Fuck the real world, Goddess," he whispered in my ear. One finger slid around to stroke the slick seam of my sex again, and my desire rekindled. "Stay with me among the stars for a little while longer."

His cock hardened against my thigh, and my exhaustion evaporated. With twenty years of heartbreak and denial between us, I supposed my cold tomorrow could wait for a few hours more.

MUCH, *MUCH* LATER, I WOKE TO THE SOUNDS OF VOICES CARRYING up from downstairs. I felt around in the darkness, expecting—hoping—to find Rafael's cool body next to mine, but did not. I wanted to ignore the disappointment that bloomed in my chest given that we'd made no promises to each other, and despite our words in the heat of passion, I had no idea where we stood. Our attraction to each other given our past was undeniable, and it would have been absurd to pretend to misunderstand his feelings for me, but that didn't change my trepidation or our circumstances. It was absurd to even consider entertaining the idea of a future when everything was so uncertain.

The voices downstairs grew louder, prompting me to kick the covers off and dress quickly. I wasn't sure what the commotion was, but given the tone of the voices, I suspected it was serious. I pinned my hair up beneath a lace cap and made for the door, only to step hard into a solid wall of man and stumble backward.

"Easy, Goddess," Rafael said, pulling me upright. "That's

twice that you've run into me. I'm beginning to wonder if it's not some ruse to capture my attention."

I bristled at his charm, still put out by waking up alone after...whatever it was that we shared.

"Well, it's not my fault you lurk outside the door of every space I occupy," I said snidely. "Perhaps it's *your* attempt to have an excuse to lay your hands on me and save me from a tumble."

His lips were at my ear in an instant. "Believe me, Mina, I don't need an excuse to lay my hands on you. Simply permission." With those devastating words, he pressed a soft kiss to my neck and held out his arm for me. "Shall we?"

I cleared my throat and willed the blush from my cheeks, hesitating before taking his arm. We made our way down the stairs together, heading toward the collection of voices emanating from Charlotte's formal dining room. The massive doors were slightly ajar, but I knocked in case the conversation was something Rafael and I weren't meant to hear. Charlotte poked her head through the gap in the door and grinned knowingly.

"Well! I certainly wondered if we'd see either of you this evening. I hope you got some rest," she teased, emphasizing *rest* as if she knew we'd done anything but.

Rafael's stoic face betrayed nothing, but I saw the flash of heat in his eyes.

"What's going on in there, Charlotte?" I asked. "It sounds like you've got an entire army of excited women in there."

"I do!" she grinned. "Won't you join us? Daphne and I are convening *les DD* to discuss what we know and plan what to do about The Order."

"And Laszlo?" Rafael asked quietly.

Charlotte nodded—her lips drawn in a tight line. She pulled open the door and waved us in.

I'd seen Charlotte's dining room decked out for countless dinner parties, holidays, and balls, and it was always impressive. Nothing, however, could have prepared me for the sight this evening. Two dozen women sat around the large table, sipping wine and nibbling on a variety of hors d'oeuvres while they chatted amiably. I recognized many of them—unlike meetings with The Order, none of these women wore masks in each other's company. Daphne sat at one end of the table, giggling through a conversation with one of Étienne's half-sisters, Josephine, famed madam of the illustrious *Maison des Nymphes*. Étienne sat on Josephine's other side, and next to him were two other women from the brothel. Across from them was the well-known Italian opera singer, Signora Russo. Antoine sat away from the table against the back wall, watching but not a part of any ongoing conversation. His eyes tracked a couple of aristocratic women I didn't know with guarded interest. Several at the table were bourgeoisie, but many looked to be peasants and commoners. Based on the number of wine glasses filled with blood, I estimated about half of them were vampires.

Rafael stilled beside me, making me wonder if he was nervous. It seemed silly to even suggest such a thing, given his status and raw supernatural power, but his face reflected a careful neutrality and his posture took on the appearance of forced casualness.

"No one is going to attack you," I whispered in his ear. "Be easy, Rafael. Many of these women are my friends."

"Your friends, Mina—not mine," he replied. "Given our history and the rumors circulating, I wouldn't be surprised if that gave them even more of a reason to despise me."

Charlotte's small smile widened, and I knew she'd heard our exchange. I clamped my mouth shut to keep from giving any more away.

"*Mesdames*," she announced. Every conversation quieted and heads turned to face her. A few curious gazes lit on Rafael, and I tensed—preparing for what, I don't know.

"Thank you so much for journeying into the chilly night to discuss our incredibly troubling and precarious situation," Charlotte said, her voice echoing through the large room. "Daphne, do you want to catch everyone up?"

Daphne stood. "As you are all undoubtedly aware, our aims have been slowly diverging from that of The Order over the past year. You're all familiar with Derais—his rather sudden and fervent religious devotion that's swaying the minds of the other men in The Order. The emissary and I have been working to bring King Louis to our cause for some time now, but our efforts have faltered. In the wake of Madame Pompadour's tragic death, it seems His Majesty has turned away from Pompadour's more liberal influences and found solace in the conservative members of the aristocracy, notably those in the church and the older courtiers in The Order, including Derais. As such, The Order has reached the height of their power thus far—their selfish tendrils have snaked their way throughout every influential structure in France. Now, they fear no one. They've already started to move against those they perceive as a threat to their power."

"Vampires," hissed someone.

"Women." Josephine chuckled.

"The bourgeois," another chimed in. "And the poor."

"Immigrants, foreigners, and minorities," Signora Russo said with a sniff.

"The backward fools in The Order are the minority," Antoine muttered from the back of the room. Everyone quieted, turning to look at him. "But they are the powerful minority."

Charlotte cleared her throat.

"All of the above," she agreed.

Daphne's mouth thinned to a tight line, and her jaw flexed. I knew she was frustrated that her work in The Order had come to naught. She'd once told me that despite her wealth, title, and connections, the only thing that would matter in the end was how she could help the people of France. *"King Louis is my cousin. If I can't convince him to consider embracing vampirekind, then I fear our cause is already lost."* Now that The Order had the ear of the king, they would boldly focus on what I always expected their true aims would be—further consolidating power within their own ranks. The Order wouldn't have to pretend to care about anyone but themselves. Rafael's words from weeks ago echoed in my mind. *How much do you know about The Order, Mina? How much have your friends Charlotte and Daphne told you? How much do they know?*

"As such," Daphne continued, silencing the whispers and chatter that had begun to circulate. "We have decided to *unofficially* sever our ties with The Order."

"They won't stand for that!" Signora Russo interjected. "Those *bastardi* will never allow you—us—to form our own group without their misguided oversight."

"Right you are, Signora," Charlotte chirped. "Which is why we're not going to tell them...at least, for now."

"What do you mean?" one of the other courtiers asked.

"It would be irresponsible for us to launch a coup without an immaculate plan and several well-thought-out backup plans. The Order will be dangerous enemies, and we want to know what they're planning every step of the way. If they believe we are beneath their notice and beneath their control, it will give us the opportunity to destroy them utterly when we make our move," Daphne said, fangs lengthening and eyes flashing.

"Daphne and I will continue to attend their summons. We

will all carry on with our current assignments with one notable exception—any information relayed to them as part of intelligence work will be somewhat altered. We will only tell them what is required for our ruse to continue, but it will not be enough for them to gain an edge. All assignments regarding blackmail, intimidation, assassination, or such will be put on hold until Daphne and I can regroup and evaluate the targets in question," Charlotte added.

"But what about the blood plague?" one of the vampires from the brothel asked. "What are we going to do about that? And vampire rights? If The Order has truly turned against us, when can we expect the stakings to start?"

"Honestly, I'm surprised they haven't started already," Josephine grumbled.

"Haven't they?" Étienne hissed sourly.

"But why all of a sudden?" another woman asked.

"Yes," the vampire from the brothel agreed. "What has changed so much that we've all been summoned tonight?"

Daphne held up her hand for quiet.

"Please," she said. "I think now is a good time for me to introduce our special guest this evening. Ladies, I present to you Prince Rafael of House Dracul of Wallachia, also known as the Beast of Gévaudan—and allegedly the devil who unleashed the blood plague upon us."

Every pair of eyes locked on Rafael, who inclined his head politely. His bland expression covered what I knew was a storm of emotions—notably anger, frustration, and barely restrained tension.

"Good evening, ladies," he murmured with a decadent smile. "I'm honored to have found sanctuary in your ranks."

CHAPTER FIFTEEN
RAFAEL

April 26, 1768
Château de Ruisseau Magdelaine

So, Duchesse Daphne had not been quite as forgiving or welcoming as Charlotte. I would press her on the matter another time—perhaps when my life and the lives of my remaining family were not in jeopardy.

I didn't think any of these women would be taken in by charm, but I would offer it nonetheless—if only so that Mina wouldn't look upon me and regret our time together. As irascible as I felt, I didn't think alienating a group of dangerous, bloodthirsty women was a sensible first step toward a future with Mina.

"Thank you, Duchesse. And thank you, Comtesse de Brionne, for allowing me to remain here given everything that has happened," I said.

Charlotte smiled and nodded, encouraging me to continue.

"Assembled members of *les DD*, I will not lower myself to address every salacious rumor you've undoubtedly heard of me or my family. I believe you're all too intelligent to be taken in given how well you understand the value of information and the power of misguided and ill-used gossip. I am here before you to plead my case, humbly asking for help, and offering what truths I can," I said.

One of the young bourgeois women piped up. "Some mighty accusations lay at your feet, Your Highness. Why should we trust you? Who vouches for you?"

"I do!" Charlotte insisted angrily, standing quickly and almost knocking her chair over. "Françoise, you little minx, who are you to question my judgment when I've known you for years and you've only just spent your first six months with *les DD*?"

"We all love you, Charlotte, but you *did* marry a man who summoned a demon and murdered several people in his quest to win Daphne's heart. Why shouldn't we question your judgment?" Françoise replied.

Charlotte's mouth hung open for a moment before it snapped shut, putting me in mind of an irate fish. Her eyes glowed with lupine power as her anger condensed.

"None of us knew what he was truly capable of," Daphne interjected, casting a warning glance at Charlotte. She winced slightly as she said, "Though, she has a point, *chérie*."

From the back of the room, Antoine growled low and quiet.

"Yes," I said, trying again for peace. "Of course, none of you know me well enough to say that my intentions are..."

"I vouch for him," Mina interrupted. Until now, she'd been silent. Always watching. Always waiting. Always calculating.

"Doctor?" the madam—Josephine, I thought she was called—looked at Mina questioningly.

"I am not a member of *les DD*," Mina said, removing her spectacles to clean them with her handkerchief. "And I am not a vampire. But most of you know me. And if you do not know me, you know of me. I do not stand with The Order. I stand for myself—for what I believe is right. I have known Rafael a long time, and I know he speaks the truth. Please, Rafael, continue."

If I'd had one, my heart would've beat right out of my chest at Mina's forthright declaration. I could not—would not—let her down. *Yet you do not deserve her*, ferocious doubt whispered to me. I brushed the thought aside for the time being.

"I did not bring the blood plague to France," I said. "And I cannot say for certain who did, but I have been hunting for the answers for a long time. I am close to the truth, but in my search, I've come up against a problem that I alone cannot solve. I believe The Order has taken my brother."

"Taken? What do you mean, taken?" Signora Russo asked.

"Kidnapped, abducted, removed by force!" Charlotte snapped, still upset at having her judgment questioned. "Do try to keep up, Signora."

The opera singer glared at Charlotte, and I fought to keep from grinning.

"It's true," Daphne admitted. "Charlotte and I saw him. The Order has abducted the disinherited Prince Laszlo and intends to try him for the genocide of French people. They are holding him responsible for the origin of the blood plague."

"Is he responsible?" Josephine asked.

Silence descended and I felt the weight of every gaze in the room. I pursed my lips, still unsure how much I trusted these women. Without their aid, I wouldn't be able to recover Laszlo, but that didn't mean I was ready to divulge the full weight of my family's history and my suspicions about the genesis of the plague.

"I'm not quite sure," I admitted. An honest answer, but not the full truth.

I was met with sighs of frustration and hisses of disapproval. Mina squeezed my arm, but I wasn't sure if it was for comfort or from the pressure to say more.

"As I said, I've been trying to track down the source. Days ago, I was led to a vampire up north who was as close to my original bloodline as I've gotten, but it wasn't enough for me to determine the true source of the infection," I explained.

"If we're to believe the blood plague comes from your family, why should it matter if it comes from you or your brother? You are complicit, if not directly responsible. This is your curse. You should be held accountable," Françoise said acidly. "Perhaps we should deliver you to The Order and let them figure out what to do with you as punishment. Then *we* can get on with finding a cure and cleaning up the mess you and your brother left."

Several of the vampires in the room hissed at her. Charlotte tensed, glaring in her direction. I noticed Mina cringe, perhaps hearing her words to me from weeks ago.

"Not all of us are so desperate for a cure," Daphne pointed out. "But one should be available, if some so choose. I believe Mina's work will deliver one to us—it is only a matter of time." Then, she turned back to me. "Rest assured, we will not be delivering you to The Order, Rafael."

She must have seen the relief flit across my face because she continued.

"But Françoise raises some excellent points. What can you offer us as proof of your intentions and willingness to serve the people of France—beyond your own obvious loyalty?" Her strange violet eyes flicked to Mina, then back at me. Her meaning was clear.

I straightened, trying to ignore the slights at my honor.

"It is true that this is my family's curse and my responsibility regardless of how it escaped the confines of my ancestral home. Since I first received word of it in France, I have stopped at nothing to find out how it arrived here. My family and I have been trying to find a cure for longer than any of you have been alive. Dr. Van Helsing can attest to that. For generations, we have hunted dead end after dead end—if you'll pardon the pun —trying every scientific potion, folk cure, religious relic, holy man, prayer, counter curse, exorcism, and more. Nothing has worked for us, but that doesn't mean I will stop searching for an end," I explained.

Daphne's eyes found mine across the table, and she smiled encouragingly. Perhaps she wouldn't be so hard to win over. Françoise, however, would not be dissuaded. She opened her mouth to speak, the frown on her lips deepening, but I cut her off.

"What none of you have yet to grasp is that this didn't start out as an epidemic or an illness for us. My family has been living with this curse—and it is that, *a curse*—for thousands of years. We have borne the brunt of this penance for sins so long ago forgotten, the gods to whom we beg forgiveness have become the dust and whispers of memory. We have seen more death, suffering, and midnights than you can fathom."

The younger vampires in the room looked away at that— likely too afraid to confront the true meaning of eternity as I spoke of it.

"And yet, there is hope," I said, looking at Mina. These words were more for her than anyone here. "There will always be hope. Hope is the universal virtue that unites humanity, even when it feeds on greed, despair, pride, ignorance, and corruption. There is hope for the future. As much depravity and evil as humans are capable of, they are capable of equal measures of kindness, compassion, and beauty. It is true that I am loyal to one in particular here, but that is because to me— after everything I have seen in all my years—she embodies the best of humanity. I will protect it for her."

No one moved, nor spoke a word. Mina's clear blue gaze was glassy with emotion, but too many at once for me to fully understand. After a few minutes of awkward silence, the sound of a tearful sniff shattered the quiet.

Charlotte waved her hand airily as tears tracked down her cheeks.

"Oh Rafael, that was so beautiful," she blubbered. "Mina, *honestly*."

A few people chuckled. Antoine stiffened and threw me a dark look.

"I don't know that I can offer you more proof than that," I said.

I looked up at Daphne again, and she grinned, showing me her full fangs. With a wink, she stood.

"Well said, Rafael," she said. "I, for one, am convinced. I will not speak for all the women assembled here tonight, but you will have my support and whatever resources I can provide." She gestured to the two empty seats at the massive dining table. Mina and I crossed the room silently and sat as we were bid.

"*Mesdames,*" Daphne continued. "Now, the fact of the matter remains—The Order has Rafael's brother in their clutches. Regardless of who brought the plague down upon France, I think it is safe to say we cannot allow The Order's warped sense of justice to dictate what happens to anyone anymore—let alone a foreign prince who may be innocent."

"We don't know that," Françoise mumbled.

"We don't know that he's guilty, either, Françoise! *Mon Dieu,* how you test me sometimes. Do you need another glass of wine or a cream puff? Anything to make your manner more tolerable while we discuss these very difficult things?" Charlotte groaned.

Françoise narrowed her eyes at the exasperated Comtesse

and begrudgingly plucked an eclair from the tower of sweets in the center of the table.

Josephine cleared her throat. "Duchesse, Comtesse, I take it you both have come up with a plan?"

"Well, *of course* we have," Charlotte said with an effusive smile.

Daphne frowned.

"We have *most* of a plan," Charlotte corrected.

Daphne chewed on her lip, her needle-like fangs coming down nearly to her chin.

"Some of a plan?" Charlotte queried. Then, after a beat—"Very well. We have *an idea!*"

Noises of disappointment and frustration erupted in the room as the news settled over the group. If the two most senior agents had been unable to formulate some course of action, I hated to think what that would mean for our chances of success. For *my* chance of success—and Laszlo's life.

"If everyone would please calm down," Daphne shouted. "We can tell you what we know, and what we want to do. Then, it will be up to us—all of us—to determine how to proceed. This isn't a lost cause, but moving against The Order will require craft and cunning unlike we've ever had to muster thus far. It will take all of us working together."

Somewhat mollified, the ladies sat back in their chairs and waited expectantly.

"If anyone here is not set in our task or this new plan of action, I would ask that you excuse yourself now. You'll be in no danger from the rest of us, but I know what we're asking, and we don't ask it lightly. You all have your own lives, and the road ahead is rife with danger. If you wish to bow out, do so now, *mes amies,*" Charlotte offered, looking pointedly at Françoise. The younger woman shrugged and reached for another eclair.

"I don't have any particular loyalty for His Highness," Signora Russo declared. "But I have loyalty to you, *miei amici*. If we are to bring down the bastards in The Order, I'm all in for a bit of fun."

When no one else spoke up or moved for the door, Mina's fingers slowly threaded through mine beneath the table. She didn't risk a glance in my direction, but the corner of her beautiful lips lifted ever so slightly, and it was enough to cheer me from my melancholy.

"We're not going after The Order just yet," Daphne said, the relief evident in her tone. I wasn't certain if she had expected her recruits to abandon her in her hour of need because she doubted them, or herself. Either way, it was comforting that she'd been proven wrong, and this band of delightful, dangerous women agreed to help me rescue Laszlo.

"We are, however, going to break into the mausoleum and —ahem—*reacquire* Rafael's long-lost brother," Charlotte finished.

"It will require many of you using your laudable feminine wiles to keep the dusty prats entertained—*distracted*—for an evening," Daphne said.

"And how are we going to do that?" Josephine asked.

A wicked grin split Charlotte's face as she looked at her. "Dearest Josephine, I am *so* glad you asked."

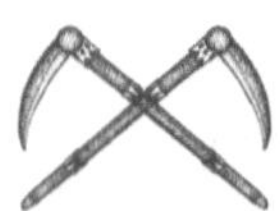

The meeting carried on into the small hours of the night, when purpling skies and the faint trills of birdsong heralded the approach of dawn. Due to the rampant exhaustion plaguing the assemblage and the necessities of the supernatural set, our meeting was adjourned before all the final details had been worked out.

I had to hand it to *les DD*—their plan was simple, bold, and brash. Of course, that meant there were about a thousand ways that it could, and probably would, go spectacularly wrong.

After bidding the other guests a good morning, I walked Mina to the door of her guest suite. She hadn't slept more than a few hours in the last couple of days, and likely less than that before my arrival. I cursed myself for keeping her up yesterday when I should have been encouraging her to rest. The dark hollows beneath her eyes gave her a somewhat frayed look around the edges, tugging at my absent heartstrings.

She paused at the threshold of her bedchamber, just long enough for me to make my decision. As she turned to me with what was certainly a "good morning" on her lips, I picked her up and carried her into my own guest room.

"Rafael," she gasped. "What are you doing?"

"Was Charlotte correct earlier when she said you hadn't been eating or sleeping lately? Were you going to lie down and rest the moment I left? Or were you going to stay up, pacing your room, flipping through your medical texts, and trying to come up with some solution to the mystery of the blood plague that you hadn't considered before?" I inquired, plopping her down on my bed.

She blinked at me, the lie taking form in her mouth.

"No—never mind," I said. "Mina, why did you allow me to take so much from you? You need rest, nourishment."

I bent to remove her slippers. She pulled away at first, frowning at me.

"I can take care of myself, Rafael," she said petulantly. "I have been doing so for ages before you came back into my life. In fact, I've gotten quite good at it."

"Yes, you're so good at it that you've completely forgotten how to address your human body's needs," I tutted, grabbing her feet once more.

"I'm a doctor, for God's sake! I know how to address my *human body's* needs," she gritted out, but allowed me to tug her slippers off and massage the arches of her feet.

"I know you do," I admitted, sliding my hands up her calves to untie her stockings and slip them down over her toes. I swallowed the burning lust building in me—as much as I desired her again, I wanted to care for her more.

"Why are you doing this?" she whispered, staring at my fingers on her legs.

"Because, Mina, I know you are strong and smart and capable, but if any of your stress or insomnia has been due to my unceremonious return to your life, I wish to help make amends. I want you to be well," I said, quietly untying her skirts and reaching up to unpin her bodice. "I *need* you to be well."

She swallowed once and, after a moment, nodded. I continued my ministrations, desperately trying to ignore the ache growing in my cock as I undressed her. Gods above and demons below, she was beautiful.

"Do you think it will work?" she murmured when I'd gotten her down to her cotton chemise.

"I don't know," I admitted. "But we will try."

I removed her spectacles and placed them on the bedside table, then reached up to unpin her glossy locks from her coiffure. They were like silk in my hands. I threaded my fingers through her hair and gently rubbed her scalp, and a soft sigh of pleasure spilled from her lips.

"Did you mean it?" she asked.

"Yes," I replied, not bothering to ask what she meant. "You are what gives me hope. You are the hope of everything for me,

Mina. A future without you would be the worst kind of Hell—but I will endure it if you still do not wish to be mine."

The words were bitter and wrong leaving my mouth, but I had to say them. Perhaps one day I would believe them. Then again, perhaps there would be hope for us yet.

Hope.

She sighed again, that soft smile tugging at her lips once more. Scooting back against the pillows, she slid her feet beneath the sheets and I tucked her in under the thick velvet coverlet. By the time I leaned down to brush a kiss to her forehead, she had fallen asleep.

"Rest well, Mina, my love," I whispered. "Tomorrow night, everything changes."

CHAPTER SIXTEEN
MINA

April 27, 1768
Château de Ruisseau Magdelaine

When the massive grandfather clock downstairs chimed six, it was a struggle for me to pull myself from the grip of sleep—and Rafael. As much as I hated to admit it, he'd been right about the fact that I was exhausted…mentally, physically, emotionally, and spiritually worn down. The rest had done me a world of good, and I woke up famished.

Rafael's strong arms encircled me like a chilly cage, one around my waist and one beneath my shoulders. His eyes were closed, but I doubted if he was truly sleeping. All the time we'd known each other, I hadn't known him to sleep much even after we'd made love. Instead, he'd hold me close, rub my back, and tell me stories of his childhood. Sometimes he'd sing to me in his native tongue, his deep, rich voice so soothing, I would swear he could cast spells like lullabies.

"Good evening, Mina," he murmured without opening his eyes. "I'm glad you slept well."

"Did you sleep at all?" I asked, reluctant to move.

"Enough," he replied. His eyes opened slowly, dark and warm and fathomless. They were like portals to some decadent circle of Hell, and I shivered with fear and desire.

"I wish I understood that aspect of the blood plague," I said. "How you can exist with the barest amount of sleep and such small requirements to feed. It seems so many other vampires require a full day's rest and at least a pint of blood per day to keep going. You only seem to need more when you shift form or use other abilities."

"My brother needs even less," he said, tucking one of my stray curls behind my ear. "And he is so much more powerful than me. I often wondered if it was because of his age, or because our mother was a newly turned vampire when she fell pregnant with him. She was much older when I was conceived."

I'd considered the line of thinking in my research. Well, my father had initially, and I'd picked up the thread after his death. Something about a born vampire made one markedly more powerful than a turned one, and it seemed that the closer one was to the true Dracul curse lineage, the more intense those powers were. Perhaps it was due to proximity to the first cursed members of the clan, and over the years, the strength of the curse waned as its effects became diluted through the blood of others.

"I've met so few vampire women who were able to conceive, and yet your mother had two. Yet another medical mystery," I said idly. Rafael tensed, and I regretted my words immediately.

"I have mourned the hope that I would ever have my own children. I know how hard it is for vampires to reproduce. I never believed I would have the opportunity," he said, the sadness apparent in his voice. "Besides, the life I live doesn't exactly make me father material."

"I think you'd make an exceptional father," I said, strangely defensive.

"Did you never want babes of your own?" he asked, stilling beneath my exploratory hands.

"No," I admitted. "I admire mothers, and I like children, but I always enjoyed my freedom. I feel too much like a mother to my work to want the responsibility. I suppose you think me selfish, though, for thinking more highly of my profession than of my biological abilities."

"Certainly not," he replied. "The impact you've had on countless lives could never be seen as selfish when it is as much of a sacrifice as it is. You never put yourself first, Mina, even when you should, logically."

I smirked. Charlotte had said similar things to me over the course of our friendship, but I always brushed them off.

"I don't find it logical to weigh my life as more important than the lives of others," I said.

"It is to me," he said softly, pulling me in for a searing kiss. When he pulled away, he swallowed thickly and caressed my cheek. "Mina, when this is all over, do you think..."

His words were cut off by a knock at the bedroom door, and the frustration in his eyes was powerful. I couldn't be sure if I was devastated or relieved that he hadn't managed to say whatever it was.

"Monsieur, Mademoiselle, dinner is being served in the dining room," one of the housekeepers said through the door. "My lady requests your presence."

The faintest flicker of hope on Rafael's face evaporated, replaced by his seductive, charming grin. I wondered if I'd imagined the expression.

"Yes, thank you," he told the housekeeper. "We'll be along shortly."

Rafael was already sliding out of bed, and my cheeks heated at the sight of his naked body. *Dieu,* he was beautiful.

Throwing a saucy glance over his shoulder as he tugged his breeches on, he offered, "It'll keep."

I frowned, certain that whatever it was, it had been important. I started to protest, but there was another knock at the door. Annoyed by yet another interruption, I stomped over to answer it.

"Oh, Mina!" Daphne exclaimed, tugging me into the hall before I could express my surprise.

"What are you doing?" I huffed. "I was just about to get dressed!"

"Excellent. I have something special for you to wear this evening, given what we're all about to undertake," Daphne said. "Don't worry. I rather think you'll enjoy this. It's incredibly practical."

She led me back to my guest room and gestured at the pile of black laying on the bed.

"Daphne." I blinked in confusion. "You're certain that's for me? That looks more like something Rafael would wear."

"Don't dismiss it just yet. Both Charlotte and I have worn breeches before, and they can be remarkably liberating. She still tends to prefer gowns, but I've always rather loved the feeling of breeches on my legs."

Atop the black buckskin breeches lay a soft, black chemise and black leather waistcoat that was positively bedecked with pockets.

"Daphne, these are *men's* clothes," I scoffed. "Why are you and Charlotte forever trying to dress me in things that are not my preference? If it isn't bloody ballgowns, it's breeches."

I hadn't told Daphne or Charlotte—or anyone, except

Rafael—that I'd dressed as a man for the entirety of my medical education. Those clothes had been baggy, shapeless, and brown and had hidden me from the eyes of every disinterested student and every pompous professor. Memories flooded back; binding my breasts every morning, sneaking baths in a nearby pond at midnight, hiding everything from everyone for two difficult years.

The thick black cloak and the black tricorne hat on the edge of the bed were at least sensible, but decidedly more masculine than I would have liked. When I picked them up and turned back to Daphne to further complain, the lightness in her expression was gone.

"Mina, tonight is one of the most dangerous missions we've ever undertaken. You've already been kidnapped once before, despite having some of the most powerful friends in France. If Rafael hadn't found you...I shudder to think what The Order would have done. It's clear to me that they will stop at nothing to get what they want and I...I feel quite betrayed. I'm so sorry, *ma chère amie*. I fear it's our friendship that has put you in jeopardy, and I cannot forgive myself for that. Especially after everything you did for Étienne and me—and Charlotte, of course," she said, diminished beneath the weight of her memories. She turned fierce eyes upon me, and they glittered with supernatural, predatory power.

"Nothing will happen to you tonight," she insisted. "We are all watching out for you and ready to protect you, but you're the only one who can help Laszlo if he's been injured or drugged—or worse. You're not an agent, it's true, but you're smart and strong and brave. These clothes are simply another layer of protection. You're less likely to be recognized dressed as a man, and if you are, these garments are equipped with various means of protection."

"I won't use weapons, Daphne," I frowned. "I appreciate

what you're offering, but it goes against everything I believe in as a physician. I only want to heal people—not take lives."

A wry smile quirked the corner of her lips up.

"I thought you might say that," she said, crossing the room to empty the pockets of the waistcoat. "And so, I have provided you with many non-violent and non-lethal alternatives."

She pulled a series of vials from one pocket. "These are fairly standard. Deadly nightshade, hemlock, various concentrations of opium, and quicksilver, just in case The Order has hired vampire guards. I'm certain you remember how harmful mercury can be to blood plague sufferers. The amount here isn't enough to kill, but it's enough to make one rather ill."

She reached into another of the waistcoat's pockets. "Here we have three small wooden stakes and two small daggers—evenly balanced for throwing, but without the practice, you might just want to hold onto them. Now, don't look at me like that, Mina, these aren't just for stabbing. Should you find yourself bound, they can be quite handy in cutting ropes. In the other pouch here, there's a garrote, my personal favorite, you know, because you can strangle someone without killing them. I know you already know how to render a person unconscious thanks to your thorough medical knowledge, but these options will help."

From yet another pocket, she produced the smallest flintlock pistol I'd ever seen. "This beauty is a new design. Small caliber, short range. If you don't want to kill anyone with it, I trust you know where to aim. Bullets, wadding, and gunpowder are in the pocket just to the left of it. Now, in this last pocket, I've created something of a miniature doctor's kit for you. Plenty of healing salves—your own recipes, of course —clean linen bandages, forceps, tweezers, a magnifying glass, scalpel. If there are other things you find you'll need in an emergency, do let me know and I'll have them added to any future clothing."

I ran my hands over the waistcoat, stunned into impressed silence.

"You thought of everything," I said, embarrassed by the tears that gathered in my eyes.

Daphne grinned. "I tried to. Charlotte did too. We were positively unhinged when we'd heard you were taken. I tried to think of everything you'd need so that it doesn't happen again."

I nodded and pulled away, but the memory of Pascal and Hubert overpowering me in the carriage made me feel weak and vulnerable. I raged at the thought. I'd always been confident in my intelligence and my abilities, but compared with my immortal friends, I was merely a liability. Daphne seemed to sense my apprehension because she offered a determined smile.

"We'll all be there together tonight," she insisted. "And I suppose if all else fails, just shout as loudly as possible."

She'd meant the words as a comfort, but the shame of them was a festering wound to my pride. Not wanting to offend her, I returned her smile. "Because a ferocious pack of werewolves and vampires will rush to my aid?"

"Of course! But truthfully, I think Rafael will be at your side before the scream even leaves your lips," Daphne said, a curious fear flickering in her violet eyes. "And may God have mercy on the poor soul who threatened you."

"I have known him too long," I said quietly, reassuring myself as much as Daphne. "I do not fear Rafael."

The terror in her eyes surprised me, given how powerful both she and Étienne were.

"I know, *chérie*. But you are the only one who does not."

We were still for a beat, the heavy confession thick

between us. Then, in an instant, her defenses were back up, and she smiled at me, dispelling some of the anxiety in the air.

"Hurry and dress. Charlotte had the chef prepare all your favorites tonight." She chuckled. "She believes if we're heading into battle, at least we'll do so well-fed." She popped off the bed with more energy than I would have thought possible, given the gravity of what we had ahead of us.

In the wake of Daphne's exodus, the room felt strangely quiet, and it allowed me time to reflect.

I regarded the unusual garments on the bed while considering how strange my life had become over the last month. Mere weeks ago, I was resigned to my quiet existence—if one could call being a vampire physician *quiet*—working, studying, researching, and finding sips of happiness at teas and dinner parties with my supernatural friends. It would be untrue of me to say that I'd been completely fulfilled...that I hadn't been touched by loneliness, or the longing that comes from the heartbreak of your first love, your first *true* love, but I'd found my kind of contentment. Satisfaction. I had a purpose, and that suited me. Perhaps I'd been too frightened, too numb to hope for anything more. Yet in the last few weeks, my entire existence had been upended. There had been a distressing number of outbursts and tears and reawakened *feelings* that my very recent past self would have scoffed at.

For the first time in years, I didn't have a plan. I didn't know what my next days or nights would bring. I didn't know the intimate structure of the hours of my tomorrow—exactly when I would wake, what I would eat, which patients I would visit, which medicines I would craft, which experiments I would attempt. Rafael's presence in my life had reintroduced chaos like only he could, and while that gnawed at the edges of my anxiety, I found myself thrilled by it. Did that mean I was ready to move beyond our past? I couldn't be sure. If I were being truthful, I didn't want to consider what our lovemaking meant for us—for me. For now, I could enjoy how his touch brought my body back to life as if from some wintry hibernation, and I wanted to leave it at that. No heavy discussions of our past devastations, our present circumstances, or our impossible future—just pleasure, plain and simple.

Even if there is nothing simple about it, my treacherous heart insisted.

I turned back to the clothes and obediently began to dress. The soft, supple buckskin of the breeches was snug on my legs and felt entirely alien compared to the heavy wool and silk skirts I was used to, but not altogether unpleasant. I appreciated the freedom of movement, though even I could see that despite the well-cut fit of masculine clothes, the shape of them on my body looked positively indecent. I assumed the thick cloak would help hide me in the gathering night, as would the hat if I pulled it low over my brow.

Sorting through the waistcoat pockets again to familiarize myself with the contents of my mercenary accessories, I grimaced at the more lethal items. Daphne included them for my protection, and I was grateful for her concern, but the thought of using them on anyone turned my stomach. The small travel kit of medical accessories could prove useful, though, and my heart swelled at her thought to include them.

Tying back my long, dark hair, I grabbed the cloak and hat from the bed and made my way to the dining room. Étienne was seated at the end of the table, sipping blood from a crystal goblet. He smiled when I entered the room.

"Well?" he asked, gesturing to my new clothes. "How do they feel?"

I blushed. "Oddly freeing, if a little uncomfortable. I feel rather scandalous."

"Excellent," he returned, his smile widening. "Sometimes it's good to be a little scandalous."

Daphne entered then and whispered something to him. He nodded and winked at me, then left. As Daphne came around the table, I saw that she, too, wore men's clothing. The form-fitting breeches, blousy shirt, waistcoat, and cravat looked stylish on her, and it made me even more self-conscious.

She approached me and placed a hand on my shoulder.

"You look very fine," she said. "Almost a proper gentleman."

"The clothes look odd on me," I muttered. "But they are well made."

Daphne tilted her head. "The clothes suit you," she countered. "But I don't think it is merely the clothes. Over the last few weeks, you've had a certain air—a glow, almost. Charlotte teases you about not eating or sleeping, so I know it has nothing to do with your health."

She brushed a loose strand of hair from my cheek and smiled fondly.

"If it were anyone else, I would say it was love."

I blanched. "That's preposterous."

The smile slipped from her lips, but her eyes carried the sparkle of mirth.

"Of course," she said. "Perhaps it's simply the exertion and excitement of the last few days."

"It must be," I answered, glaring, wishing to be anywhere but beneath those intense, amethyst-colored eyes.

"It would be absurd to suggest that you'd found love within mere weeks with the man who broke your heart twenty years ago, who was *not* the villain you believed him to be, and who has come back to claim you once more," she continued. "You're much too sensible to fall for his charms again. Humans and vampires make difficult pairings if you do not wish for immortality. You know that, of course. He is handsome and honorable, I believe, but his past...well, you know. Some women have a hard time settling down with rogues, even if they are reformed. Still, he would make a fine match for any supernatural woman."

The thought of Rafael with another woman kicked bile up into my throat, and I swallowed the instinctive swell of anger with force.

"He would, of course," I said with a tight smile. "A fine match for a supernatural woman. Clearly anyone but me." The words came out bitter and dripping with misery. *Of course I don't deserve him. I'm just some lowly human.*

"Oh?" Her sharp gaze pinned me in place, seeing through my lie. Mercifully, she carried on as if I hadn't said the words. "I've never known you to be interested in marriage or immortality," she said airily, walking back to her seat at the end of the table and picking up Étienne's abandoned glass of blood. "I suppose you worry a husband would force you to stop working and that marriage would be terribly dull. And that immortality comes with too many sacrifices and too few benefits."

I didn't say it, but Daphne had put her fingers on two precise reasons why I'd been so afraid to consider a future with Rafael. I pursed my lips, wishing this exchange would end.

She sighed as she sat down. "It would be untrue of me to say I didn't miss a warm, sunny afternoon now and then. The hum of birdsong and insects in a summer meadow. The glitter of sunlight on freshly fallen snow. The dazzling blue of a cloudless sky."

I wasn't particularly attuned to the natural world, but every time I had considered immortality, I shied away from it like a coward.

"Of course," I said. "Your world is marked by blood and darkness and death."

"So it is," she agreed, with a knowing smile. "But so is yours."

I opened my mouth to argue, but upon reflection, realized that she was right. Even if I wasn't a vampire, I'd kept to a supernatural schedule for so long, I couldn't remember the last time I'd seen a sunny afternoon. And in my profession, blood and death were as common as they were to any vampire. It was an odd realization and one that gave me pause.

"On the other hand," she said, violet eyes fixed on the red swirling in her glass. "There is beauty to be found everywhere, and supernatural senses have much to offer. Sometimes, when it is truly quiet in the small hours of the night, I could swear I hear the stars singing."

A floorboard creaked behind me, and Daphne's gaze rose above my shoulder.

"Rafael," she said, her sly smile returning. "I do hope you haven't been waiting there long."

Dread pooled in my stomach. I prayed he hadn't heard our conversation, but from the fiery look in his eyes, it was obvious he had.

Merde.

CHAPTER SEVENTEEN
RAFAEL

April 27, 1768
Château de Ruisseau Magdelaine

When I entered the dining room, two things became excruciatingly clear to me. The first was that Mina was wearing breeches. *Gods above and demons below, this must be some sort of test.* The second was that I suspected Daphne had known I was outside the dining room and expected me to hear every word of their conversation.

Nursing the gaping wound where my heart would have been made it a touch easier to try to ignore the discomfort of my hard cock pressing against my breeches. I couldn't help but stare, taking in the way the supple buckskin caressed her round ass and shapely legs as my hands had done a day ago. The men's clothing showed off every curve of her body in a way that made my mouth go bone dry. I felt my eyes darken to black and red and my fangs lengthened, startling me with the ferocity of my desire. Altogether inconvenient given Mina had just confessed she thought I'd make a better husband for someone else.

"Rafael," she said, her voice pitched high with panic.

"I'll just go see where Charlotte is," Daphne said, downing the last of her blood and hurrying from the room. Mina's gaze cut to the retreating duchess—also clad in men's attire—as if she would rescue her from the looming storm of my anger.

The door closed quietly behind her, but the sound was like cannon fire in the tense silence that stretched between us.

"What Daphne said...I didn't mean..." Mina fumbled over the words.

Frustration pulled my nerves taut. Maybe it had been naïve of me, but after the intimacy we'd shared, I'd sensed a change in her. A softening. I dared to hope it meant we'd be able to work through some of the things that parted us, but I'd been fooling myself. How could I have expected her to leave behind a past that she felt defined her? She'd told me herself. Following my false betrayal, she'd forged a life of ambition and solitude. I didn't fault her for that, but it was devastating that my absent heart had become entangled in a mere physical distraction for her. Despite that, I would be with Mina in any way she would allow—even if it meant never having her completely. That heavy knowledge made me the world's greatest fool.

Pain took root in my chest and seemed to wind throughout my body, irritating me like thorns beneath my skin. The pitying expression on Mina's face cut worse than a thousand harsh words. I stalked to the end of the table where Daphne had left the decanter of blood and poured myself a glass.

"Be easy, Mina," I said, draining the glass and pouring myself another. I had to get a handle on myself—on the raging emotions warring in my head. With the smooth, salty tang sliding down my throat, my ire lessened, and I felt my eyes shift back to normal. I sighed, strangely fatigued given that I'd slept and fed more in the last day than I had in the previous week.

"You promised me you wouldn't invade my mind—my privacy," she said quietly.

I cocked a brow. "I did not invade your mind or betray your privacy. I was merely answering a summons. I was unfortunate enough to overhear what I suspect the duchess wanted me to hear."

Mina tilted her head, confused. "What do you mean? Daphne wouldn't do that. She wouldn't purposely..."

"Wouldn't she?" I snapped. "To protect you, I suspect, from me."

"I don't need protection from you," she replied.

I rushed forward in a blur of supernatural speed, pushing her back into the heavy wooden door.

"Are you so certain?" I growled. "Perhaps she is right. Perhaps the rumors are true. Maybe I am a hedonistic rake— selfish and bent on serving my needs. A murderer and a devil, summoning demons and using hellish magic to torment humans while I infect the world with my cursed plague. Is that what you think of me? Is that what you think I have always been—what I've become? Is that why I am only good enough to warm your bed?"

Her heart pounded in her chest, but I could tell it was from excitement, not fear. I dropped one arm to her waist and swept my fingers from her leather-clad hip to her ass and lifted my knee to part her legs. Her blue eyes widened, and a gasp of pleasure escaped her lips, testing my restraint.

"Perhaps you do need protection from me, Mina. You already know how I want you—what I would do to get you. Maybe the devil in me that bays for your sex will one day bay for your blood. It seems even your friends mistrust me—fear me—and they have no idea what I can do. I could make you my willing slave, Mina. I could mesmerize you, compel you to strip for me, force you to your knees to suck my cock until I said stop. I could have you bouncing naked on my lap, your breasts in my hands and your perfect little clit stroking my shaft and even then, I could invade your mind and keep your release at bay. Could you imagine that, my Persephone? Endless days and nights of sex without an orgasm, all because I might have a torturous whim."

Fire sparked in her gaze, and her cheeks grew pink. Her breath came in panting huffs and her lust made me wild. I pressed my knee higher into her groin and felt the damp heat pooling between her legs. I grinned wickedly, my fangs long and sharp.

"I can smell your desire, little goddess, and it tells me I wouldn't even need to ask. I wouldn't need to compel you. I could just take it." I leaned forward and licked from her collarbone up to her delicious throat. The tips of my fangs grazed her skin, sending shocks of pleasure along my nerves—exquisite torment.

"I could take it like I could take your life, beloved. One slip of my fangs and I could bring you to Death, taking away your sunshine and your summer afternoons. I could turn you against your will and tie you to me for eternity. Perhaps I'm tired of waiting for your forgiveness. Perhaps I'm still the spoiled, selfish, reckless prince. Perhaps I will change my mind and give up caring for the hope of humanity because you are the only human worth saving, and you despise me."

I shifted my knee, and she moaned slightly, her eyes clouding with emotion.

"I don't," she whispered. "I don't despise you." Her breath was coming quickly, ragged and raw.

"You do," I said, resigned. "You may like what I can do with your body, but you do not want me, Mina. After everything, you have found your own path, and it is not through the underworld with me."

I pressed a lingering kiss to her throat, loving the feel of her pulse beneath my lips.

My thoughts clanged and crashed and rattled through my skull. I wanted her with a need so powerful, it dwarfed every thought. Every emotion. Every ancient, eternal piece of me.

I could take much from you, love, but I won't. No matter what, I will give you what you desire. If you consented to be mine, I would burn this world down and rebuild it stone by stone, brick by brick to suit your tastes. If I had a heart, I would cut it out and give it to you, if you wished to possess it. If you wanted the end of every vampire on earth, I would stake them all without a thought.

Words I could not—would not—say anymore.

A tear slipped down her cheek, and I reached up to wipe it away.

"If your wish is that I give you up—well and truly—I will leave you to your peace and never darken your doorstep again."

I didn't tell her it would kill me to do so.

She swallowed, intent on saying the words that would probably damn me to an eternity of misery.

"I…"

The door swung open with a loud thud, smashing into the opposite wall. I briefly entertained the idea of ripping out the throat of the person who'd done it.

Merde, does no one knock in this household?

A young woman stood in the doorway, bloody, bedraggled, and panting. She choked out a sob and looked around wildly. Mina pushed off the wall and hurried over to her.

"Charlotte!" the young woman yelled. "Where is Charlotte? I have news for her."

Charlotte rushed into the room behind the woman, a whirlwind of dark purple skirts and the acrid scent of fear.

"Nanette! What has happened? Are you injured?" Charlotte gently pushed the woman down into a chair and motioned to Mina to look her over.

"No, I am fine. This blood is not mine," Nanette replied. "I escaped. But I was there—at the graveyard. I was watching from the trees. The vampire Laszlo is not alone. The Order has another, but it is a woman."

"What do you mean?" Daphne asked, coming into the room with Étienne and Antoine on her heels. "They have a woman? You are certain she is a vampire? Is she with The Order or have they captured her?"

Fear and apprehension whispered through me.

"She is a vampire. At first it looked like she was with them—she was yelling at two masked men as they walked toward the mausoleum, but something happened," Nanette said, pausing to take a sip of the water that Mina offered.

"What happened?" Charlotte pressed.

"I couldn't see exactly. The woman said something that upset the men she was with, and the argument escalated. One of the men attacked her, and even with her vampire strength, they overpowered her and dragged her into the mausoleum by force. It was awful. After that, I thought the coast was clear. I climbed down from my hiding spot, but one of their hired thugs must have spotted me leaving, because he chased me around the graveyard. When he caught up with me, we tussled, but I broke free and managed to lose him a few streets later."

Mina dabbed a clean cloth across a small cut on Nanette's eyebrow, but that appeared to be the worst of her injuries. Charlotte and Daphne exchanged a look.

"Did you recognize the woman?" Daphne asked.

Nanette shook her head. "Never seen her before. She was pretty, though. Dark hair, dark well-made gown. She was definitely French."

"We must find out who this woman is. If The Order is starting to round up vampires off the street, we're in serious trouble," Charlotte said grimly.

"That doesn't make any sense," Daphne argued. "They wouldn't choose any vampire at random. Our first action must be to find out who this mystery vampire is and what The Order wants with her."

A heavy sense of foreboding weighed on me when I answered.

"She is Marguerite. She is Laszlo's wife."

Everyone turned to regard me.

"How do you know?" Charlotte asked.

"That's a rather vague description for you to be so certain," Daphne said.

"I hadn't seen Marguerite in twenty years before this past week," I said, fighting my annoyance at the interfering duchesse. "Laszlo's trail led me to Dunkirk up north. When I was there questioning one of the older vampires about his maker, Marguerite appeared."

"What did she say?" Mina asked, focused on me now that Nanette was somewhat recovered.

"She asked me for help. She told me Laszlo had been taken by The Order and she asked me to get him back," I said. "I stayed at their meager townhouse to shelter from the day, but when I awoke the next evening, Marguerite was gone. Vanished without a trace. I still have not determined how much I trust her...or her story."

"Why didn't you bring this news to us sooner?" Charlotte demanded. They were the first words of frustration I'd heard from her, and it grieved me to wonder if I'd lost my only other ally.

"I couldn't be sure that she was involved," I replied evenly. "And forgive me, but I do not answer to you or your organization."

"Why do you suspect she is involved?" Mina asked.

"How much do you remember about Marguerite, Mina?" I scoffed. "She was a selfish, entitled human with her sights set on my brother and when she got what she wanted from him, she threw him to The Order. Probably told them he was the cause of the blood plague."

"Why?"

"Perhaps she is tired of him. Perhaps it is about money. Without Laszlo, she will inherit whatever my father left him."

"But your father disowned Laszlo," Mina argued, her brow furrowing in confusion.

I laughed bitterly. "True. But if there's one thing my family has never had much use for, it's wills. It might seem strange to you, but when you expect to live forever, you don't really think about leaving your worldly belongings behind. After my father was assassinated, I discovered he'd never officially disinherited Laszlo. As the eldest son and heir, he inherited what's left of my father's holdings, but no one has been able to find him to give him his settlement. And naturally, if Laszlo dies, the assets that have been moldering away in various banks and vaults in Hungary will pass to his wife."

"Would Marguerite know that? If you only discovered it after your father's death, how would she know that she stood to gain anything?" Charlotte pointed out.

"That much is unclear. But as far as I know, no one communicated with Laszlo after he ran away. There was no request for formal abdication—Hell, no one even knew where to find him to tell him Father had been murdered." I tried to explain things with forced casualness but talking about my family meant *thinking* about my family, and that always brought me to a dark mood. I didn't hate my father, exactly, but he'd been distant from my earliest memory. Laszlo was the favorite—the true heir—and I was the unexpected, unwanted extra. My wretched behavior in my younger days was the only escape I had, but it further drove the wedge between my father and me. Even after Laszlo's betrayal, there was never any gratitude at my willingness to step up and take over—just resentment that Father was left with the unacceptable spare to continue his brutal legacy. When he was killed, I grieved not for him, but for the relationship I always wished we might have had.

"So," Daphne hedged. "We continue with our original plan. Only this time, Rafael, you will be responsible for Marguerite, as well. If she is a prisoner, she is to return with us. If she is in league with The Order..."

"If she is responsible for Laszlo's kidnapping, I will kill her," I growled.

"We don't know that she is," Mina said anxiously. "She could have been in trouble at the cemetery."

"Ah, Mina, always looking for the best in people—even when there is very little to be found," I said, still angry beneath my teasing smile. "So delightfully human."

She straightened and glared. "Better than being a cynical old bloodsucker."

Everyone turned expectant eyes on me, waiting to gauge my reaction and probably expecting me to fly into some monstrous rage. I was almost sorry to disappoint them.

I laughed heartily at her insult and was rewarded with the slightest smile on her lips.

"Guilty as charged," I admitted. Then, with more gravity, I added, "But I'll be surprised if Marguerite isn't the one orchestrating Laszlo's kidnapping in an effort to regain her freedom and any lingering wealth she feels entitled to."

"Forgive the impertinence," Charlotte interjected. "But is there any lingering wealth? If you were on the wrong end of a coup, I assume most of your holdings have been seized. I would expect Marguerite would draw the same conclusions."

"We're not returning to Wallachia for any crown jewels or royal residences, but yes, there is a considerable fortune that my brother is owed. As I said, it is unclear whether he or Marguerite are aware of that fact," I replied.

Daphne nodded. "Knowing your sister-in-law, how do you think we should proceed?"

"As you said. Carry on with your original plan. I'll deal with Marguerite," I said.

Everyone seemed to agree, but there was palpable unease in the room now that we had another variable to consider. As the room emptied and we each steeled ourselves for the next steps, Mina stayed me with a hand on my arm.

"You cannot kill her," Mina insisted. "Rafael, you must promise me. You don't know what she's been through, and you don't know that she's at fault. You go into this with your own prejudice, and it will end badly for everyone."

Anger and hurt made me peevish, my brittle temper snapping.

"Why do you care? You don't know her, Mina, any more than you know Laszlo. She might be the cause of the blood plague—of all that suffering you've been fighting to hold back. You should be begging me to put an end to her and free the world from the curse of the plague. Your life would be so much simpler then, wouldn't it?"

The last thought was one I'd meant to keep to myself, but it was out now, souring the air between us.

"And anyway, she isn't your family nor your responsibility.

You can carry on with your part of the plan and then, when this is over, we can all move on."

"What are you talking about? Move on?" Mina narrowed her eyes.

"It's what you want, isn't it? You've been clear with me from the beginning—you made your life and it's better without me in it. I can respect that, Mina. We can leave what we've enjoyed behind, and you can return to your clinic and your research," I said.

"Damn it, Rafael, would you stop trying to determine my life for me?" she shouted.

Anger made her face cold and storm clouds gathered in her sky blue eyes. Her jaw clenched as she faced me, fierce and frustrated. I took an involuntary step back.

"Ever since our failed elopement, you've been deciding on our course of action without talking to me about it. You alone decided to stay and take up your family's mantle when Laszlo left. You forced me from your world after inviting me in, left me in bleak silence for twenty years, then determined you would come back, and we would have a future...without ever stopping to wonder if that's what I wanted. You expect it to be easy, for me to be pliant—you expect that because I still have feelings for you and desire you, that it erases all the pain and hurt and memories? That my feelings for you solve all the problems that live between us? And when I don't immediately uproot everything I've built over the last two decades, you determine it must be because I want nothing to do with you and I do not care for you, and all I want is your body?"

She advanced on me, jabbing her finger in my chest with each crushing point.

"You admit I am smart and capable, and yet you won't even do me the courtesy of letting me make my own decisions. You make them for me under the guise of love because you are too afraid of what I will say and do if you let me have my choices," she spat. "Still the spoiled young prince! You, Rafael, are too afraid of hard work. You don't want the arguments, the responsibility for your actions, or the ownership of the pain you knowingly caused me. You want to move forward without paying the price. You want a future with me without healing our past. You want to find the cause of the blood plague so you can prove it's not your fault. You want to blame Marguerite for your brother's departure from your life without stopping to consider if your poisonous father or your youthful indiscretions had a hand in it. You want to absolve me of the responsibility of having to say no to you and risk breaking your heart when you wouldn't afford me that consideration from the beginning."

"I..." I opened my mouth to argue, but she held up her hand.

"I am not finished!" she continued. "You want me to agree to be with you forever without admitting that it would require a sacrifice on my part—that if I *don't* want to make that sacrifice, it must mean I don't love you enough. You are drawing conclusions without examining all the evidence before you, which I can promise you will always lead you to the wrong answers. You say you are a scientist now, Rafael—a botanist. What evidence do you have to make these theories? And what right do you have to make any kind of choice in my stead?"

God, she was magnificent. Her eyes were blue fire, and the pink flush of outrage colored her cheeks. She was like a sunrise in her rage and I loved her all the more, even as she cut me to ribbons.

"Then what?" I asked, my voice low. "What is it that you want from me? If not my love, my protection, my hope...what?"

She closed her eyes and exhaled.

"Time," she answered. "The one thing you have more of than anyone, Rafael. Just *time*."

CHAPTER EIGHTEEN
MINA

April 27, 1768
Château de Ruisseau Magdelaine

THE DAMNED FOOL STARED AT ME, TOO STUNNED TO REPLY. BEYOND frustrated, beyond exasperated, and more fatigued than I'd been in a long while, I stepped back and turned toward the door.

"You could do me the honor of allowing me some time to work through these events. You had twenty years to think and plot and wait. I had *nothing*, Rafael. Nothing! No word from you, very little news of your family, no support while I mourned the loss of our relationship and the deaths of my parents, no rationale for your decisions—nothing. You showed up in Gévaudan a few months ago and approached me mere weeks ago. It's rather a lot to take in, and it's been incredibly difficult. Since you have all the time in the world, perhaps you'd lend me some," I said.

The words came out harsher than I intended, but I was hurt by his actions. I could understand if he was losing patience with me given that he'd waited twenty years to confess everything, but he failed to grasp that this was all still new for me. I was tired of feeling pressure from him to move on, and I was tired of feeling *less than* my supernatural friends because I was simply human. My pride smarted at being coddled by Daphne and Charlotte for this all-important mission, and I was done with people trying to manage me *for my own good*. I'd had enough of that with my mother, God rest her soul.

Well, no longer. Perhaps it was the breeches that gave me the courage I needed, or perhaps I'd simply reached my breaking point. Whatever it was, I would no longer stand for it.

Rafael's dark eyes softened, and his gaze fell. A lock of raven hair draped over his forehead, reminding me of him as a young, well, *younger* rake. My fingers itched to tuck it back behind his ear, to place my warm palm against his cool cheek and kiss the downturned corners of his beautiful lips, but I didn't. My need to touch him—to be near him was almost overpowering, but this time I was listening to my head, not my heart.

Rather than sit in the path of temptation, I left Rafael to his thoughts and headed for the front hall. With everything we had ahead of us tonight, it was time for me to regain my focus.

Charlotte, Daphne, Étienne, and Antoine entered the hall shortly after I did. The air in the room was heavy with anticipation—even Charlotte was quiet and introspective. Each of us was dressed similarly, in snug black breeches, black shirts, black waistcoats, black hats, and black cloaks. At a great enough distance in the black of the night, it would be difficult for any human to tell us apart. Vampires, however, were another story. I hoped The Order didn't employ too many—it could prove tricky for our work this evening.

The grandfather clock in the hall struck eleven, and Rafael

emerged from the dining room. I avoided looking at him, partly because I wanted to keep my mind clear and partly because tendrils of guilt whispered through me at my outburst. Had I been too hard on him? *No.* No! If he was upset with me for speaking my mind, that was his problem—not mine.

Daphne cleared her throat. "Is everyone feeling well? Are we all together?"

Silent agreement all around.

"Good. To the carriage, then. Charlotte, Antoine, we shall see you soon. Good luck and be safe." Daphne patted Charlotte on the shoulder and threw Antoine a determined glance. Without another word, there was a nauseating explosion of flesh rending and fur and claws knitting together, and the two massive wolf creatures that had been Charlotte and Antoine raced out the front door in the direction of the cemetery.

"I think, perhaps, I might be more useful flying alongside the carriage," Rafael said quietly. "I'll keep an eye on things from above."

I shuddered, remembering the massive bat demon I'd seen him become in my opium haze.

"As you wish," Daphne said with a shrug.

I turned to him uneasily, but he didn't spare me a glance as he walked down the front steps. In the blink of an eye, he'd shifted into a small, normal looking bat. *Rather cute*, I thought.

Daphne's eyes widened a bit at the transformation, and I remembered she'd only seen Charlotte and Antoine shift before. But she kept her thoughts to herself and blew Étienne a kiss as he perched atop the carriage in the driver's seat. Daphne and I climbed inside. Étienne uttered a gentle command to the horses, and we lurched forward. Rafael had flitted off into the night, but I sensed his presence nearby.

Even in the ink-dark interior of the carriage, I knew Daphne was staring at me. As the carriage trundled on, shafts of light from the full moon outside filtered in through the windows and I noted her pensive expression.

I suspected she'd heard everything Rafael and I had argued about inside. In a household full of supernatural beings, the walls had ears—and claws.

"What?" I snapped.

"I didn't say anything," she said defensively.

"I can feel you staring at me," I argued. "Out with it, Duchesse."

She sighed. "You seemed very angry with him."

"Did you bait him?" I asked.

I could see moonlight glinting off her fangs as she smiled—answer enough.

"Why?" I asked, anger rising. "Things between us are complicated enough. I don't need your help to muddy the waters any further. Is it because you dislike him? Hate him for what he is—what he has done?"

"No."

Genuine shock stuttered through me.

"Good," I said. "Because you shouldn't. You said it yourself. He is honorable. Perhaps he had a difficult past, but who hasn't?"

"I do not hold anyone's past against them, Mina." The chill in her tone reminded me that she, too, had been through enough trials to last the rest of her immortal life, and yet here she was, barreling into more.

"Are you aiming to drive a wedge between us because you don't approve?"

"Certainly not. That would be absurd," she laughed.

Irritation climbed up my spine. "Then why?"

Another sigh—softer this time. "I was simply trying to feel you out. And him."

"It is no affair of yours," I said tartly.

"You're right," she agreed. Then, more gently, "Mina, I will be honest with you. Before Étienne and I realized how powerful our love for each other was, it took an act of near Herculean willpower for either of us to entertain the idea of a future together. We loved each other by then, of course, but neither of us wanted to acknowledge it and accept what it would mean. It was no small thing for me to declare myself to him and to likewise accept him. Beyond the vast differences in our worlds—our lives—we faced more than simply prejudice. And I paid the highest price for my love of Étienne—my mortality. But I have never looked back or wished for a different choice."

I fidgeted, uncomfortable with the emotions Daphne laid bare before me.

"Love is sacrifice, Mina, or it is nothing. It is not always easy. But when your soul calls so strongly to another, the alternative is worse than death. If you hadn't come to us and made us realize that a future together was possible, we would have carried on living dull half-lives, lonely and pining for each other. It was your intervention that helped us find our way in the dark."

I nodded.

"And so you think to do the same for me?" I asked, understanding dawning. "You try to—what is the expression—set a cat among the pigeons? Stir things up so we can get over our past and be together."

"I wouldn't presume to tell you what to do," she said. "But I will give you the intelligence I have collected."

I waited.

"Rafael loves you, Mina. He loves you so fiercely, I fear what he would do if something were to happen to you. End the world, I think," she continued. The gravity of her tone told me she wasn't exaggerating.

"He has told me as much," I admitted. I didn't tell her that his words frightened me—not because I feared him, but because I feared I couldn't match his passion. *Me. Cold, calculating, logical Mina.* Of course I loved him. I never stopped loving him, even when I hated him. It wasn't enough.

"You don't doubt his devotion to you," Daphne said, face illuminating ghostly white in a shaft of moonlight as the carriage turned down the cobblestone street blocks away from the cemetery. "Is it that you doubt your devotion to him?"

I didn't answer. She couldn't know what it had been like the last twenty years—the loneliness, the grief, the rage. The cold kept those fires of misery at bay. I found comfort in the cold because feeling anything else was too much pain.

"You love each other," Daphne insisted, gentle but firm.

"It has been a long time," I said, "since I have allowed myself the luxury of that thought."

"The fact that it holds true means something. If you still love him after all these years, after the awful things he did, that is a powerful kind of love."

More likely, it meant that I was warped. I'd clung to the memory of our love even when Rafael abandoned me for his family and his kingdom. Clung to the hope like a beaten dog returning to its abusive master. And then, miraculously, when the pain and hurt from that betrayal had become too much, I'd found the cold within me. It had been so easy—too easy—to shut everything else out. I didn't want to tell Daphne that, or Charlotte or Rafael, for that matter. I couldn't admit that I was afraid of what love looked like after spending so long being comfortable in the cold.

I struggled against the lump in my throat. Humiliating tears pooled in my eyes, and I dashed them away before they could fall.

"It is not enough." Even with more time, could I forgive

him? Even with all the apologies and declarations and penance, if he somehow surpassed my unforgiving nature and we could move on, he was still immortal and I was human. With everything between us—our past and the reality of time itself—love wouldn't be enough. *I wouldn't be enough.*

Daphne cocked her head as the carriage slowed.

"Perhaps not now. But it's a start."

The inside of the carriage suddenly seemed too small—too warm. The pressure of expectation weighed on me, boxing me in. Why did everyone expect me to simply move on? To simply *be fine*? To forgive and forget and throw myself headfirst into a relationship with a man I loved and hated in equal measure. To give up everything I'd worked for and start anew. It was bad enough Rafael was here, waiting and hoping and *expecting*, and now Daphne and Charlotte had thrown their lot in with him. It left me no room to breathe, no space to think.

I lunged for the door, worried I would heave my guts up all over her fine upholstery. As soon as I threw open the door and gulped the steadying, cool breaths, I heard her final statement on the matter.

"Mina," she said, low and stern, as if she'd plucked the very thought from my mind. "*You* are enough. It is why he has come for you after all these years. It is why we fight tonight. It is why we will all die to protect you."

Just as Charlotte had said. Just as Rafael had said. But I couldn't escape the truth—tonight, I was a liability. I wasn't the master healer in her clinic, the bold woman breaking the rules of a top university to acquire the best education, the preeminent supernatural physician sought out by kings and foreign courts and vampires worldwide. I was simply the human who needed protecting. I wanted to scream.

I frowned and jumped down from the carriage. It had rained lightly throughout the day, leaving mud puddles glinting with moonlight in the carriage ruts. Étienne had driven past the cemetery to an overgrown, tree-lined lane to park the carriage as we waited for word from Charlotte and Antoine's patrol.

Étienne jumped down to help Daphne emerge from the carriage, and I grimaced at the sounds of their tender kisses behind me.

"I may not have vampire hearing, but that is loud enough for human ears," I complained.

Étienne chuckled and came to stand beside me. Daphne was occupied taking various weapons out of the box at the back of the carriage, and Rafael, it seemed, was still off surveying us from some aerial perch. While we waited, Étienne nudged me with his shoulder, as affectionately as a brother.

"She's right, you know," he said softly, casting his eyes to his mate. Daphne was oblivious to us, checking the powder and shot in the twin flintlock pistols she wore in a harness around her waist.

"I swear upon all that is holy and unholy, Étienne, if you say anything else to me about the conversations that were meant to be private *or* my...situation...with Rafael, I will fill your veins with quicksilver and leave you writhing on the floor," I warned. A headache of annoyance had begun to build between my eyebrows.

He laughed again and held up his hands in defeat. We waited another few minutes in companionable silence.

"Do you know how he learned his other abilities?" Étienne asked quietly. "I have learned only the simplest illusions. Yet he seems to ooze power."

"I don't even know what all his abilities are," I admitted. "Suffice it to say that the ones I do know of are truly horrifying."

"One wonders why he needs *les DD* to help him retrieve his brother," Daphne said casually as she came to stand beside us.

"Perhaps it is because of your dazzling company," came that rich voice from the disembodied night around us.

Rafael materialized from the shadows.

"No, that is a very good question," I said. "Why can't you simply go in and take him?"

"I suspect the cell where Laszlo is being kept is warded with some holy power, or spell," Rafael said.

"How could you know that?" Étienne asked. "Have you been inside?"

Rafael shook his head. "No, but it would take something very powerful indeed to contain my brother. Very powerful and very, very bad."

Anxiety swept through me like winds across a field, caressing my nerves and tightening my muscles.

"How powerful is he if he managed to be captured?" Étienne wondered.

"That's what truly worries me. Either he is wounded and unwell, or whatever means they have for subduing supernatural beings is straight from the depths of Hell. Either way, it's unlikely that I would be able to save him alone—even with my *gifts*."

The wind began to whip up, colder than I'd expected. I tugged the thick wool cloak tighter around me, wishing for the fire in my study or a hot bath. The air smelled of damp earth and fresh rain, and I smiled despite myself.

"What's so amusing?" Rafael all but whispered, coming to stand on my other side.

I tensed, trying to forget everything Daphne had said on the ride over here. That familiar millstone of expectation pulling me down. The self-doubt and comforting cold. The fear of being a liability—useless. *Less than.*

"That scent," I replied after a moment. "I think I like it more than flowers. The wet mud after the rain—it means the promise of spring. It is the scent of hope to me."

He inhaled deeply. The moonlight on his face was a soft blue caress, highlighting parts and throwing others in shadow. His ancient vampire eyes glowed faintly, giving him an ethereal appearance. With his stunning, cold beauty, he might have been a haughty angel.

He remained in profile, standing next to me a few feet away. Whether it was because he wanted to respect my space after my tirade or because he dwelt in his own melancholy, I didn't know.

"You will be fine tonight," he said. "In there." He nodded toward the mausoleum.

My temper flared. "I know," I snapped. "Everyone here is on the lookout for me. Everyone will protect me. Weak, human Mina will be watched over and cared for."

"No," he said firmly, turning to me. "Not because of us. Because of you. You were right, Mina. You are strong, and smart, and capable. You are all you need. You will be fine because...you will be fine."

Daphne and Étienne had wandered away from the carriage, drawn toward a stand of trees a short distance away.

"I'm sorry for how I behaved earlier," he said. "For how I have behaved this whole time. You have every right to your anger and frustration. For all my immortality, I struggle with patience when it comes to you. You sunk tenterhooks into my soul long ago, and my single-mindedness in pursuit of yours has consumed me. I've told you I would give you anything, so I will give you what you ask—time. After tonight, I will wait for your summons. I won't come to you until you are ready."

I blinked. I hadn't expected him to agree so easily, given how hard he'd been fighting for me. It was what I wanted, wasn't it? I found myself nodding to him, heard myself thanking him, but something dark and despondent snaked through my chest.

I didn't have much time to examine the thoughts swirling through my mind because at that moment, two massive Hell-touched wolves bounded in from the trees where Daphne and Étienne had been skulking.

"No patrols?" Daphne asked.

Charlotte barked.

"Very well. That's...unexpected."

"Do you think it's a trap?" Étienne whispered.

"Likely," Rafael said, lifting a shoulder casually. He didn't seem particularly concerned, but Daphne tensed, scanning the area as if she could detect some unseen threat. Her hands went to the pistols strapped at her sides.

"What choice do we have?" I asked.

"Change of plans. Charlotte, you and Antoine stay out here on guard. Étienne, Rafael, and I will go in first. Mina, I don't know what we're walking into but...I'm sorry. You'll have to wait in the carriage."

"What?" I almost shouted. "Absolutely not. If Laszlo is hurt, time may be of the essence. You might not be able to move him. I'm going with you."

"It's too risky," Daphne said. "I'm sorry. But something feels...off. They tried to come for you once, Mina, I won't let them grab you again."

I made an outraged sputter, looking to Étienne and Charlotte for help. Étienne winced and refused to meet my eyes, rubbing the back of his neck with his hand. Charlotte merely whined and licked my land.

"If Mina wants to come, she comes," Rafael growled. He took a step toward Daphne, and Étienne tensed, hand on the wooden daggers at his waist.

"Please, Mina," Daphne begged, frowning. "We need to get moving. We don't have much time."

"Fine," I gritted out. "But we are going to have a *serious* discussion about boundaries and friendship when you return."

I stomped back to the carriage, disgusted by my petulance and embarrassed by my mortality. I couldn't face Rafael as they all turned toward the cemetery, easily vaulting the eight-foot iron fence. I watched them dart among the headstones until they came to that wretched mausoleum entrance of The Order's subterranean hideout. With a sharp tug and a metallic groan, the door swung open, and I watched with frothing anxiety as the living darkness in the tomb swallowed them entirely.

CHAPTER NINETEEN
RAFAEL

April 27, 1768
Cimetière des Innocents

OF COURSE, IT WOULD BE A TRAP. HOW GOOD OF A TRAP, THOUGH, remained to be seen. Tearing my lingering focus from Mina's well-deserved sulk in the carriage, I reached out with my senses as Daphne, Étienne, and I descended into the yawning gloom of the mausoleum. We climbed down a staircase until we reached the dank hallway below, which reeked of wet rot, old sweat, and greasy smoke from tallow candles. I paused at the foot of the stairs, uneasy.

"What is it?" Daphne whispered.

"Beyond the hallway," I said, puzzled. "I can't sense anything."

"So?" Étienne prodded.

"I can't hear anyone through the walls," I explained. "I can't smell the blood of any living thing or touch the consciousness of anyone."

"We're beneath a graveyard," Étienne retorted. "Why would you?"

"Because," I said impatiently. "That means no one is here. *No one.* Not just guards or prisoners, but rats, insects, and every other cold wriggling thing that makes the deep earth its home."

"How is that possible?" Daphne asked, taking half a step forward.

"It isn't," I said. "It means this *is* a trap. It means there is some kind of dark magic at work here that affects my abilities. It means that beyond this hallway, every other supernatural gift I possess is effectively useless."

"That settles it," Daphne replied. "We're turning back. I'm not risking our safety. Tomorrow, we'll regroup and come up with a different plan."

"Are you certain?" I asked. "If you're not prepared to carry on..."

"We'll come back, Rafael," Étienne insisted.

"If you wish," I said, affecting an air of disappointment. My inability to sense Laszlo worried me more than I cared to admit, and I was reluctant to leave without getting some idea of what The Order had planned for him. Resentment gnawed at me. I didn't want to be here; I wanted to be holed up in my castle with Mina. The sooner I could put an end to this mystery, the better.

"Then we should return to the carriage," I said.

I sensed the relief flowing from Daphne and Étienne, and could only hope they would forgive me for what I was about to do. We walked silently back up toward the mausoleum entrance. The moment they exited into the moonlit graveyard, I slammed the tomb door closed behind them and barred it with one of the tall candelabras inside.

"What the devil do you think you're doing?" Étienne shouted, banging against the iron door.

"Go back to the carriage and keep Mina safe," I replied. "It's better for everyone if I face this alone."

"We're not leaving you here," Daphne hissed. "Mina will have my head!"

Étienne swore beneath his breath, and by the sound of it, heaved his body into the door. The metal clanged and groaned. I knew the door wouldn't keep them out for long, which meant time was of the essence. There were several soft metallic clicks —Daphne loading her pistols in the dark. I hurried back down the stairs in case she tried to shoot her way through the barrier.

I moved forward swiftly and silently. With every step, I reached out again and again with my supernatural senses, hoping I'd been wrong—that I wasn't stumbling blindly into Death's waiting embrace. Each time, I felt the same thing—a void of feeling, sensation. As if I was coming to a precipice and was about to tumble off the edge of a map.

The corridor ended in a large door, cast in something like iron, but...not. It was much thicker than the one in the grave-yard above and while this one felt like it had been fashioned recently, the material it was hewn from felt ancient and rare. I placed my hand against it and recoiled almost immediately. The cold that leeched from it was unearthly and *wrong*.

This strange material must be some kind of prison door. Now, I was certain Laszlo was inside. I only prayed he was alive.

The massive door swung open easily, as if it had been waiting for me to arrive. Every instinct screamed at me to stop —go back—go no further, but I silenced them. I was here for answers—and for my brother.

I entered a large underground study with a great table in the center. Aside from the stacked bookshelves lining the walls, there were maps of Paris and charts of Europe, all covered with cryptic codes and pins. Curiosity needled me. What was The Order's master plan? Was it truly as simple as eliminating every vampire and maintaining their consolidation of power? Who would be the scapegoat for their evil deeds when all the vampires had been wiped off the map?

Suspecting Laszlo would be somewhere further underground, I reached out again with my supernatural senses and found them severely diminished, as though wandering through an empty void. If there was a secret dungeon underground, it would be well hidden. Searching for any kind of clue, I noted a conspicuous lack of dust in front of one of the bookshelves lining the wall. Running my hands along the edge of it, I found a catch and pulled. The bookshelf creaked forward, revealing a hidden archway leading even further into the darkness.

The floor was damp stone, and I heard the faint drip of water below. Despite my muted senses, at the edge of my awareness was something dim—familiar. A soft, shuddering breath and a wracking cough split the silence and I raced down the stone steps.

"Laszlo!" I hissed. "Is that you, brother?"

"My god...Rafael? Is that you?" His voice was weak and hoarse, and icy rage settled in my gut when I realized he had to have been starved and badly beaten to sound so diminished.

The small circular room was lined with seven cells. All were empty, save one. I rushed forward and gripped the bars, then pulled back as if burned.

"The bars," Laszlo huffed. "They are the same as the door."

"What is it?" I asked.

Laszlo had been sitting in the back corner of his otherwise empty cell. He struggled to stand and shuffled forward to clasp my arms through the bars.

My stomach dropped. Laszlo had once been so tall, strong, and handsome, taking all the best parts of our parents without the weak chin and sloping shoulders the other side was prone to. But here before me, he had wasted away to a skeletal corpse. Skin stretched over his bones and his long, black hair hung in greasy threads over his forehead. Fresh cuts, purpling bruises, and open festering wounds indicated he'd been tortured extensively, but hadn't been able to heal.

"How is this possible?" I muttered. "You can't have been here so long. How have you not healed? Why have you not ended these fools with a thought?"

Laszlo shook his head with great effort. "They know things, Rafael. They know enough to keep me in this weakened state. The inner door and the bars of my cell interfere with my abilities, as I'm sure you learned."

"We must hurry, Laszlo. Who holds the keys to your cell?" I asked, darting around. I scanned every surface for a keyring or latch that would open the cell door but saw nothing. "And where are they keeping Marguerite?"

"Marguerite is here?" Laszlo asked, stunned. "When? How?"

"You didn't know? The traitorous bitch! I knew something was off. I went to Dunkirk to find you and she approached me there, took me to your townhouse and spun me some tapestry of falsehoods about you being taken against your will by The Order. But how could they have found you? How could they have subdued you?"

A crash echoed from above. I hoped it wasn't The Order coming to ensnare us all in their wretched net. I paused in my hunt for the key to Laszlo's cell to brace myself for my enemy, who I could hear running down the stairs above me.

A blonde head poked around the doorframe, and a sigh of relief whooshed out of me.

"I'll have you know Étienne and I are *very* put out, Rafael," Daphne grumbled. "This is a horribly ill-advised idea, and if we get into trouble down here, it's entirely your fault." She inclined her head at Laszlo and smiled. "Your Highness."

He eyed me questioningly.

"It's a very long story," I answered. I looked back at Daphne. "Étienne? Mina?"

She waved my concern away. "The only reason I'm down here is because I convinced them to wait in the carriage while I came down to fetch you." Her eyes sparkled when she added, "And I don't fancy being in your shoes when Mina gets a hold of you. I don't think I've ever heard her use that language."

I winced. "Best for us to hurry, then. I'm looking for the key to this cell."

"Oh, damn the key, Rafael, let me see if I can pick the lock."

She produced a small roll of leather with half a dozen thin, metal picks of varying size and shape. As she knelt before the lock, I came back to Laszlo.

"What happened? And where is everyone tonight?" I wanted to know.

"We were wondering why they would leave you unguarded. Do you know when they will return?" Daphne asked.

After a few tense moments, there was a soft, metallic click and Daphne let out a triumphant laugh. She yanked the door back, hissing when she touched the metal, and Laszlo fell forward into my arms. He stumbled, nearly dragging me down with him.

"Just give me a moment," he wheezed. "I haven't much strength left."

"Rafael, we will need to carry him! We must get out of here before The Order returns," Daphne pressed.

A piercing sense of foreboding sliced through me just as I picked up the sounds of a struggle above me. Daphne whirled around; her face drained of color.

"Étienne!" she screamed.

She ran for the door in a blur of speed but staggered back just as she reached it. Two young vampires marched in, carrying the unconscious emissary between them. There was a mighty gash on his head spilling thick, black blood, but he was otherwise unharmed. The vampires tossed him in one of the cells. Before the enraged duchesse could launch herself at her love's captors, Marguerite appeared in the stairwell behind them.

"Easy, Duchesse," she warned. "I wouldn't want anything to happen to your friend here."

Terror gripped my body, almost swallowing me into oblivion. Marguerite tugged Mina forward, bound, gagged, and bleeding from her nose. She kicked furiously at Marguerite, connecting with a satisfying *thwack*. Marguerite grunted and dropped Mina to the ground, where she landed with a sickening crack. She stilled, but I could still hear the beat of her heart—alive, but unconscious. I made to run toward her, but bands of iron wrapped around my waist and held me in place —*Laszlo*.

Stunned, confused, I turned to him. "Laszlo! What are you doing?"

His thin lips cracked on a sad smile.

"I'm sorry, Rafael—truly I am. But they said it was you or us."

I stared, uncomprehending. He couldn't be—*couldn't be*—

betraying me again. Not after all this time. Not after everything I went through to find him. To come here and release him.

"Unhand me, you absolute clod! Do you have any idea who I am?" The outraged bellows of Charlotte's voice drifted through the staircase next, followed by the roar of rage coming from Antoine.

"Yes, Comtesse de Brionne," said a soft voice that sent chills down my spine. "But I'm afraid titles don't impress the likes of us very much."

"I wasn't talking about my title," she snarled. "I meant that the moment I get out of here, I'm going to rip your throat out with my teeth and spill your insides with my claws."

Several more vampires trudged in. Charlotte was utterly nude beneath what looked like a borrowed cloak, her wrists and ankles shackled in the same peculiar metal as the cells and the inner door. Antoine, pinned between four vampires, was led in behind her, similarly bound. The vampires shoved them into the cell next to Daphne and Étienne, closed the doors, and marched back out of the room. In their wake, a cloaked, masked figure emerged. He was tall and lean, with silvery hair and the sloped shoulders of idle aristocracy. He reeked of expensive perfume that could not hide the stink of rancid hair pomade, sweat, and cognac.

"Monsieur Derais," Charlotte chuckled darkly. "I know you're not intelligent enough to try to carry out some villainous plan all on your own. Where, pray tell, are your compatriots?"

The gentleman sneered. "How like you, Comtesse, to swiftly come to the wrong conclusion. We are not the ones plotting a coup."

"*Mon Dieu,* have you been drinking? What the Hell are you on about? No, you know what? I do not care. Simply release my friends and I, and I shall endeavor to forget this whole misunderstanding happened," she said airily.

I had to hand it to her—she was putting on a spectacular performance of the entitled aristocrat, given I could scent her fear.

"What is this all about, Derais?" Daphne cut in. She'd cleaned Étienne's wound and was wrapping it with a strip of clean linen from some secret pocket.

Monsieur Derais seemed to have some ounce of respect or fear for the duchesse, because he frowned apologetically as he approached her cell.

"His Majesty wants someone brought to justice for the blood plague. He believes the growing restlessness of the commoners can be...*redirected*...toward a shared enemy. We know the plague hails from the Dracul curse, and frankly, we don't care who initially brought it over the border. We will present the king with both brothers and have him try them publicly for execution. Crimes against humanity—and the crown," Derais said matter-of-factly.

Laszlo turned to him, shock written on his gaunt face.

"You said we would go free! My wife and I—we could return to Dunkirk after we brought Rafael to you! It was promised!"

"You fool," I snarled, shoving Laszlo to the ground. "You believed the word of these cowardly maniacs?"

"I'm sorry," Laszlo mumbled, his voice a strangled sob. "I just wanted to return home with Marguerite. They ambushed me in Dunkirk. After days of torture, they sent word to her and offered the bargain. If we could bring you out from hiding, they would let us go."

Derais whirled on Laszlo, a cruel smile lighting his face. "You don't expect us to let you continue roaming our country, poisoning everything with your vile infection. You and your blasphemous family and wretched blood offspring will burn on earth before burning in Hell. The Order will see to it. *I* will see to it. You and all your kind will be punished."

"You have done more to poison this country than vampires ever did," Daphne growled. "I regret that I was blind to your true aims for so long. I only hoped to steer you toward a more moderate and peaceful existence between human and vampire alike."

Crouching to better meet her furious gaze, Derais sneered and spat through the bars of her cell. "Filthy *sanguisuges!* There was never going to be a peaceful existence between vampires and humans. Vampires are an abomination—a crime against God. We will cleanse your kind from our country just as God cleansed the wicked from the Earth with the great flood."

From his cell, Antoine stretched out his long legs and grunted. "Sounds pretty blasphemous to me."

"Right you are, *mon cher.* Derais, you cannot simply hold us here. Daphne and I have the protection of the king. He would be furious if he found out you were holding us without just cause," Charlotte pointed out.

Derais rose and crossed back to stand above Mina, then tried to shift her with his foot. Rage ignited in my blood, first white hot, then fathomless black.

"You will *not* touch her," I snarled, my voice coming out like a demon's. Derais raised a supercilious eyebrow, challenging me.

"You think the king can save you? You were breaking in to release our prisoner, who represents the greatest threat to mankind. I think His Majesty would find that was cause enough," Derais replied.

Mina began to rouse herself with a groan, clutching at her head.

"Doctor, so glad you could join us," Derais offered, malice

sparking in his gaze. "As much as we have enjoyed your services, I'm afraid they are no longer required. We won't need doctors for supernatural threats after we manage to eliminate them entirely."

He tugged a pistol from his waistcoat pocket and hauled Mina up from the floor by her hair. I reached deep into myself to transform, to mesmerize—anything—but was entirely impotent. *Almost human.* At her yelp of pain, I screamed in abject horror.

"Derais!" I shouted. "Stop! I will give you anything—do anything. Please do not hurt her. She is innocent. She is human. She is *good.*" The words caught in my throat, and I hated myself for the begging in my tone, but I would do it for her every time. "Please."

Derais looked at me for a moment—considering.

"No," Mina whispered, looking at me. "Rafael, no. I...I'm sorry. For everything. I just...thought we would have more time to figure things out, but...I love you."

Tears of blood leaked from my eyes, and the more I wanted to scream and rage and unleash brutal violence, the weaker I felt.

"I will not say goodbye to you again, Mina," I said. "Derais, please. I will serve you. I will help destroy your enemies. I will give you wealth, land, armies...*Anything.*"

The pause of deliberation was enough for a breath of hope. In one swift move, Mina stamped hard on Derais's foot. He screamed, dropping the pistol and releasing Mina's hair. She leapt up and ran for the door, taking the stairs two at a time.

Derais shrieked at Laszlo. "Go after her, Dracul, and I *might* spare you and your wife."

"No, Laszlo! Brother, please!" I shouted, launching myself at Derais.

But Laszlo was off like a shot, hobbling up the stairs after

Mina. I had Derais in my hands, but I felt the sharp edge of a blade at the back of my neck. Marguerite stood behind me, holding a short sword.

"Let him go, Rafael," she said, her voice trembling. "He cannot grant us safe passage if he is dead."

Blind rage gripped me as Derais smiled. I knew Marguerite would behead me with one stroke if I so much as breathed wrong. Seething, I let go of Derais and stepped back slowly.

"Hear me now," I growled at him. "There is no place on earth you can hide that I will not find you. I have visited torment on lesser men than you for lesser injustices, so believe me when I say that you, Derais, will reap what you sow. I will have you begging for death when I've only just begun with you."

A flicker of fear passed over the older man's face, and he swallowed but stood and squared his shoulders.

"Powerful words from a powerless vampire." He sneered. "Step back, Dracul, into that cell there. Yes—those bars that feel so strange to you? That's Judas silver."

I would have said it was impossible, but my inability to access any of my powers proved it was true. Even now, I could feel my supernatural strength siphoning off, draining every-so-slightly, like a trickle of water from a cracked pitcher.

"What's Judas silver?" Charlotte asked, uneasy.

"Surely, you remember the story," Derais scoffed. "Judas betrayed Jesus to the Romans for thirty pieces of silver— blood money that led to the death of our Lord and Savior. Even if you and your kind are sinners for succumbing to the temptation of the blood plague's power, I'm certain you recall how well that played out for humanity's greatest traitor."

"*Mon Dieu,* Daphne, I forgot how melodramatic Derais could be," Charlotte droned, rolling her eyes. "Look, if you're going to execute us, just get it over with. I don't need the torture of Bible study before I die."

Daphne snickered and Étienne stirred in her lap. She stroked his bloodied hair idly, no doubt trying to comfort him and quell her fear.

Derais's face twisted in anger, but he continued.

"Well, what happened to those thirty pieces of ill-gotten silver? Cursed, they were. Tainted. They left the mark of evil on everyone and everything they touched. They disappeared from legend for a few hundred years, only to resurface during the Crusades. When people slowly realized what they were, they were collected and kept in a lead vault in the holy land. The Order formed sometime after that, and then the blood plague came to France, and my holy brothers agreed the ultimate test of the silver's effects would be to pit it against the greatest, most powerful threat to our world—the House of Dracul."

He paced, seething in righteousness as I slumped to the floor. The more he spoke, the wilder the gleam in his eye became and the more rabid his tone. Flecks of spit flew from his lips as he continued his tirade.

"I secured the unholy treasure myself this past year at great personal cost, but it was worth it. Now, we finally have a means to eliminate every supernatural creature from the face of the earth. Once we had the cursed silver, it was almost *too* easy to find ways to use it—to smelt it down, mix it with other metals, and turn it into powerful weapons against blasphemous threats."

"You are mad, Derais," I growled. I tried to fight the rising nausea and weakness snaking through my body. "You and your Order are twisted. If you wish to protect humanity from its greatest threat, you should start by hanging yourself."

Derais crossed the room and closed the cell door, locking me into Laszlo's old cell. Placing the keys in his front pockets, he gestured to the door and motioned for Marguerite to leave. She flicked one glance back at me, regret written on her face.

"I'm sorry, Rafael," she whispered. "But Laszlo is all I have."

I wanted to hurl an insult at her, to scream and rage and wrap my hands around her delicate neck, but the sound of Mina's screams split the night, and my horror froze me in place.

CHAPTER TWENTY

MINA

April 27, 1768
Cimetière des Innocents

Faster and faster I ran, swerving between trees and dodging shrubs and puddles. Laszlo had come staggering out of the mausoleum, obviously weakened from his imprisonment. Otherwise, I would have already been caught—or dead.

He gained ground ever so slowly, and I knew I had to do something to gain the advantage. But the farther we got from The Order's headquarters, the more he seemed to recover, as if his strength was slowly finding its way back to his tormented bones. Sheer terror had me in its thrall, and I couldn't think—couldn't puzzle my way out of this one.

"Doctor, please!" he called from behind me, closer than I would have liked. "Please, you must understand! I don't want to hurt you! I just need to do as they say, and they'll let Marguerite and I go!"

I wouldn't be able to hide from him, and I couldn't outrun

him for long, but that meant my only recourse was to stand and fight.

Impossible. Even weakened, Laszlo was probably stronger and more powerful than Rafael, and it was only a matter of time before he caught up with me and hauled me back to The Order for my execution.

I stumbled on the root of a large tree and nearly went down, but as I twisted to right, I heard the faint clink of glass from my waistcoat. *The vials in my medical kit. The pockets! The weapons!* Realization slammed into me as I hurdled a low shrub —Charlotte and Daphne had given me everything I needed to defend myself; I simply had to find the right time and place to use it.

I groped blindly through the pockets, trying to remember which ones held what. I plucked the vial of quicksilver and a small wooden stake from my waistcoat, held them out, and then slowed to prepare for my final stand.

Laszlo was almost upon me, but he stopped after seeing the items in my hands. I knew they wouldn't be enough to kill him, but if he was still weak, they would be enough to delay him considerably. I brandished them before me.

"Let me go, Laszlo," I warned, desperately trying to catch my breath.

He shook his head slowly.

"You know I cannot do that," he said. "If I don't take you back, they will kill Marguerite."

"If you take me back, they will kill me," I pleaded. "And they will not let you go, Laszlo. You will take me to them, and they will kill you, anyway, and Marguerite. They will kill my friends. And they will kill Rafael."

My voice broke on his name.

"I have to try," he choked out. "I must try for Marguerite.

She has been through so much. I cannot leave her there with them."

"You are damned either way," I said. "But if we work together, there might be a way to save us all."

"How?"

I sighed, hating myself for advocating the death of anyone, no matter how evil. "We could take them down *together*."

He stepped toward me. "What do you mean?"

I backed up. "You and Rafael are more powerful than all The Order put together. The two of you could go through those men like a hot knife through butter."

Laszlo huffed a laugh. "Surely you saw the vile things their witchcraft does to vampires. With that, we're weaker than human. Besides, killing them would only prove the humans right about us. The Order would be martyrs, and we would be the monsters everyone already suspects we are. There would be no doubt in anyone's minds."

He had a point, but I wasn't ready to give up. Pain throbbed in my ankle, and I wouldn't be able to outrun him. I had to try to reason with him.

"So we tell everyone the truth about The Order. How they've lied and stolen and controlled all along. Make everyone see them as the power-hungry manipulators they truly are."

He slowed, considering. From the tree above us, an owl hooted softly. We both tilted our heads toward the sound. I desperately wanted to believe it wasn't an ill omen—that they were watching over us, offering hope. *Hope.*

"Please, Laszlo," I begged, playing every card in my hand. "I've spent the last twenty years hating Rafael for abandoning me and serving penance for his mistakes. Now that he's come back into my life, I'm not ready to have it all end before we can set things right. Frankly, I'm not even ready to forgive him. I love him, but I just...need more time. We all need more time."

Turning his gaze from the owl to the fallen tree at his side, he scrubbed his hands across his face, and he sat down hard.

"It was never supposed to happen," he said, his voice drifting absently on a gentle wind.

I waited, still palming the quicksilver and wooden stake in case he decided our parlay was at an end.

After a beat, I asked, "What wasn't supposed to happen?"

His dark eyes—so much like Rafael's, yet weary and sad—lifted to mine.

"Marguerite was pregnant when we fled Wallachia," he said.

The news hit me like the shock of cold from winter's first frost.

"But—that's impossible. Humans and vampires cannot reproduce," I argued.

"Yes, that's what we've believed all along. My ancestors and now the modern vampire...it simply does not happen. And yet, Marguerite grew with my child while we made our home in Dunkirk."

Logic compelled me to ask the impertinent question.

"You're certain it was yours?"

A dark, rasping chuckle issued from his chest.

"I wasn't at first, but when the pregnancy began to show signs of the curse, it became evident. I had not planned on eloping, but when she told me about the babe, everything in my life became clear. I would not allow my child to live in this world of darkness. I would not allow my father to corrupt the only good thing in my life. So I did the only thing I could think to do—I packed up as much as I could without drawing notice, and we ran."

I watched Laszlo as he spoke, the despair plain on his face and in the set of his shoulders. He ran his fingers through a patch of damp grass at his feet, and I tried not to stare at his long, lethal claws trailing through the dew.

"We traveled around for a while, trying to hide from the men my father sent after us, but eventually I had to kill them. We couldn't keep running. We went north as far as we could, but she was so weak then. We stopped at Dunkirk to shelter and rest for a while—she was so ill. I had to turn her then, you see. She would not have survived the birth of the child if it was, in fact, a blood drinker."

I considered going to sit on the log next to him but thought better of it. Instead, I crouched where I was, ready to jump up at the slightest twitch of his movement. The owl above us had fallen silent, as if sensing the heaviness of our conversation.

"Marguerite's condition during the turning left her weak, and even when she completed the transformation, she was weaker than most vampires. But she survived—that was all that mattered to me. And the babe in her belly continued to grow, unharmed by her change of state. When my daughter was born, nothing in the world had prepared me for how much I would love—could love—another being. I'd loved my parents, but feared them, and I'd loved Rafael, but we had grown apart after our childhood. Marguerite was the first person who made me believe I was more than a monster or some ancestral obligation. And then she gave me the one thing that I'd never felt worthy of having—a love so pure, I would have done anything to keep it. To protect it."

"A family trait," I offered.

A sad smile tugged at the corners of his lips. Thinner than Rafael's lips, but the same shape.

Rafael. Hold on, Rafael.

"For a few years, we existed in bliss. We were living meagerly, but one of Marguerite's sisters came to stay with us to help care for our daughter. Lucy. My little Lucy, sweet starlight of my life."

He gasped out a painful sob, and a tear of blood spilled down his cheek.

"I should have seen it coming. Could have prevented it if I'd been smarter or faster. But it was an accident, my little Lucy biting her aunt. She nearly drained her—too young to know how to stop in the grip of a blood frenzy. When Marguerite found her sister, almost dead, and Lucy at her throat, she panicked."

Pieces started to fall into place. "Marguerite turned her sister, rather than let her die."

"It was forbidden," Laszlo said. "It is forbidden for any of the Dracul family to turn another, except for our mates. It was a way to ensure the curse was contained to our family."

"What happened to Lucy?"

"Marguerite's sister did not take to the turning well. It was painful and messy. When she awoke as a vampire, it was...*wrong*. She was wrong—broken. I don't know what happened, if it was because she was the first outsider to undergo the change, or perhaps because Marguerite was weak when she tried to turn her. Whatever it was...she awoke angry —and hungry. In her wrath, she killed Lucy and nearly killed Marguerite. She fled into the countryside before I returned home. I have not seen or heard from her since, but we looked. How we looked! After burying Lucy and caring for Marguerite during her recovery, my grief was too heavy for me to consider vengeance."

My heart broke at Laszlo's confession, for the loss of his daughter and the near loss of his mate—his wife. The blood plague hadn't come to France because of a malicious, corrupt vampire nor his greedy, selfish wife—it had simply been an accident. A true tragedy, brought about by terror and confusion and grief. I felt sick.

"I'm sorry," I whispered, unacknowledged tears falling down my own cheeks. "I cannot fathom the depths of your loss."

He nodded. "It does not get easier, even with time," he said. "Time does not heal wounds, as they say. In my experience, time simply earns us more wounds so that we cannot focus on the pain of one for too long."

"Time grants us perspective," I said. "But that is all."

Laszlo offered a half smile and opened his mouth to say something, but a distant crash echoed through the woods. He was up before I could blink, panic glittering in his eyes.

"It is Derais!" he hissed.

"They will stop at nothing, Laszlo. Even if you give me to them, you and Marguerite do not stand a chance. Then, they will come for every vampire in France. It will be genocide!"

Desperation and anger warred in his expression.

"Please, Laszlo! I have spent my life trying to help your kind. Do not let my work be in vain. Do not let your brother pay for the shattered dream of your family—it was no more his fault than Lucy's."

He took the words like a blow, wincing as they landed.

"Dracul!" came Derais's shouts. "Dracul, you better have my prize in your filthy claws, or I will remove your pretty wife's head."

Enraged, Laszlo roared into the night. The sound was horrifying and hellish, filled with anger and pain and torment.

"Run," he commanded, the sound guttural and inhuman. His form began to shift, bones breaking and sinew snapping and skin ripping away from his body. For a moment, I stood there and watched, transfixed by the shapeshifting. In a heartbeat, he had finished, and I couldn't help the scream that climbed its way up from the pit of my stomach.

Where Laszlo's gaunt, sagging human form had stood now appeared a true monster from the lowest, most nightmarish circle of Hell. He looked like the devil himself, with spindly, garish sets of fangs—his eyes, black puddles of darkness that glowed with a faint red light. Massive bat wings sprouted from the upper body of a creature that was a demonic shadow of the wolf creature Rafael could become. A thick, scaly tail whipped around his powerful legs and long, razor sharp claws erupted from his fingers and toes.

Run, he said again, this time in my mind.

I didn't need to be told again. I took off, weaving through the trees until I came to the low wall on the opposite side of the cemetery. I crouched behind a massive oak tree with the cemetery at my back. The moonlight dappled silver on the ground, and I heard Derais's threatening shouts at Marguerite and Laszlo.

Given that he'd just shifted into an eight-foot-tall monster, Laszlo seemed to be healing more quickly than I'd expected. I didn't know what he intended to do, but I wasn't prepared to question it just yet.

Derais stormed into the clearing where Lazlo and I had been. He dragged Marguerite behind him and threw her to the ground—her head making a sickening crack against the fallen tree. Laszlo roared and rushed to her side. She struggled to rise and reached for him.

"You had her! You had her and you let her go!" Derais screamed. "You filthy beasts, we should have slaughtered you where we found you."

Laszlo picked Marguerite up from the ground, shielding her with his enormous wings. I watched in horror as Derais slipped the pistol from his pocket and aimed at Laszlo's back.

"No!" I shouted, rushing forward. Anger and horror propelled me forward, and no small amount of stupidity. "Please! Don't kill them!"

Laszlo whirled around, a low growl spilling from his throat.

"Please," I begged Derais again. "Just let them go!"

Confused, still enraged, Derais turned to me. "My dear Doctor, why the Hell should I? They're abominations—they should all be wiped off the face of the Earth."

"They're not," I insisted. He turned the pistol on me, and I froze. "They're cursed, as you say. But the plague was not their fault—it was an accident, and they have suffered enough. They did not come here with malice in their hearts. If you do believe in God and divine justice, you must also believe in penance and forgiveness. The Draculs have been paying penance for longer than any of us have been alive. Leave them, Derais. Let them go home. Let them live."

For one heartbreaking moment, I thought he would listen. But Derais hissed out a breath, madness clouding his eyes.

"The Order is the right hand of God, and I am acting on his behalf."

The shot cracked the silence of the night in the same instant that Derais screamed. I staggered back with the force of being hit but didn't understand how. Laszlo had Derais by the throat, and Marguerite was slumped on the ground, sobbing those strange vampire tears of blood. Slowly, cold seeped through me, and it became difficult to draw breath.

How strange.

A phantom pain throbbed in my chest and at last, I looked down to see a sticky wetness spreading down my new waistcoat.

Understanding dawned.

"I've been shot," I huffed, stunned. I took a step forward, then my legs failed, and I crumpled onto the damp ground.

There was a strange rushing in my ears, and I was suddenly exhausted.

Mina.

It was Laszlo in my mind again.

Mina, you have been shot in the heart with a powerful bullet—one made from Judas silver. You are dying. Do you wish for me to save you?

I opened my eyes, unprepared for the shock of seeing Laszlo's demon form looming above me.

"Save me? From death?" My voice was strangely distant.

Yes. You asked for time. Do you still wish for it? I can give it to you—all the time in the world. I can turn you, Mina, if you wish.

"But the sunshine..." I said thickly. I didn't want a life without sunshine. No, that wasn't right. I didn't want a life without Rafael. I didn't want to die without Rafael. Curiously, Daphne's words drifted through my mind. *Sometimes, when it is truly quiet in the small hours of the night, I could swear I have heard the stars singing.* She was right—my life had always circled blood and death and darkness. Even without Rafael in it, that was where I took comfort. It was never the lightness of a summer afternoon or a lemon-yellow gown. The darkness in my life was mine—it was me. It wasn't because of Rafael. He was the only thing that brought me true joy and passion, and who gave me the ability to value life as much as I did. And with remarkable clarity, I knew my answer.

Yes, Laszlo. Give me more time. Give me darkness. Give me a chance at a future with Rafael.

The terrifying demon nodded once and bent his head to my neck. He raised his wrist above my lips and sliced his arm open with one long, sharp claw, and black liquid copper slid over my tongue and down my throat. Then he bent his head, and his lethal fangs found my throat—his claws digging into the bullet wound in my chest at the same time. I would have screamed from the agony, but my vocal cords no longer worked. Eternities of pain crashed through my body, igniting every nerve in a symphony of suffering, and then a cold, silent darkness descended, and I knew no more.

CHAPTER TWENTY-ONE
RAFAEL

April 28, 1768
Cimetière des Innocents

"Rafael, stop trying to wrench those bars apart; they're not going to move," Charlotte called to me from across the dungeon. "We have to come up with another plan."

"Damn it, why can't I pick this bloody lock?" Daphne shouted, discarding her fourth bent hairpin onto the floor.

I ignored the lot of them and heaved my shoulder against the hinges in the door, near feral with desperation to get to Mina. To keep me sane, I fantasized about all the ways I would torture each surviving member of The Order and punish Laszlo and Marguerite for betraying me.

The insistent throb of pain in my head and spreading weakness in my limbs sang the Judas silver's song. Each time I flung myself at the bars, the pain echoed louder and louder, but I wouldn't—couldn't—sit in this pit and do *nothing*.

Noises drifted down from the stairwell, and I scented

blood. When I realized whose blood, I collapsed to the floor, screaming.

To my horror, Laszlo filled the doorway, covered in blood. Marguerite leaned on his shoulder, and in his arms, he carried *her*.

My reason for existing.

But it was wrong—she was wrong. Her beautiful throat—the one that I'd lavished kisses upon and drawn laughter from—was ravaged. There was a gaping wound in her chest, right above her heart. *Her heart*, which no longer beat.

Daphne and Charlotte screamed as they saw the lifeless body of their friend hanging limp in the arms of a naked, bloody Laszlo.

"I am going to kill you, Laszlo!" I screamed. "I am going to rip you apart! What have you done? What have you done to my Mina?"

Tears of hot blood streamed down my face as I shouted and sobbed.

Marguerite pulled something from her skirts and came to my cell door.

"I gave her time," Laszlo said.

"What the fuck does that mean?" I choked out.

"She asked me for more time, brother, and so I turned her."

The room went silent and began to spin.

"Derais shot her in the heart with a Judas silver bullet," Marguerite said softly. She brandished the key and slipped it in the lock. "She was dying, Rafael. Laszlo offered to turn her, and she agreed."

For one shocking moment, there was only the faint sound of water dripping somewhere above.

"She—she is turning?" I whispered, not believing it. "I don't believe you! What have you done to her? Where is Derais? I'm going to end you all!"

My screams of rage had turned to sobs as I stared at the family who had betrayed me.

"Forgive us," whispered Marguerite. "If you must have vengeance, visit it upon me. Laszlo wanted no part in this. He only wanted to protect me. He could not save Mina from Derais...from the bullet. He could only turn her. Forgive him. *Forgive him.*"

For once, I did not sense any treachery from her. I felt only grief. Lifting my eyes to Laszlo, I saw the same look of regret and haunted sadness.

Could it be? *My Mina—turning.* Her summers and her sunshine, my spring goddess. My Persephone, doomed to a life of darkness and death.

The cell door swung open, and I pushed Marguerite aside to go to Laszlo. He gingerly handed Mina's limp body to me. I cradled her in my arms. In the distance, I heard Marguerite unlocking the doors of Charlotte and Daphne's cells. They came to stand at my side.

"If she is turning, we will need a safe place for her to heal and be reborn," Marguerite said.

"Where is Derais?" Charlotte asked sharply.

"In pieces too small to be found," Laszlo replied.

Daphne and Charlotte exchanged a look.

"Well, I expect neither of our homes will be particularly safe after tonight. Once The Order returns and finds Laszlo and Marguerite gone and Derais...erm, *indisposed*...they will come for us, and they know where to find us," Charlotte said.

"Where can we go?" Étienne asked. "I don't want to risk my sisters' safety by hiding out with them."

"My home," I said. "You may stay at my home. It is outside Rouen."

Daphne nodded. "We are grateful, Rafael."

"And us?" Laszlo asked.

"You must come. We have much to discuss," I replied. My voice sounded hollow.

He nodded and reached for Marguerite's hand. We filed silently up the stairs, exiting through the mausoleum. The deep indigo of the night sky was beginning to lighten to a soft pewter as we made our way toward Daphne's hidden carriage. Once outside the influence of the Judas silver, Charlotte and Antoine shifted to their wolf forms to run alongside the carriage. Étienne and Laszlo perched atop the driver's seat, while Marguerite, Daphne and I carried Mina between us in the carriage.

The ride was an exercise in patience. Every bump and shake of the carriage jostled Mina's body and sent fresh spikes of fear through me—what if Laszlo had been too late? What if Mina didn't react well to the blood plague? Would the effect of that poisonous bullet prevent her from turning, or turn her into something else entirely? What if she regretted her choice?

What if she found she had eternity waiting for her, and even then, decided it was not enough time to heal from the pain I'd caused her? She'd chosen life after death...but what if she didn't choose me?

By the time my ruined castle came into view, I was deep in my melancholy and the sun was almost at the horizon. I hadn't been this close to the sunrise in a long time, and it was almost impossible not to admire the soft oranges and pinks and dusky purples of the sky.

"Cutting it a bit close, brother," Laszlo grunted, coming down from the driver's seat.

Charlotte and Antoine padded up next to us and shifted back to human form.

"Well, this is charming, but you seem to be missing a roof, Rafael," Charlotte observed.

"The entrance is at the top of the tower. Laszlo and I will

shift and fly you all up. I'll take Mina first, and then come back for the rest of you," I said, not bothering to wait for their acknowledgement. I exploded into my large bat form and picked up Mina's body in my claws. Behind me, I heard Laszlo change as well, and saw him grab Charlotte and Marguerite in his beastly hands.

We entered the tower, and I summoned Guillaume, explaining everything as quickly as I could. Though I was loathe to do it, I handed Mina's cold, still body to him and leapt back up the tower to pick up Daphne and Étienne. Laszlo was on my heels with Antoine in his claws just as the first rays of sunlight crested the horizon. I threw the stone door in place just in time. Exhausted beyond words, I led our group through the halls of my home, assigning them guest rooms as we went. I instructed the household staff to bring blood and fresh meat to everyone, as well as draw hot baths.

"Rest for the day, my friends," I said. "We will dine together after sundown. Then, I will be happy to show you the rest of my home. Please be comfortable here. If you should need anything, my staff will gladly attend to you."

I bowed stiffly and headed on swift feet to the guest room where I'd had Guillaume bring Mina. Already, the maids had come in and removed her bloodied clothing and changed her into a simple cotton chemise. She was tucked into the large bed while one of the maids stoked the fire in the fireplace. The young girl wasn't surprised to see me arrive, but merely rose and inclined her head.

"I've made her as comfortable as possible," she said forlornly. "But her wounds..."

"She will recover," I said. "She is cursed now."

The maid's eyes widened, and she nodded quickly, then hurried from the room.

Exhausted, depleted, I came to the side of the bed and fell

to my knees. Here, alone, I let my despair and fear wash over me as I clasped her hand.

"I never wanted this for you, Mina," I whispered, bloody tears coming hot and fast. "I never wanted you to have to leave your world behind for me. How I have tainted you and your future—all because I could not bear to be apart from you. All because I was afraid of hurting you. And no matter how much I wanted to protect you, you still ended up here. Forgive me, my love. Please forgive me. I will spend the rest of eternity earning your forgiveness, even if you wish to banish me from your sight. I will give you all the time in the world to come back to me. But please, Mina...please come back to me."

Her breathing had stilled, her limbs lay stiff and cold—a sign that her mortal body was dying. Even as I hoped the transformation would go well and she would recover quickly, I still mourned the death of her human self. It was the Mina I'd fallen in love with, the Mina I'd dreamed of marrying, the Mina whose blue eyes turned silver like a storm at sea when she was angry. The Mina who loved little almond cakes and small bouquets of yellow daisies, even though she would never admit such small romantic gestures delighted her. The Mina who fought harder than everyone for what was right. The Mina who had the strength for others when they fell to weakness. Ever logical, ever curious, ever questioning, ever loyal and loving Mina.

I wasn't sure how long I stayed there on my knees at her bed. It felt like a few moments and an eternity at the same time. Eventually, Charlotte came in—somewhat rested and restored, and damp from a bath. She told me to sleep and feed, which I refused until she insisted that Mina wouldn't want me to deteriorate at her bedside when nothing could be done.

"Besides," she said. "If she wakes, I hardly think you'll

want to greet her looking like *that*. Do have yourself a bath, Rafael."

She crawled into the bed on Mina's other side and withdrew a romance novel from her skirts. She began reading out loud as if Mina was awake, even though I was sure she knew Mina would have been too embarrassed to read something so salacious.

Despite my melancholy, the ghost of a smile played about my lips, and I allowed Charlotte some time to grieve for the woman that we both loved. I expected Daphne would be along in time, as well, which gave me a measure of comfort while I dragged myself into my bedchamber. There was a bath waiting for me and two large decanters of blood, which I devoured. The Judas silver had leeched much of my strength, and the blood helped to restore some of it, as would a few hours of rest.

Sending a silent prayer to my long-abandoned gods for Mina's health, I quickly washed and slipped beneath the covers. It wasn't long before sleep wrapped me in its drugging embrace and pulled me under.

I woke to the sounds of bare feet padding toward my bedroom door. Before the knock came, I threw on my banyan and rushed to yank the door open. Daphne stumbled back a step, startled.

"She—she's awake," she said.

Without another word, I ran to the guest room where I heard Charlotte chattering excitedly and soft, rasping laughter from Mina.

Mina.

She was sitting up in bed, her long dark hair thrown over her shoulder and her blue eyes sparkling. She looked a touch pale and drawn, but considering she'd come back from the precipice of Death, she looked remarkably well.

The relief I felt staggered me, stealing my strength almost

as much as the cell of Judas silver. I gripped the door frame and took a steadying breath, determined not to collapse and come apart. Charlotte looked up and saw me, and fortunately had the good grace not to tease me at that moment.

"We'll talk later," she promised Mina, winking at me as she and Daphne left the room. In the silence that followed, I could only stare, unsure if I was dreaming or if this was truly happening.

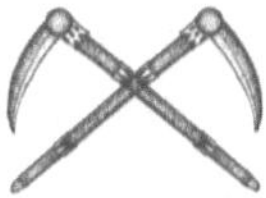

MINA

THE SENSATIONS THAT ASSAULTED ME WERE INTENSE ENOUGH TO BE painful. The sounds and smells and uncomfortable awareness of thoughts from everyone in the household pressed against my consciousness until I wanted to claw my brain from my skull. Slowly, my new form became accustomed to the riot of stimuli, and with effort, I found a place of quiet stillness in my mind. It was falling asleep in a dark cave, then suddenly waking up in the middle of the busiest square in Paris.

Once the shock wore off, I was left with the waning embers of hope and the gnawing doubts about what had befallen Rafael and my friends back inside The Order's mausoleum.

Some strange, new instinct had me closing my eyes and stepping out from the quiet place in my mind and reaching out —listening. I heard people moving in the household. I heard birdsong in the world above me, the soft sounds of wind across the grass, and the burbling of a distant stream tripping its way over river stones. I found myself open to vast amounts of sensory information, and if I was careful and mindful, I could home in on one being at a time. It wasn't like reading another person's mind, but if I focused hard enough, I could perceive the shape and feeling of an individual's thoughts. In this household, it was a heady mixture of fear, love, relief, and worry. When my mind drifted to Rafael, the sense of his grief, shame, and regret broke my heart, but the persistent pulse of love from him was a soothing balm.

Most of the vampire turnings I'd seen, as well as Charlotte and Antoine's werewolf turning, had taken place over the course of days—weeks, in some cases. And yet, mine had taken place over the course of a few hours. It could have been from the strength of Laszlo's blood and his proximity to the curse, but I wasn't certain. I'd need to speak with him—and soon.

RAFAEL

Mina tilted her head—a soft smile appearing on her lips.

"You are not dreaming," she murmured.

I froze.

"You can—read minds," I said slowly.

"I can…sense…thoughts," she replied, her brow furrowing. "It is strange. I feel very strange, Rafael. Everything is more intense."

"You're alive. You survived death and the turning," I stated, stunned.

"Yes," she acknowledged, softly.

Emotions surged and I stumbled, gripping the door frame for strength.

"I thought you were dead," I choked out.

She tilted her head, considering. "Technically, I was," she replied. "And now I am...not. It's a very odd thing." Her eyebrows pinched together. "When this is over, I will need to update my notes and my medical texts. I fear I got a few things wrong in my understanding of supernatural anatomy." She held up her formerly human hand and stared at it as she grew long, lethally sharp claws.

Her logical assessment of the miracle of her rebirth unlocked me, and I smiled.

"It will be like this for a few days as your body learns to adjust to your supernatural senses," I said softly. I crossed the room to sit next to the bed in the chair Daphne had occupied.

Mina reached for a pitcher of water on the nightstand and a pewter cup.

"Allow me," I offered, pouring her a drink. I tried not to stare at her—to evaluate what else was different about her supernatural form from her human one. She seemed the same, if a little worn out and on edge.

"It is not what I expected," she blurted out, massaging the place between her brows that usually held her tension.

I bit my lip, trying to keep from peppering her with questions or launching my body at hers and covering her skin in worshipful kisses.

"Oh?" was all I replied. "What did you expect?" *Why didn't you want me to turn you?* The traitorous, selfish thought whined in my ear like a mosquito of self-doubt.

She sighed, pursing her lips. After a moment, she began.

"It's not that I never considered turning, Rafael. Of course I did—for you. But that was years ago, and I spent the rest of my life convincing myself that I didn't need to become supernatural to prove that I had value—that I was worth something. At first, after you sent me away, I wanted to be enough for you. And then, when I had soothed some of my hurt, I wanted to be enough for myself." She reached for a small glass of blood on the nightstand that had been kept warm by the low flame of a candle. Curiously, she sniffed at it, lifted it to her lips, and drank greedily. When she was finished, her eyebrows lifted in surprise. "Fascinating!"

"Mina, you have always been enough for me. You have always been worth more than ten of me—a thousand of me, even. When I sent you away, I thought I was protecting you from my father's wrath. I never considered that I was protecting myself from the pain I feared I would feel when we were separated by time. Perhaps I didn't want to approach you to find a solution together because part of me believed it was futile, since you did not want to turn. For that, I am sorry—I will never stop apologizing for getting things so wrong." I stood to refill the glass of blood from a crystal decanter.

"My anger at you has protected me, as well, Rafael. But when I was lying there on the ground, feeling my life ebb away, there was peace and...clarity. I held onto my anger because it was a shield. Yet the only thing it protected me from was finding happiness and closure without you. I think, on some level, I didn't want to heal from our wounds because it would mean having to let you go. And even though we have been apart for the last twenty years, I think I have always lived my life alongside yours. Keeping to a nightly schedule, immersing myself in work benefiting vampires and vampirekind, forming relationships with supernatural people...the proximity to blood, death, and darkness...it has been my life even without you. I was never one for spring flowers and sunshine. I would have always found the night—and found you in it, waiting for me. The threads of my entire being have been interwoven with yours from the beginning."

I was speechless—devastating grief and overwhelming hope warring in me like the forces of nature building a hurricane. I opened my mouth to speak, but she pressed a gentle finger to my lips.

"When I was dying, I wanted more time, but not for me. For you. We spent so long apart, and I couldn't believe things were over now that we'd found our way back to each other. I realized I still wanted the same things I always wanted, but for the first time ever, I could see you standing next to me in my dreams of the future. I want the happiness being with you gives me. I want the joy and love we forged years ago. I want the life we dreamed of back when we were too young and naïve to know the cruelties the world had in store for us."

I sucked in a breath.

"What are you saying?" My chest ached with longing to hear the words from her lips—words I'd dreamt of every night since we separated years ago.

"I love you, Rafael. I cheated Death to be with you. I defied the laws of nature to stay on earth and claim you as my own. I have carved out my place in the darkness so that together, we can be our own light."

I closed my eyes and leaned forward, touching my forehead to hers. I threaded my fingers through her hair and thanked the gods—every one I could name—for answering my pleas.

"Mina, my goddess, my Persephone, has finally come to the Underworld."

"Rafael, my devil, my wintry Hades...I have always been here." A tear slipped down her cheek—not blood, but a soft, glowing silver.

I pressed my lips to hers, so softly, fearing this was all a dream that would fade away with the dying light of sundown.

The gentle kiss deepened, and she laced her fingers behind my neck, pulling me down to cover her body. Her soft, pink tongue licked at the seam of my lips, igniting volcanic lust buried in me. The leash of my holy restraint snapped. I pulled back quickly, the question hovering on my lips.

"Mina, are you certain—do you feel well enough to..."

Blue fire sparked in her eyes and in answer, she ripped my clothes from my body with a flick of her wrist.

CHAPTER TWENTY-TWO
MINA

April 28, 1768
Château du Diable

I WAS STARTLED BY THE SHARPNESS OF MY CLAWS AND THE STRENGTH in my fingers—I'd need to be careful. Unused to this odd supernatural body and its new, inner workings, I pulled away slightly, intimidated and hesitant.

Rafael smiled softly and straddled me, tugging the chemise up over my head.

"Say it again, Mina," he purred, his eyes liquid pools of jet.

"I love you," I murmured, feeling more contentment than I had in the past twenty years. Perhaps even longer.

He closed his eyes for the briefest moment, then lowered his body to mine and buried his face in my neck.

"If I heard those words from you every day until the end of time, it would not be enough," he said.

The soft brush of his lips on my collarbone sent a ripple of fire through me, and I arched toward his luscious mouth. I felt him smile against the skin on my neck, and his tongue slid out

—licking and exploring my jawline and my earlobe. Every feeling was so intense, as if my nerves had doubled, and my brain struggled to keep up with the delicious torture from the lightest touches. He dropped kisses on my cheeks, forehead, eyelids and chin before my need urged me to yank his mouth to mine and plunder it thoroughly.

The slickness of his tongue tangling with mine sent heat spiraling straight to my core. My nipples tightened, and I felt painful pressure in my gums as fangs lengthened in my mouth. I pulled back, my hands flying to my teeth. Rafael and Laszlo had two sets of fangs, more than other turned vampires, but I had...*Mon Dieu.* All my teeth had become fangs. Embarrassment and confusion battled against my lust, but Rafael dropped back on the bed as if he had all the time in the world. Perhaps we did.

"It's all right, my darling," he said, stroking one firm hand up my arm. "That's perfectly normal. It will take you some time to get used to them. Do not fear them and do not be ashamed of them. Every vampire's fangs are different. Yours are beautiful—dangerous and lethal. Impossibly erotic."

I nodded, running my tongue across the sharp points. His red pupils flared with the movement, and he crawled forward again, predatory and excited.

"Would you like to continue? Or would you prefer we waited until you've had more time to adjust to your new form?"

I didn't even pause to consider the question. I offered an encouraging smile and beckoned him closer. When he'd wrapped me in his arms again, I rolled him over and pinned his hands above his head, emboldened by the way he'd looked at me with my new, disconcerting teeth. For the first time ever, I had no trouble pinning him to the bed. My strength matched —and possibly surpassed—his own. The thrill in his eyes and the wild grin on his lips was a heady rush of power, and I found myself drinking it in greedily.

I slid my hands down his pale, muscled chest, tickling the soft, dark hair beneath his belly button and nestling his hard cock. I leaned down to twirl my tongue around his nipples and loved every muscle in his stomach that tightened, every harsh breath he sucked in, every filthy word he hissed when I trailed my lips and tongue and claws lower.

When I wrapped my fingers around his impressive length, he bowed off the bed and snarled at me.

"Mina," he groaned. "Please."

Tentatively, I licked the smooth skin underneath. A litany of words in a language I didn't recognize exploded from him in a bestial growl. I couldn't help but chuckle, reveling in this newfound sense of power and control.

"I wonder how much you held back from me because you were afraid of damaging my human body," I said idly, taking him into my mouth completely. I sucked gently, swirling my tongue from the base of him to the salty tip. He almost came up off the bed, but I pushed him back down.

"Gods above, please," he growled. "You are killing me. I need you, Mina."

"Did you?" I asked, encircling him with my hands.

"Yes," he almost sobbed. "I had to. I couldn't—I didn't want to hurt you."

"Hm," I replied, curiosity peaked. I released him and straddled his hips, positioning my ready heat above him. His gaze flew to mine, his fangs glinting in the candlelight. I'd seen him in the throes of passion before, but never like this—he was a wild animal straining at the end of a tether. It would only take one word to set him free.

"Don't," I said, surprised at the tone of command in my voice. "Don't hold back this time."

The leash snapped—the beast was free. He grabbed my hips, sliding his thumbs forward to gently part my sex and dip his fingers in the wetness between my legs. He slipped one finger to the apex of my pleasure. I tilted my head back and moaned in satisfaction, and the sound made him feral.

He thrust up into me, filling me, fitting like something that had been missing for a long time. We stilled for a moment, and then he began moving, slowly at first, then faster and harder as he lost himself in the primal pleasure of it. As the heat at my core spun out through my body, Rafael pushed me back down on the bed, rolling me to my side. His hands found my breasts, and he pinched my nipples, then snaked one hand back down to rub tight circles on the bud of pleasure that threatened to ignite my entire body. Faster his fingers worked, harder and harder he thrust, until all the years of longing and need and hope and love condensed into one perfect moment of absolute, earth-shattering joy, and I came apart around him. He was quick to follow me over the precipice, growling an animal *"Mine!"* as he sank his fangs into my neck and shuddered with release.

I collapsed back against him, then turned around to offer him a satisfied kiss. The curious expression on his face made me pause.

"Mina, your eyes," he whispered. "They're silver."

"What?"

He reached toward the nightstand and pulled a small mirror from the drawer. Just as his eyes filled with black and red, mine appeared filled with silver, with glowing moonstone-colored pupils in the center.

"Interesting," I murmured. "I've never seen a transformation like this before."

"Nor I," he said. "They're beautiful, darling. They suit you."

"You haven't? Doesn't that worry you?" I asked, unease threading through me.

His dark chuckle vibrated through me as he pulled me against his naked body.

"No. Hours ago, my only worry was confronting eternity without you. Given what we know about Charlotte and Antoine's turning—how the plague changed with them—it does not surprise me that it would change again in you. You are the strongest person I know. Laszlo's blood is the most powerful supernatural blood on earth. You died with a Judas silver bullet in your heart. All these factors could explain why you are...*different.*"

"I shall have to perform some experiments," I said, feeling apprehensive.

Rafael kissed my forehead and I felt a wave of love pulse from him.

Hm, I could get used to this. Well, I supposed I'd have to. I nuzzled against Rafael's strong chest and wrapped my limbs around his body. A vague awareness of another presence alerted me of the incoming intrusion just before the knock sounded on the door.

"Why is it every time I get you in bed, the world outside beckons insistently?" he complained.

"Probably because the only time we make love is when we're facing earthly peril," I said wryly. "Perhaps you should work on the timing of your romantic overtures."

I stood somewhat unsteadily, my legs unused to their new strength and speed. I wobbled over to the chair where the blue silk dressing gown had been placed and shrugged it on. When I turned around, Rafael was already dressed in his customary crimson banyan with gold dragon embroidery.

"It's like watching a little fawn find its legs for the first time," he smirked. "Adorable."

I narrowed my eyes and stuck my tongue out at him like a petulant child.

He rushed to me with supernatural speed, pinning me against the wall. Caged between his arms, lust ignited in me again.

"Be careful with that tongue, goddess," he growled through lengthening fangs. "I have plans for it later."

I laughed and pushed past him, making my way to the door. I felt the tug of a ghostly thread of connection and knew exactly who was standing on the other side of the door.

"Laszlo," I greeted, offering him a small smile.

He looked much recovered after being kept in The Order's dungeon. He had obviously found rest, nourishment, and a bath—his hollow cheeks had filled in some, and his lips had a touch of color. His long black hair hung down his back in a thick braid and he wore a bright green banyan with a gold dragon, similar to Rafael's. Now that he was free from the horror and filth of his dim cell, it was easy to see the similarities between the brothers. They shared the same aquiline nose, the same faintly almond-shaped eyes, and the same shaped lips. But where Rafael's eyes were almost black, Laszlo's were a warmer brown with delicate rings of green in his irises.

He bowed formally, and I waved the gesture away. I opened the door and waited for him to enter. Rafael frowned and sat in a plush chair next to the fireplace.

"Come in. I know we have much to discuss," I said.

His gaze flicked to Rafael.

"Would you prefer we were alone?" I asked.

"Absolutely not, Mina," Rafael said. "The last time I left the two of you together, things didn't end very well for you. I'm staying."

Laszlo winced slightly but nodded.

"As you wish, brother," he said. His voice was warm and

rich, unlike the despondent roughness from the previous evening. He walked to the fireplace and sat in the chair next to Rafael, leaving me the remaining seat on his left. Before sitting down, I picked up the glass of blood from the nightstand and drank deeply. My new, vicious thirst was somewhat mollified.

"Can I offer you some refreshment?" I asked.

"I would be honored," he said.

"Thank you for granting my request," I said quietly, handing him a glass. "For turning me. I know you are forbidden from turning anyone who isn't your mate, and I want you to know the sacrifice is not lost on me."

Rafael was silent, assessing us.

"I have wanted to turn others," Laszlo admitted, swirling the dark red liquid in his glass. "Marguerite is not the first woman I've loved. I've lived lifetimes longer than even Rafael, and no matter what they say, it never gets easier to watch the humans in your life wither and die. But I've never broken that rule. I have never turned anyone except for her. And I did so out of sheer desperation." His eyes cut to Rafael, the silent question on his face.

Rafael shook his head. "Never. I kill and drain when necessary, but I have never turned another. I would have turned Mina had she asked."

The edge in his voice drew my attention, but there was no animosity in his expression.

Laszlo tilted his head to regard me.

"I knew you were something special, Doctor—even before I offered you the choice. You spent your entire human life trying to help my kind and solve problems that were not yours. You atoned for mistakes you never made. You speak of my sacrifice, but it is you who has lived as a martyr to our curse." He drained the glass and stood to place the empty crystal on the mantel. "And make no mistake—it *is* a curse. You will have Rafael to coax your happiness through eternity, but you must be prepared for the loneliness of time."

"All of my friends have been turned," I replied. "I felt more lonesome as the last lingering human in our group. It grieved me to think of aging while they remained trapped in amber—looking down on my slow decay with pity."

Laszlo shook his head slowly. "I speak not of company, though that is part of it. When you have been alive for hundreds and hundreds of years, young one—only then will you understand. You will see the world change in ways you are not prepared for. It is a sad thing to look around you and feel as ancient as naught but the mountains. The older you get, the harder it becomes to...*understand* people, places, things. You become a living relic—ancient and sacred. Something meant to be enshrined in a tomb, not walking around, witnessing the relentless march of days."

I was stunned, overcome by the gravity of his words.

"I pray you retain this zeal you have for life, Doctor. This passion! Do anything—*anything*—to keep it. Do not fall victim to the melancholy of millennia when you cease to feel rapture at the miracles of the world. The growth of a tree. The birth of a human baby. The moon and the tides. The true curse we bear is not that we must live like parasites, surviving on the blood of others. The curse is that we must exist with more loneliness than anyone can bear over countless lifetimes."

I nodded, my emotions caught in my throat.

"You had gifts before you were turned, Doctor: kindness, intelligence, compassion, strength, loyalty. These gifts are better than anything you could have gained from your turning—though I suspect those will reveal themselves to you in time. Respect the rules of our curse. Honor your gifts. And do not forget to keep the candle of your humanity lit."

He came to stand before me, then kneeled to take my hands

in his. The smile on his face was small and heartbreakingly sad. I wondered if he'd had a full smile since the death of his daughter.

"You will do many great things. Trust in yourself. Trust your instincts. Let the blood tell you what it wants you to know. I have the utmost faith in you, Doctor Wilhelmina Van Helsing."

I blinked back tears—the same strange silver ones that I'd cried before.

"Marguerite is recovering," he said, turning to Rafael. "We thank you for your hospitality, brother. I know you have no reason to offer it. We will not stay here overlong."

The shadow of disappointment crossed Rafael's face, but he lifted a shoulder in forced nonchalance.

"You will do as you please," he said. "But we should all agree upon what needs to be done about The Order. If everyone is feeling up to it, I will have sustenance brought to the greenhouse and we can discuss the matter there."

Laszlo's brows hitched up. "The greenhouse?"

If Rafael had been capable of blushing, he would have been as red as a beet.

"Yes, I...well, I'd like to show it to you. I think you'd appreciate it," he stammered. The boyish need for approval from his big brother made him seem so human, the sweetness of it almost shattered me.

Laszlo nodded appreciatively.

"I am certain I would," he said, walking back to the door. "I'll rouse Marguerite and we'll await your summons."

Rafael threw me a glare as his older brother closed the door behind him, but I flung myself at him before he could deny his embarrassment.

CHAPTER TWENTY-THREE
MINA

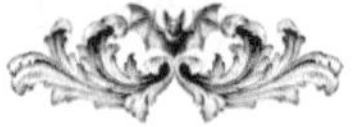

April 28, 1768
Château du Diable

I WAS COMFORTED TO SEE EVERYONE RECOVERED WHEN WE GATHERED in front of the greenhouse. The mood was subdued, but there was a palpable sense of relief. Étienne had given me a brotherly once-over, checking to make sure the gaping wound in my chest and my savaged throat had completely healed. Once he was satisfied, he began telling me all the best places to get good blood—even *virgin* blood—which I knew had peculiar healing properties. Antoine, for his part, materialized before me and threw his arms around me for quite possibly the most unexpected embrace of my life. Even Charlotte looked at him as if he'd grown a second head for a moment, then some understanding seemed to dawn on her, and she patted his back gently.

"I'm glad you're alive. Er, undead," he said. "I was—am—unprepared to lose another...friend."

Charlotte had told me about the loss of his sister and

nephew—it had been one of the things that set their love story in motion.

"Thank you, Antoine," I said, touched by his admission. I'd wanted siblings when I was a child, and it seemed that now, throughout everything we'd endured together, I'd found them.

"Yes, yes, we're all glad Mina isn't worm food," Charlotte scoffed. "Darling, have you tested out your abilities yet? Can you change shape? Do you subsist on blood, or meat, as well? Can you fly like Rafael?"

"I don't know," I admitted. "I am becoming aware of some gifts. Others feel...possible, but I haven't tested anything yet."

"Yes, well, you have time," Rafael encouraged.

"Perhaps," Daphne said, warning in her tone. "The Order will strike again, hard and fast. We need to come up with a new plan."

Charlotte suddenly noticed the carved wooden door in front of us and the beautiful reliefs of Hades and Persephone.

"Rafael," she said, intrigued. "Is that...Mina?" Now that she said it, the resemblance was impossible not to notice.

He coughed.

"I don't believe it!" she shrieked, laughing. "Honestly, Mina, it's so romantic I could die all over again. Antoine, my love, why haven't *you* ever had a door carved with my likeness as a goddess?"

Rafael covered a smirk and opened the doors, once again revealing the exquisite underground greenhouse. The gasps and whispers of appreciation added a little bounce to his step, and I was glad for my friends—as mismatched as we were.

In the back of the greenhouse, tucked beneath several massive tropical trees, sat a large circular table. It had been set with pitchers of blood for the vampires and dishes of raw meat for Charlotte and Antoine. The sun had only just set, and the warm sherbet of the sky cast the entire space in a delicate pink and purple glow. Two maids set about lighting candles and torches along the walls. We all sat down around the table for our bizarre little dinner party.

Rafael offered me a glass of blood, but Charlotte's raw steak smelled equally enticing. I reached out to pluck a cube of meat from her plate and sampled it—*heavenly*. She raised a brow at me, and I shrugged. Yet another new trait for me to log.

Daphne downed her glass and stood.

"As I said, they will come for us again. They will not stop, but they will not be stupid, either. The way I see it, we have two choices. We can eliminate the threat or try to turn the king against them. He's the only person with power over them," she said.

Laszlo chuckled. "With the greatest respect, Duchesse, The Order has existed in some form long before your king. They will spring up again whether he agrees with their politics or methods—or not."

"I agree," Rafael said. "Laszlo and I have left them alone for long enough, and they came for both of us. They came through all of you to get to us. It is time for them to understand who they're dealing with."

"Does that mean impaling?" Charlotte whispered to Marguerite.

Marguerite paled and scooted closer to Laszlo.

"The Draculs are right," said Antoine. "I never wish for violence, but we cannot risk them coming for any of us again."

"Mina, your judgment has weight here," Étienne said over the low din of conversation. "Laszlo and Marguerite suffered terribly at their hands, but your human life was effectively ended by their cruelty."

Charlotte turned to me. "Darling, I know you didn't want to get involved with them before. I know you never trusted them. But I also know how you feel about killing. If you wish for us to find another path, I will stand with you."

All seven sets of eyes fell upon me, but for once, the weight of expectation didn't feel like an impossibly heavy yoke around my neck. Charlotte was right—I didn't want the killing. I wanted humans to have as much of a chance at life as vampires did. I feared a future with Rafael and me on the run—like Laszlo and Marguerite. I didn't want to hide away from the world, constantly looking over my shoulder for threats. I considered the people around this table—the pain The Order had caused them, directly and indirectly. I wanted futures for my friends as much as I wanted my own. I knew what my answer would be.

"It should be swift. Quick, clean kills. If we are to do this, it must be thorough—we must find everyone in their network. We should act when they are all together, otherwise word could travel and some of them might slink off to hide away in their little holes," I said decisively.

Daphne's eyes widened in surprise, but Charlotte grinned fiercely and patted my hand.

"Fortunately, *mes amis,* I happen to know exactly when that will be," Charlotte said.

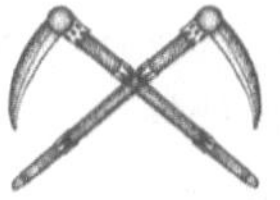

Over the next few weeks, we remained at Rafael's home, falling into a kind of routine. Daphne, Rafael, Antoine, Marguerite, and Étienne began to sketch out a rough plan, while I worked with Charlotte and Laszlo in the evenings to connect with my new supernatural gifts. Laszlo helped me learn the basics of blocking out or shielding the persistent mental connection to others and taught me ways to focus that strength to mesmerize and control. The idea of controlling another person turned my stomach, but he said it was important for me to learn both the reach and limitations of my power.

Rafael *did* enjoy when we retired, and he allowed me to bend his mind to my will. Actually, we'd both enjoyed that rather thoroughly.

As the May days marched on and the nights warmed up, finally shaking off the long, cold spring thaw, we drew nearer to the evening we'd planned for our final mission with The Order. The mood in the house was thick with tension.

One evening, to escape Daphne's incessant pacing and Antoine's worrisome brooding, Charlotte and I went outside to the grounds above the castle for a bit of fresh air. We wandered through the secluded forest nearby and when we came to the edge of a clearing, she shucked her gown and tossed it to the side.

"Now," she began. "The key to shifting forms is to find that place within yourself. It is your inner animal—your inner beast. You must call it forth. Allow your human shape to fall away. Do not fear the pain. It is uncomfortable, but brief."

With that, she shifted into her wolf form, exploding in a blur of skin and fur and bones. When she was done, she tilted her head back for an unearthly, horrific howl. Then, she sat on her haunches and watched me expectantly.

"I don't think I have an inner beast," I said.

Charlotte growled and laid down.

You do too. Now, hurry up—I want to go for a run.

The benefit to my mental connection was being able to communicate with her when she was unable to speak.

"Very well," I agreed, laughing. "I'll summon forth my animal self—if only for the sake of science."

I closed my eyes. I stilled my thoughts, allowing the rise and fall of my breath to calm the ever-present power simmering beneath my skin. I thought about werewolves and bats and demons—everything I'd seen in my work with supernatural creatures. I turned inward and searched. The deeper I went, the darker things became, as if I'd stepped into Rafael's Underworld and found myself amongst the monsters. There, at the edge of my consciousness, knelt something...*primal.* I reached for it, stroked it, and imagined picking it up and throwing it over my shoulders like a cloak.

Pain exploded in my body. Wrenching, scraping, splitting, breaking, burning pain, and then just as suddenly as it started, it stopped. I stood, uncertain of what to expect. When I opened my eyes, the first thing I saw was Charlotte cowering, tail tucked between her legs.

Mina? She tentatively pushed against my consciousness.

That was incredibly unpleasant, I answered.

I looked down at my limbs and suddenly understood her fear. I hadn't shifted into a wolf or a small bat—I'd shifted into the eight-foot-tall bat demon that Laszlo had turned into when he bit me. But that meant...

Yes! I rolled my shoulder muscles and felt them—massive leathery wings. I flexed them tentatively and spread them open, then took an experimental leap from the ground. I soared through the air.

Stop showing off, Charlotte challenged. *Is that all you can do?*

I landed back on the ground with a thud. Stilling my mind again, reaching for that inner place, I shifted once more. This time, the pain wasn't quite so bad, but I heard myself howling when the transformation finished.

That's more like it, Charlotte said, wagging her tail. I looked down and beheld giant paws tipped with long claws—a wolf form.

Hold on, I bid her. *I want to try one more thing.*

This time, when I centered myself, I went back to my inner darkness. I let go of my thoughts and expectations, focusing instead on that raw, primal power. As I neared it, I could sense the pulse of it; ancient, dark, patient. I extended my thoughts to it and let it take root.

No pain this time. Simply...*quiet.* I lost track of my physical sensations. When I came to my outer awareness again, Charlotte was calling for me.

Mina! Where have you gone?

I am here, I answered.

She turned to me, trying to track my scent on the wind.

What are you? she asked.

I don't know, I replied. I saw the grass below me and drifted low to the ground. As I neared it, the grass began to wilt away, recoiling into the soil. All that was left behind was a faint silver sheen. Charlotte noticed and whined.

I can see you—faintly. Like a soft, silver cloud, she said. *But I don't know what you are. It's wreaking havoc on my lupine senses.*

I stared at the fallow ground that I'd touched.

Charlotte, I think—I think I am Death.

Hours later, we returned to our rooms just as the sun was rising. I'd told my companions about my strange new abilities, anxiously waiting for fear and disgust. Instead, they comforted me and offered me blood and raw meat to restore my depleted strength.

"It must be from the Judas silver," Rafael said. "It would

explain the eyes, the tears... Brother, have you ever seen anything like this? Or heard of it happening?"

Laszlo shook his head. "Rafael and I can turn into mist, but it's just that—mist. Closer to weather than anything else."

Étienne chuckled. "Simply marvelous. The only one of us that has a real problem killing anything has become the embodiment of Death. I suppose that's one way Fate will stop you from taking advantage of these *gifts*, Mina."

"You know," Daphne hedged. "This does present us with an opportunity. Of course, it's probably too dangerous to even consider given how little we know about this ability."

I knew exactly what she was about to say—I'd considered it myself.

"I'll do it," I said.

"Do what?" Rafael asked, concern in his tone. "What are you talking about?"

"I'll go into the mausoleum alone," I said. "If The Order are all assembled, I can eliminate them with one fell swoop. None of you need to risk putting yourselves in jeopardy again, given how we know the Judas silver affects you."

"Absolutely not!" Rafael insisted, rising from his chair. "We have no idea what will happen if you try this on humans, and we know even less about how you will react to the Judas silver door when you're down there. If the worst happens in either instance, you will be down there *alone* and at their mercy. And I think we all know just how *merciful* The Order can be. I'm sorry, Mina, but you've already died once at their hands—I will not let that happen again."

"Rafael's right," Charlotte added, placing her hand on my arm. "It's too dangerous."

"I appreciate your concern," I said. "But it's my decision to make."

"Mina, please," Rafael beseeched. The pleading in his tone

shook the foundations of my resolve, but I knew what I had to do to keep my friends safe. What I had the power to do.

"If it makes you feel better, you can come with me and wait outside in the cemetery," I offered. "If something goes awry, you can swoop in and rip out as many throats as you like. As it stands, I am the only one who can go in alone and do what needs to be done."

"You don't know that," Rafael argued.

"The bullet," Antoine said suddenly. "Laszlo, what happened to the bullet from Mina's chest?"

"I ripped it from her and threw it on the ground in the woods," he said. "I wasn't sure if she would be able to turn with it lodged in her heart."

"What if we retrieved it?" Antoine asked. "And used it to see if the Judas silver affected her as it does the rest of us?"

"It's not a bad idea," Daphne agreed. "Mina, Rafael, what say you? If we manage to find the bullet and it doesn't affect Mina's abilities to shift, then she goes in alone. We will be there, of course, right outside in case something goes wrong."

"No," Rafael said firmly.

"Yes," I agreed. "Rafael, you must give me a chance. Just once, let me be the one to protect you. Almost all my life I've been surrounded by powerful, supernatural beings and I've always been the weak one—the one to watch out for, to keep an eye on. Now that things are different, let me try to be the strong one for a change."

"You have *always* been the strong one," Rafael insisted, but I heard an undertone of defeat in his voice. "But I know you, Mina, and I know how fruitless it is to try and stand in your way when your mind is made up. I will stand by your decision, even if I do not like it—or agree with it."

I squeezed his hand. "Thank you."

"It's daylight now, but as soon as the sun goes down, we'll send someone to retrieve the bullet," Daphne said.

"I'll go," Marguerite volunteered. "I know where we were in the woods when the doctor was turned. Besides, it was mine and Laszlo's actions that brought us to this place—we are far in your debt."

Daphne nodded. "Very well. We could use a report, as well, to see if anything has changed around The Order's headquarters over the last few weeks. You will not go alone, Marguerite. Étienne will go with you."

Étienne grinned at her and saluted.

"Good. Well, I'm sure we're all exhausted. Let's adjourn for the morning and get some rest," Charlotte suggested.

I blew out a breath. My explorations with my abilities had sapped both my physical and mental strength, and by the time Rafael and I made our way to his bedchamber, I was nearly asleep on my feet. Blessedly, he helped me undress, slipped a clean chemise over my head and tucked me into bed.

I watched as he pulled his shirt and breeches off and slipped into bed naked. The crease in his brow and the tight set of his mouth was enough for me to roll over and lay my hand on his chest.

"Do not be cross with me, Rafael," I said.

"I'm not cross," he argued. "I'm worried."

"You are both," I replied. "Would you love me as much if I were simpering and biddable?"

He wrapped strong arms around me and pulled me into his embrace.

"I would love you in every way, in every world, in every afterlife," he sighed. "But that doesn't mean it is easy for me to let you walk into danger."

I yawned and his hands drifted to my low back, caressing and stroking.

"I understand," I said. "But you will be there. You can always save me if things start to go awry."

He chuckled and the sound hummed through my very bones. The sensation soothed me deeper into sleep, and I almost missed his final words as I drifted off.

"Mina, you've never needed me to save you, but I will always be there to try, anyway."

CHAPTER TWENTY-FOUR
RAFAEL

May 20, 1768
Château du Diable

I woke some hours later with Mina's lush, shapely ass cradling my insistent erection. As much as I wanted her—needed to feel that connection between us—she needed sleep. She was still learning what her new abilities demanded from her body. I thought back to my youth, when my abilities had begun to manifest and stifled a laugh. What a terror I'd been.

Mina shifted back against me, and I tensed, desire building in my body.

No, I chided myself. *Let her rest.*

She sighed in her sleep and arched against me, lightly rubbing her breasts against my arm. I fought against the onslaught of wild heat that raged in me, desperate to think of anything but burying myself in her and claiming her again. *Mine. After everything, she is mine.* She moved again, her soft skin pressing against the hard ridge of my cock, and when I bit back a groan, I heard a soft explosion of laughter.

"Torturous minx," I growled. "How long have you been awake?"

"Long enough to enjoy a little torment," she chuckled, rolling over to face me. She leaned forward and captured my mouth in a passionate kiss, sucking my lower lip between her fangs. The friction was like a jolt of lightning.

I moaned into her mouth and reached between her legs, slipping one finger through her wet heat. I shuddered when her hand snaked down to encircle me, then she angled her hips to slide me inside of her.

I swore—ready to die from the perfection of it. Of her. Of us together. I pushed myself up over her, nudging her legs apart and thrusting into her again. Her soft moans grew louder, and I wondered if I'd ever heard anything so beautiful.

"No matter what happens," she said, wrapping her legs around my waist to grant me deeper access. "I will always be yours, Rafael. You will always be mine."

"Mine," I grunted, already so close to release. I reached down between our legs to stroke that sensitive spot above our joining. She bowed up off the bed and I seized the opportunity to bend down and capture her right nipple in my mouth. When I gently sucked and then grazed the underside of her breast with my fangs, I felt her pleasure draw up and shatter, and she screamed as she came apart. I followed her over the edge, thrusting into her, swearing against gods and demons alike that I would destroy anything that challenged me for her.

"I love you," she whispered, placing a hand against my cheek.

I touched my forehead to hers and kissed her again, softly. As if I could bottle this moment and cherish it forever.

"I love you," I replied. "I have always loved you, Mina. I will die loving you."

She smiled at that. "Hopefully not too soon."

I chuckled, drawing her into my arms again.

A few moments later, there was a soft knock on the door.

"My lord," Guillaume said from the hall. "The lady Marguerite and the emissary have returned."

That familiar pit of worry opened inside me again, but I told him we would join them shortly.

"We should go," Mina said, rising to dress. "I'm anxious to have this done with."

I nodded, unsure of what to say. I'd had some of her clothes brought into my wardrobe, and I watched as she adeptly laced her stays, tied on her skirts, and pinned her bodice in place. The gown she'd selected was one of my favorites—an ethereally soft midnight blue velvet, embroidered with stars in glittering silver thread.

She caught me staring as I stumbled into my black shirt and breeches.

"Fitting for the queen of the underworld, no?" she teased.

I grinned. "I shall endeavor to be worthy of you, Your Highness."

We finished dressing and made our way to my laboratory, where I'd told everyone to gather. I had enough equipment here to allow Mina to test whatever she wished and had several supernatural remedies on hand, just in case.

Charlotte lifted a brow as we entered.

"I do hope you're taking some time to actually *rest*," she said. "Though by the look of things, I'm not so sure about that."

Étienne laughed. "I'm sure we all remember what our early days after turning are like. Once you recover and grow accustomed to things, then the *hunger* sets in—in more ways than one." He winked, and Daphne rolled her eyes.

Laszlo and Marguerite entered, clutching a small lead box.

Marguerite placed it onto the main worktable in the center of the room and grimaced.

"It was where we expected to find it," she said. "Nothing seems different about the area itself, but as we made our way back, we overheard a couple of vampire guards keeping watch over the cemetery."

"Were you seen?" I demanded.

Étienne laughed again. "How insulting! I may not be as old as you, but have some respect for me compared to a couple of freshly turned mercenaries. We were all but invisible to them."

"What did you hear from the guards?" Charlotte asked.

"Our homes are being watched. The Order has been hunting the agents of *les DD* that they know of, but it sounds like your warning letters arrived in time and they've all gone to ground. With no one to question and none of their leads playing out, they are forced to sit and wait for us to make our move," Étienne replied.

"They will be waiting for us," Marguerite said, a warning in her tone.

"What do they know of Mina?" Daphne asked.

Marguerite shook her head. "Nothing. When The Order arrived back at the mausoleum that night, they discovered Laszlo's and my cell empty and Derais's blood in the woods. They believe we turned on Derais and fled with Rafael, but they don't know anything about Mina. They are watching her clinic, but they don't know the extent of her involvement."

"Good," Mina said. "That will at least give me the element of surprise."

We all stared as she reached forward to pick up the box. When she opened it, everyone took an involuntary step back— the poisonous feeling of the Judas silver bullet repulsed us all.

All but Mina.

She tipped the bullet into her hand and stroked it, then held it up to her face to get a better look.

Antoine paled, and Charlotte clapped a hand over her mouth.

"What do you feel?" I asked, my voice a breath above a whisper.

Mina stared at the lump of silver in her palm, warped where it had met her vital human organs. She narrowed her eyes and glared at it, and we all watched in astonishment as the ball began to melt into a puddle of liquid metal in her bare hand.

"I feel—*kinship*," she replied in a strange voice. The silver liquid pulsed and flexed, moving around her hand as she willed it with some secret power. She closed her eyes, and then the silver was absorbed into her skin. When she opened her eyes, they were that same silver with moonstone-colored pupils. She smiled—but of all the ways I'd seen Mina smile, I'd never seen her look like this.

"I'm ready," she said, her voice sounding distant and ethereal.

Daphne raised her brows and cleared her throat. I would have sworn I heard a tremor of fear in her voice, but I might have imagined it. "Well, we have a few things left to do," she hedged. "Charlotte, let's send our messages to the remaining agents of *les DD*. Étienne, you send word to our staff and Charlotte's that they're not to return to our homes over the next few days—we don't know what will happen, and I don't want any of them getting caught up in The Order's collateral damage if something goes wrong."

"Send your messages," Mina said in that strange, other-worldly voice. "But The Order convenes tonight, does it not?"

"Yes, but we weren't planning on going in until they meet

next week," Charlotte said, staring at Mina with a mixture of admiration and horror.

"I will go tonight," Mina said.

Daphne and Charlotte exchanged a look.

"If you're certain…" Daphne began.

"Yes," Mina replied. "Come on horseback, or in a carriage, if you wish. I'm going to fly."

She turned to me, her strange silver eyes glittering in the low light of the laboratory. She smiled again, but this time it was closer to a true Mina smile. She closed her eyes for a moment, and then when she opened them, her eyes were back to their normal sapphire blue.

"Care to join me?" she asked, as if nothing bizarre had happened.

"You must be joking," I replied—too unsteadily. "What the Hell was that?"

"I'm not entirely sure," she said. "But I don't feel any ill effects from the silver."

"Mina…" I began, but she held up a hand to stay me.

"Rafael, yes. You and I will run a barrage of experiments on my abilities when this is over. However, we face a more pressing threat. I'm going to deal with that first. Are you coming?"

The silence that fell over our companions was tense, as if everything hinged upon my ability to allow Mina to lead us into battle. *Mina, my Mina.* The one person I'd fought so hard to protect, and the one person who needed my protection the least—even before she'd been turned into a supernatural creature with god-like powers. *Goddess.* I sighed, swallowing the shredded remains of my pride, and inclined my head.

"Lead the way, Persephone."

WE STOOD AT THE CRUMBLING EDGE OF THE HIGH TOWER, FACING southeast toward Paris. Charlotte and Antoine prepared to shift, tying their clothes in a bundle around their shoulders. Daphne, Marguerite, and Étienne would be on horseback, which was less conspicuous than a carriage, but would also save their energy from having to run the distance. Laszlo, Mina, and I would fly.

The sun had set, turning the night sky the same soft midnight blue as Mina's gown. As Laszlo and I began to disrobe prior to shifting, she eyed us anxiously.

"I'd hate for you to ruin that gown when you look so fetching in it," I purred, hoping to ease some of her nerves. "Laszlo will turn around, so you needn't worry about him."

For once, my brother's raspy chuckle split the silence.

"As lovely as you are, Doctor, trust that I only have eyes for my beloved Marguerite." He bundled his clothes and tied them to his waist, then turned to face the opposite direction.

Satisfied, Mina undressed in haste. When she was down to her stays, I stepped over to help her unlace them.

"Everything is going to be okay," I said in her ear. "We'll all be there together. Trust your instincts. They've served you well thus far."

She nodded, then twisted back to give me a perfunctory kiss on the lips.

Fear and anxiety fought to take hold, but I refused to let Mina sense them from me. As much as I hated to stand aside and let her take on The Order alone, I knew she could do it.

"Ready?" I asked when she'd finished undressing.

She offered a tight smile.

"As I'll ever be."

MINA

WHEN THE PAIN OF THE TRANSFORMATION EBBED, I LOOKED AROUND. The sight of two massive, hellish wolf creatures and two—no, *three*—enormous bat demons would have shocked even the most unshakeable person. A bubble of manic laughter burst in my chest, coming out as a warped growl from behind my fangs.

The Judas silver pulsed in my blood, whispering to me to do terrible things. *Betray. Punish. Kill.* When I'd first encountered it inside Rafael's laboratory, I'd sensed it immediately. It wasn't repellant to me as it was to the others. Rather, it seemed to call to me...coaxing, enticing, seducing. I could feel it sliding through my body along my muscles and bones, tempting me to unleash power I'd only recently become acquainted with. *Very well.* I would use it. I would let it feed me to bring down The Order—to help me ensure they would be stopped from their dangerous campaign against the sufferers of the blood plague. And then, I would purge the haunting silver power from my body and bury it in a place where no one could find it again.

I stretched out my wings and kicked off the ground, soaring high into the night sky. The air cooled as I ascended, and the wind buffeted me mercilessly until I found a warm air current that propelled me forward. I felt Laszlo and Rafael at my sides as we careened over the treetops, and I allowed myself a few moments of joy at the novelty of this new feat. I was flying! Despite the strange and sometimes uncomfortable feelings my new abilities gave me, this felt like a true miracle.

As I sped on, I saw the distant shapes of Charlotte and Antoine below me, running all out through the woods. Daphne, Marguerite, and Étienne were on their heels, their horses kicking up a fine mist of soft earth and gravel in their wake. We traveled faster than I'd ever believed possible, spurred on by our collective desire to protect ourselves, our friends. Our people.

When the suburbs outside Paris came into view and we closed in on the little forgotten cemetery, my stomach clenched at the thought of what I was about to do—what I was prepared to do. I'd never willingly ended a life before, and here I was, cozying up to the idea of taking out two dozen men. I considered the fact that they believed they were doing what was right for the people of France, that many of them had families, that not all of them were perhaps...*evil.* Knowing these things, doubt rooted in my gut, despite the hissing, brutal encouragements from the Judas silver slithering between my nerves.

We touched down in the small, wooded area just outside the cemetery. My heart pounded with the memories of running from Laszlo and Derais—the pain and fear of my death and turning. Within minutes, Charlotte and Antoine arrived at our chosen rendezvous and split off to survey the area around the cemetery, looking for threats. Daphne, Étienne, and Marguerite raced in and dismounted, then tied their exhausted horses to a nearby tree.

Rafael, Laszlo, and I dressed in silence as I reached out to Charlotte. Our mental connection had proven the strongest—aside from mine with Rafael—and it was easy for us to communicate without me having to break through mental barriers to read her mind. She sent me a comforting wave of reassurance.

I turned to Rafael. His beautiful face was impassive, but I could see the angst sparking in his eyes. Without a word, I pressed my lips to his, infusing the kiss with as much love as I dared. I needed him to understand that I would come back to him...that I would always come back to him. This wasn't goodbye.

Taking one final breath of resolve, I smoothed my hands down my lovely midnight gown and walked into the cemetery. Behind me and around me, I felt gentle brushes of strength, hope, and gratitude. It helped to settle my stomach and calm my raging nerves. It temporarily tamed the vicious bloodlust the Judas silver inspired.

When I reached the mausoleum, I paused at the door and listened. Beneath me, I heard muted voices arguing, snarling, deriding each other. The men of The Order were here, convening below. As I opened the heavy door to descend into the tomb, a wave of surprised rage emanated from the forest.

It seemed The Order's vampire mercenary guards had shown up. Before I could drop my hand from the door and turn to help, Rafael sent a pulse of reassurance to me.

We will be fine. Go, my love. Finish this.

In the distance, I heard a horrifying, unearthly scream, followed by a wet, crunching sound, and then eerie silence. More screams, then—but not from Rafael or my friends.

Another wave of ease, this time from Charlotte.

All is well. Go, Mina! We have your back.

I rolled my shoulders, threw open the door, and descended into the black maw of the tomb.

CHAPTER TWENTY-FIVE
MINA

May 20, 1768
Cimetière des Innocents

I walked down the stairs, listening for clear threads of the conversation from the members below.

"No sign of them! How can that be? They cannot have fallen off the face of the earth!"

"Unbelievable. If His Majesty would only allow us more resources, we'd be able to cast a wider net and broaden our search."

"His Majesty doesn't *officially* endorse anything we do, and I doubt he would condone the hunt of one of his cousins."

"It's not my incompetence that led us here. Whose idea was it to allow the women to join? I swear, they're more of a curse than the damn blood plague."

I considered shifting then but felt one last bubble of hope lift in my chest that maybe, *maybe*, there was another way.

When I reached the inner door at the end of the hallway, the silver in my veins vibrated with energy at the proximity to the silver inside the door. I willed it calm for the moment, then knocked firmly. The men on the other side stilled.

The door opened a fraction, and a man with salt and pepper hair and a black domino mask looked me over. Surprise and recognition lit in his brown eyes, and I thought I remembered him from the last ball I'd attended at Versailles, but I couldn't be sure. He waited expectantly—eyes wide.

"Good evening," I said. "I'm here to negotiate with you."

Laughter deepened the wrinkles around his forehead and mouth, and the hollow sound filled me with a white-hot stab of anger.

"Well, I suppose we should hear you out," he replied. "Do come in, Doctor."

I entered the room and beheld the disapproving sneers beneath two dozen domino masks. I'd seen more than a few of these men before and knew they kept their masks merely for the sake of tradition.

A second man approached and smiled, offering me a seat at the large round table in the middle of the room. Gradually, each man came to the table and sat down, at least indicating a willingness to listen. I considered that a positive sign.

"Gentlemen," I began. "You know me—you know who I am. I'm here to negotiate on behalf of a few individuals: the House of Dracul, the Comtesse de Brionne, Captain Antoine de Valle, the Vampire Emissary and his wife, the duchesse—"

"Yes," the second man interrupted. "We are aware of the identities your friends. Get to the point. What is it you're requesting, and what is it you're offering?"

"I'm requesting the full cessation of your campaign against the sufferers of the blood plague; the vampires. I'm requesting the protection of my friends and their families. And I'm requesting the absolute and total dissolution of the shadow dealings of The Order," I said in a cool, even tone. "For this, you will be allowed to leave here with your lives. You will be allowed to return to your families...and bask in the sunlight."

Laughter erupted around the table. I waited with waning patience for their response.

The second man spoke again.

"You cannot be serious," he replied.

"Respectfully, I am not known for my sense of humor," I shot back. "I'm afraid you must decide now. Renounce this foolish campaign and fight for peaceful coexistence or suffer the consequences of your actions."

The first man flicked his gaze to two younger men waiting against the walls. They moved toward the door, barring anyone from leaving—attempting to barricade me inside.

"*Respectfully,*" the man scoffed. "We are charged with protecting our king and our people. You come in here attempting to parlay with us to allow our country to fall under the ruin of some foreign bloodsucker? How utterly idiotic. You haven't even come with anything worth bartering—our *sanguisuge* dogs are outside right now, sniffing your lot out. They're armed with something very special, Doctor. Perhaps you've seen its effects on that wretched Dracul filth."

My heart pounded. I looked around the room, making eye contact with each of these self-righteous men. Gently, I pressed against their minds, hoping to find something...*anything*. A crack in their resolve. The faintest tendril of self-doubt. Willingness to change.

Despair took hold of me when I came up empty.

I stood from the table, and one of the men behind me moved away from the door to put his heavy hand on my shoulder, trying to force me back into my chair. I turned around, finding the man's gaze in the gloom.

"Do not touch me again," I warned.

Yes, hello, the silver whispered in my blood. *Have you come to threaten me?*

"We know more than you think, Van Helsing," the second man continued. "We know you're the younger Dracul's little whore. We know of your father's failure to find a cure for the disease. We know your hellcat friends are plotting to infiltrate and dismantle our Order from within. We have the weapons we need to take them out and end the line of bastard monsters in its entirety. God works through us, and we are fit to damn you all to the fires of Hell."

"I've never been a particularly religious woman," I answered. "But I do know there is no God here. You serve your own aims, and your actions are guided by fear and greed. It is not too late to change. Simply say the words, and I will spare you."

Again, riotous laughter filled the dark little space.

"I've heard enough of your madness," the man said, waving a hand in dismissal. "Take her below. At least we can use her as bait to trap that bastard Dracul and his filthy brother. Send out word to the bloodsuckers—we move against the homes of the comtesse and the duchesse tonight. Burn everything. No survivors."

The man at my back moved forward, reaching for my shoulder again.

My heartbeat drumming a war cry in my ears, I closed my eyes and let the silver take hold. Pain fractured my bones and flesh apart, but only for an instant. In one breath, I was sitting at the table, having a calmly insulting conversation. In the next breath, I was without form, a shapeless silver mist, driven by the need to protect. *Hunt. Kill.*

Amid the exclamations of surprise, I slid up my aggressor's extended arm...corrupting, breaking, poisoning. I watched as he screamed—a bloodcurdling sound—and collapsed to the ground as his heart sizzled in his chest. *Dead.* I went to the next man by the door, slithered down his open mouth, took root in his stomach and exploded outward in splinters of cursed silver.

Shrieks and terrified shouts echoed off the damp stone walls as I drifted through each man at the table, still searching for those dim threads of hope, still finding nothing but rage and hatred. The scent of scorched flesh and fresh blood and shredded skin permeated the room as I worked, ending life after life. At last, I came to the man who'd spoken so cruelly to me.

I shifted back to my human form, suddenly naked, but altogether uncaring.

"Holy Mary, Mother of God," the man screamed, falling to his knees in prayer. "Protect me with your divine mercy. Save me from this unclean spirit—this demon from Hell!"

"You know," I said, stepping forward to haul the man up by his throat. "I would have been happy as a simple vampire. I would have turned to be with the man I love. We would have lived together happily, working toward finding a cure. Hoping that in that time, hearts and minds would change. But it was you who changed everything. Your hatred and fear took on a life of its own, and because of that, Derais ended my human life. I died with a Judas silver bullet lodged in my heart and came back as what you see before you. Maybe you think I am an abomination—perhaps I am. But this..."

I summoned the Judas silver from my blood, and we watched as it pooled into the palm of my hand, rising through my skin.

"This was by your hand," I murmured. I squeezed my hand closed, pressing the silver into a small lump.

"Anything," the man whispered, tears running down his cheeks. "I will give you anything to let me live. Money. Power. Influence!"

I sighed, letting my mouth full of fangs lengthen.

"All I ever wanted was peace," I said forlornly. "But instead, you brought me war."

I sank my teeth into his throat, drinking until I felt his pulse still and his soul depart. Letting his body fall to the floor, I stepped back to survey the damage. The gory carnage turned my stomach, and I immediately retched. Numbly, I climbed back up the stairs, scanning the dark corridor for the faint glow of moonlight.

As I stepped onto the grassy earth outside of the mausoleum entrance, I fell to the ground. Heaving sobs wracked my body, and I screamed—agonized by the destruction I'd wrought. I was dimly aware of a pair of strong arms grabbing me, holding me steady, encircling me with faint waves of comfort, hope, love, gratitude.

Time ticked by, and I felt the individual presences of my friends—my family—standing close to me. Charlotte draped a soft woolen cloak over my shoulders and eventually, I peeled my face away from Rafael's damp shirt.

No one spoke.

"It is done," I muttered. "The Order is no more."

Daphne nodded, rubbing a hand down my back.

"I'm so sorry," she whispered. "I'm sorry for what you've endured."

"I will spend my eternity wondering if it was the right thing to do," I replied, my voice oddly calm.

"Oh, it was, darling, it was!" Charlotte insisted, throwing her arms around me. "You've done more for the people of France than all of us. And you've protected us all—you've done what none of us could have accomplished."

I looked up into her warm brown eyes, finally noticing the blood caked to her face. I whirled around, taking in the blood on *everyone.* Faces, hands, and clothes were shredded, bloody messes.

"I take it that was The Order's mercenary gang?" I asked.

Awkward silence descended, along with a tension I recognized as reluctance for them to tell me the truth. To avoid worrying me.

Antoine shuffled at the back.

"Not really much of a gang now," he rumbled. "Just a collection of spare parts."

Charlotte threw an exasperated look at him, but he simply shrugged.

"They came out of nowhere, really," she defended. "Caught us by surprise. And you know what they say about surprising a predator."

"I'm sorry I wasn't there," I replied. "I should have sensed them coming."

"You had more important things to do," Rafael said. "And we had it covered. You're not the only one with special gifts."

Étienne spat in the dirt behind Daphne.

"You weren't kidding, Rafael," he coughed. "Vampires taste *terrible.*"

"I told you not to swallow," Laszlo said.

Suddenly, Charlotte erupted with laughter. For the briefest moment, everyone looked at her in horror.

"I'm so sorry—do forgive me. I know it's inappropriate, but that's simply the filthiest thing I've heard Laszlo say."

"I didn't mean it like *that,*" he insisted.

Charlotte laughed even harder. Then, surprisingly, Marguerite joined in, covering a ladylike giggle with her blood-soaked hands. Étienne started up, and then Daphne, until everyone was in a collective bout of hysterics. Eventually, the absurdity of it hit me, and I joined in.

Rafael squeezed my hand, sending a wave of assurance through me.

When at last we recovered, I jerked my head back toward the mausoleum.

"I wanted to burn it," I said. "But I didn't know if there was anything down there that you thought was worth saving, Daphne."

She tilted her head for a moment, considering. "We can always come back for the Judas silver. As to the rest...I think it's time for a fresh start, wouldn't you say, Charlotte?"

"Oh, most definitely. Antoine, darling, you're so good with fire. Would you do the honors?" she asked, handing her mate a flint.

Antoine disappeared into the tomb for a few moments, and we heard the soft hiss and crackle of flames, followed by the acrid scent of smoke curling up from the mouth of the tomb. Antoine returned a minute later, looking a shade paler than before. He caught my eye and nodded—an acknowledgment of the devastation I'd wrought.

"For heaven's sake, I'm starving, and Daphne and I don't have any staff right now—we sent them all on holiday until we could get things sorted out with The Order. Rafael, darling, be a dear and have us over for a little longer, would you?" Charlotte asked, attempting to pin her wild brown curls back into her coiffure, and failing.

Rafael chuckled, the sound tugging at my scarred heart.

"What say you, Mina? Are you ready to go?" he asked.

Overcome with exhaustion, grief, and the sudden desire for an hours-long bath, I nodded.

"As I'll ever be. Take me home," I said, allowing him to help me to my feet.

We walked away from the mausoleum, pausing once to turn back as the flames expanded, licking the sides of the tomb. I was struck by the image—thinking it looked like the mouth of Hell. In some ways, I suppose it was.

Charlotte and Antoine shifted into their wolf forms and bounded off, followed by Daphne and Étienne on horseback. Laszlo opted to ride with Marguerite this time, so they set forth on a much slower course, leaving Rafael and me at the back.

"Are you well?" he asked.

"No." I shook my head. "But perhaps with time, I will be."

"I will be here with you. I will help you every step of the way," he said. "And now, at last, time is on our side."

I gazed up into his dark eyes, so full of hope and the promise of love for years to come, and for the first time in years, I felt like he was right.

I pulled him down for a tender kiss, and we prepared to shift together.

"Ready?" he asked, shooting me an encouraging smile.

I grinned back at him. A bit damaged, perhaps, but ready to begin healing—as we were, together.

"As I'll ever be."

EPILOGUE
MINA

October 31, 1768
Château du Diable

"For the life of me, I'll never understand why you didn't want a spring wedding," Charlotte opined, staring out the windows at the driving rain. "This weather is absolutely ghastly! It's one thing to have a nighttime wedding—I mean, obviously—but why not in the spring with all the flowers blooming? Or in the summer, when the temperature is more pleasant for all our human friends?"

"You'll see," I said with a smile. "It's a bit of a surprise. It was Rafael's idea, actually."

Daphne paused her ministrations with my hair, holding one errant curl aloft.

"Rafael helped plan the wedding?" she asked, stunned.

"In truth, he planned the entire thing," I admitted, a little chagrined.

"I don't believe it." Charlotte chuckled. "Are we all going to strip naked for a blood orgy and impale some priests for entertainment?"

"Laugh all you want," I smirked. "But he was most insistent. I suppose I didn't help matters by complaining every time he asked for my opinion on fabrics, flowers, or the guest list. He has such a romantic streak in him, I feel a bit guilty about not doing more."

Truthfully, it had taken me some time to recover mentally after the events of the previous May, and the weeks after the downfall of The Order had been busy and dark. We were relieved to not have to worry about the safety of our friends for the time being, but no one knew what would happen when King Louis learned about The Order's demise. The court had covered up the news of the aristocrats' deaths by blaming a random vampire gang for the violence, though the gossip from my bourgeois and commoner patients was that no one truly believed any of the stories coming out of Versailles.

For a time, we all were content to lie low and see how the dust settled. I'd gone back to the graveyard to recover the remains of the Judas silver and had it tucked away in a vault in Rafael's—*our*—home. Charlotte and Daphne continued to lead *les DD* in the efforts to undo much of The Order's more nefarious deeds, and they worked diligently to right a great many wrongs. It would be a long road for all of us.

And then, as the days wore on and we found a new sort of normal, I realized how lucky I'd been—how lucky *we* were—to have this second chance. Admitting as much to Rafael had resulted in a bout of fevered lovemaking that ended with a marriage proposal. Not content to wait another moment, he'd begged for my hand in the throes of bliss and came apart beneath me when I'd said yes. From that evening onward, he was a whirlwind of loving motivation—determined for us to marry as soon as possible and with as much fanfare as I'd allow.

I'd stalwartly refused to let Rafael hire servants for me, especially to dress me for a wedding. It felt too intimate to have strangers come in and gawk at the fiancée of the devilish Beast of Gévaudan. By way of compromise, he enlisted Charlotte and Daphne to help, and they were only too happy with the arrangement.

Charlotte came to admire Daphne's handiwork and wiped a tear from her eye.

"Is it that bad?" I teased.

"I'll have you know I practiced this style for a month!" Daphne replied.

Charlotte sniffed and smiled. "She did! You should have seen it. Every lady's maid from her household and mine walked around with the same coiffure for weeks."

Daphne grinned and pulled me up from the chair, twirling me around to stand before the large mirror in the bedroom.

Though I wasn't prone to vanity, I couldn't help the catch in my breath when I saw my reflection. Daphne had swept my dark curls up into a beautiful twist on top of my head, allowing a few loose strands to frame my face. She'd pinned dozens of tiny, jeweled flowers in, which made my head sparkle beneath the candlelight.

Charlotte had overseen the design of the wedding gown, and it was sheer perfection—elegant yet simple. The fitted bodice and flared, flowing skirts were the lightest shade of blue, like the color of sky seen through a wispy cloud. Small flowers were embroidered across the bodice and hem in shining silver thread.

For a moment, no one said anything.

"You look like a queen," Charlotte finally blubbered, fanning her face to keep the tears from streaking her makeup.

Daphne grasped my hands and squeezed.

"She *is* a queen," she said, her voice thick with emotion.

"I look…" I struggled to find the right words that would encompass my joy and gratitude, the love for my friends, and the astonishment I felt at looking so splendid. "…pretty."

"Pretty?" Charlotte shrieked. "Mina, *chérie*, you look well beyond pretty. You look enchanting, gorgeous, stunning, angelic—like perfection itself. It's no wonder Rafael's loved you for twenty years."

I bit my lip to keep my emotions contained.

"I love you both," I murmured. "Truly."

Daphne and Charlotte threw their arms around me, and we held the embrace until Guillaume's light knock broke the emotional silence.

"The guests are seated and waiting," he said.

"Are you ready?" Daphne whispered.

I nodded. "As I'll ever be."

Guillaume led us down the hall toward the sunken greenhouse and paused, waiting for my nod. With a steadying breath, I gripped Charlotte's and Daphne's hands, and Guillaume threw open the door.

Getting married in the greenhouse had been Rafael's idea, and though I'd had my doubts about the practicality of it, I didn't have the heart to relay them to him. I merely let him plan and plot, and now laughed at how wrong I'd been to doubt him.

The greenhouse was positively aglow with candlelight, and flowers trailed along every surface of the marble pathway. It looked like an enchanted fairy garden from a children's storybook. A string quartet played heartbreakingly beautiful music off to the side, and rain delicately tapped on the glass ceiling while wedding guests murmured quietly to each other. I closed my eyes to memorize the sound. It was one of the most wonderful things I'd ever heard.

Daphne and Charlotte kissed my cheeks and found their seats with Étienne, Antoine, Laszlo, and Marguerite. I scanned the room and saw all *les DD* agents were in attendance, along with a few of my better-known patients. Rafael stepped into the aisle ahead of me, and when our gazes met, the world fell away.

"Oh," he breathed, shock freezing him in place.

"Is that all you can say?" I whispered, teasing. "Oh?"

The spell rooting him in place broke, and he smiled more broadly than I'd ever seen. The wave of love and joy I felt from him was almost enough to drown me.

"You're the most exquisite creature I've ever seen, Mina. You look ravishing," he rumbled, his eyes flooding with the black and red of his desire.

A suit of black silk hugged his body perfectly, with delicate touches of silver embroidery that matched the details on my gown. His black hair was tied back and though his face was a mask of calm happiness, beneath the peaceful expression I sensed the wildness of his emotions—excitement, impatience, hunger, lust, and a flicker of annoyance that he couldn't lift my skirts and take me right here. I loved him even more for the duality.

His cool hand slipped into mine, and he gestured at the altar built in front of the waterfall where we'd first sat together. I gazed up into his dark eyes, happier than I'd ever been.

"Are you ready, Rafael?" I asked.

He winked and led me forward over the flower-strewn path.

"As I'll ever be."

BONUS EPILOGUE
MINA

February 6, 1769
Venice

"If that man looks at you one more time, I'll take great pleasure in plucking his eyes from his skull," Rafael grumbled, glaring at the scientist sitting in the front row of the lecture hall.

I turned to see who had drawn my new husband's ire and swallowed a laugh—Signore Bianchi was in his seventies and likely squinting through cataracts.

"You have nothing to worry about, my love," I soothed. "I can assure you his interest is purely academic."

"Mina, you think every man's interest in you is *purely academic*. You don't see what I see—the heat in their eyes as their unworthy gazes slide over your body. The interest sparking in their faces when they listen to you speak. Even when they know I'm here with you, they cannot keep their lustful thoughts hidden," he growled. "My fangs ache to rip out their throats and offer their blood to you as tribute, my goddess."

A heady swirl of violent desire made my focus waver, but I

cleared my throat and adjusted the tight neckline on my modest gown. As much as I loved carving out my place in the scientific communities across Europe, part of me longed to be done with the lecture circuit—to simply spend my evenings in bed with my dark prince, learning all the ways we could find amusement in each other's arms. With each stuffy academic event, I felt more guilt at dragging Rafael along when we were supposed to be on our honeymoon trip around the world.

"I appreciate you attending tonight's lecture, but you've heard the material a hundred times already—you must be bored. Why don't you go explore the city, or take in an opera? I'm sure the Carnivale fêtes would prove most diverting."

"If you think I'd rather spend my evenings carousing with a lot of sweaty, drunken revelers instead of watching you deliver hour-long talks on the metaphysical properties of supernatural blood types...clearly you are mistaking me with the man I was twenty years ago," he smirked. His hand snaked around my waist as I collected stacks of notes and illustrations.

"Besides, when you speak passionately about your work, your cheeks flush and you nibble on that delicious bottom lip. It is *unbearably* erotic. It makes me think of all the things I'm going to do to you as soon as we get back to our rooms..."

A gruff cough interrupted us.

"Doctor Van Helsing, your research is *most* inspiring," the older scientist said. He bowed stiffly and I worried that he might topple right over, so I reached forward to help him.

"Signore Bianchi, thank you," I said. "It's an honor to make your acquaintance. I enjoyed your book on foraminifera and have read it many times. May I present my husband, Rafael of House Dracul? Darling, Signore Bianchi helped persuade the academy to invite me to speak."

Rafael inclined his head, offering a lethal smile.

"Thank you, Signore, for arranging this evening on my

wife's lecture tour. Your correspondence has brought her much joy and it is, of course, my life's pursuit to keep her happy," he charmed. "I hear your cabinet of curiosities is unparalleled in this part of the world. At some point, I would dearly love to see it."

Signore Bianchi preened and smoothed a gnarled hand over the vanishing forest of gray hair atop his head.

"I do boast a very comprehensive specimen collection," he said, warming to the attention. "I should be delighted to invite the two of you to visit me in Rimini. I wonder—would you be willing to donate to my ever-growing collection?"

Confusion drew my brows up. I felt Rafael stiffen next to me.

"Donate, Signore?" I asked. "I'm afraid my husband and I don't have many specimens. A botany lab of some note, but nothing that would interest a collector like you."

"Well, ah, I'm most interested in samples of your blood—the both of you," Signore Bianchi replied. "The both of you are rather rare specimens yourselves. You should both be examined. Studied! The blood of an elder Dracul must have such interesting properties. A true prize for any collector."

Nausea rolled through my gut as the realization solidified. I hadn't been invited here to discuss my research or my life's work—I'd been invited here because of our reputations as mere scientific oddities. Staring into the older man's expectant face, I allowed myself a gentle push against his consciousness. *Interest. Curiosity. Greed. Disgust.*

My heart sank.

"I'm afraid that's quite impossible," I heard myself say. "The research my husband and I do on the blood plague is... well, we prefer to keep it *in house*, so to speak. I do thank you for your interest, and for the invitation to lecture this evening."

Lip curling in displeasure, Signore Bianchi stepped forward

to argue—to insist, no doubt. Before my curt retort had time to fully form on my tongue, Rafael moved in front of him.

"I suggest you find the exit, Signore, or the only blood sampled tonight will be yours," he growled, flashing a threatening amount of fang.

The older man paled and wisely determined not to press his luck. He hurried over to a knot of older men, hissing whispers of outrage.

"I take it the late reception of sherry and coffee is no longer on offer," I mumbled, gathering the last of my notes and books. I was keen to distract myself from the blooming disappointment growing like a parasite in my chest. Rafael seethed at my elbow, barely containing his rage as we made our way from the academy lecture hall and into the winding streets near the Piazza San Marco.

The narrow alleys along the canals were choked with tourists for Carnivale, and while their boisterous joy lightened my mood somewhat, it was clear Rafael didn't share my amusement. Guilt threaded through me—all his life he'd been an outsider, a *thing* to be feared and reviled, and despite the inroads he'd made recovering his reputation over the last few months, people still thought of him as a monster. A *creature*.

He was a lost prince to a fallen kingdom, and my academic work had put him in the path of yet another insult tonight.

When we reached the sprawling piazza, revelers in masquerade finery crowded around market stalls selling wine and sweets, cheap trinkets, and garish masks. Musicians and theater troupes drew small crowds, and my sharp supernatural eyes caught several young pickpockets weaving through the unsuspecting groups, lifting purses from oblivious marks.

"Would you like a gelato before we head back to our rooms, Rafael?" I offered, hoping to assuage some of my guilt. "My treat, since you've been such a patient, supportive husband allowing me my academic pursuits on our honeymoon."

He grunted and frowned, but led me over to a vendor selling the delicious confection. *Oh yes, he was definitely upset.*

I dug through the pockets of my red brocade gown, fishing for my coin purse, but Rafael sighed and insisted on paying. Anxiety almost curdled the iced cream in my hands at his sour temperament.

"That was meant to be my peace offering," I said quietly as we found the darkened edge of the square. Torches and braziers guttered with flickering orange light, but neither my vampire lover nor I needed it to see our way along the canals.

We ate our treats in silence for a few moments, until finally, Rafael regarded me with arched brows.

"Peace offering?" he echoed. I watched as his tongue swiped a lick of the swiftly melting lemon cream and something low in my belly clenched.

"Yes, I..." My voice was a touch breathless, and I swallowed. *Focus, Mina.* "I'm sorry for what Signore Bianchi said. For how he treated us—*you*. But that's not all...I'm sorry for taking away from our time together for all these silly lectures and society events. It's far from fair, but I just...well, I hadn't been asked—*allowed*, really—to lecture much before but after I turned and we got married, the invitations poured in, and I felt a bit like the belle of the ball."

The last of the gelato eaten, Rafael crumpled the paper cup and tossed it into the nearest brazier. A devastating smile tugged at the corners of his mouth. With excruciating slowness, he drew a finger across my lower lip to wipe an errant drop of cream, then sucked it off his finger. Lust exploded in my veins—far from a slowly stoked fire, much closer to a destructive volcanic eruption.

"And I've never been the belle of the ball before, you see?

Not that it matters, but...Oh, I'm rambling," I squeaked out, still staring at his delicious mouth, my thoughts a dizzying jumble of embarrassment and desire.

"Have you finished?" he asked patiently, slowly forcing me back me against a wall.

I nodded, my breath coming in excited pants.

"You have nothing to apologize for, my darling. Every time I have the privilege of watching you teach others about your work, I fall in love with you all over again. You are brilliant, and it grieves me that you haven't had every opportunity before now. If this was all you wanted to do with your supernatural life, I would happily consent to follow you everywhere just so I could carry your books and ink your quills..." he pressed his hard length against my belly and nipped at my earlobe. I whimpered. "And feast on your divine cunt while the pathetic scientists and physicians who scorned you go back to their sad, lonely laboratories and stroke themselves over the pretty doctor they cannot have."

I was going to go mad with the force of my sexual need. My heavy breasts and peaked nipples strained beneath the bodice of my suddenly too-tight gown and desire soaked my under-skirts. Rafael chuckled, grinding against me and ghosting kisses up my neck. *Dieu, if he is quick, I will have him right here.*

"I don't need you to make amends, my love," he whispered against my heated skin. "I need you to *scream.*"

My knees buckled and pressure built in my gums as my monstrous fangs lengthened. My blood burned in my veins—I needed Rafael with a dangerous ferocity, and I knew just how to unlock his demonic side.

"Make me," I challenged, reaching for the falls of his tight black breeches.

He pulled back slightly, his eyes a flood of black and red possessiveness.

"What?" he growled.

"Your hearing is impeccable, husband," I taunted. "Is it comprehension you lack? If you want me to scream, you'll have to make me."

The lust in his gaze sharpened to a knife point, stripping me bare of my bravado. I watched several expressions dance across his face as he fought to control the wicked things he kept leashed out of consideration for me. But I knew who I married—who I cleaved my eternity to.

"Do you understand what you're asking for, my Mina?" he ground out, anxiously flexing his trembling hands on my waist.

I nodded. "I do."

He closed his eyes and shuddered against me; a desperate moan wrenched from his lips. When he opened them, there was an unhinged excitement glowing in his gaze.

"Should you wish me to stop, you'll need to say *almond cake*. Agreed?" he rasped.

"Agreed. Touch me, Rafael, before I go mad with want," I begged, leaning forward for a kiss. Before my lips could make contact, he pulled back and threw me over his shoulder. I shrieked as he ran down the darkened canal at supernatural speed until he reached a small private dock. He set me down with heartbreaking care, gesturing to a sleek black gondola bobbing in the water ahead.

"Surprise," he murmured, tugging my hand toward the impressive watercraft. A small cabin sat perched in the center of the boat—a *felze*, I thought they were called.

Confusion stole some of my passion away, and I turned to him quizzically.

"Are we going somewhere?" I asked.

"Well, we can go anywhere we want. I had it made for you, my love. Come, let me show you," he said.

"You bought me a boat?" I replied, stunned. "Rafael, the expense!"

He waved away my concern and helped me step down into the beautiful gondola. Intricate carvings decorated the bow and plump pillows studded the seats. As he led me forward, he pulled up the rope tying us to the dock and with a swift motion, poled us into a wider part of the lagoon. Once we neared a small island a short distance away, he abandoned the oar and opened the door of the cabin. Inside was a plush bed— just big enough for two—with a navy blue silk coverlet and an avalanche of pillows. Candlelight flickered from small sconces along the walls, and a tray of sandwiches, sweets, and two full decanters of blood sat against a bench in front of an open window.

"Oh, Rafael," I breathed. "This is wonderful. How unbearably romantic!"

When I turned to thank him, I gasped at the hunger in his eyes. His fangs lengthened over his lower lip in a predatory smile, and he backed me into the cabin until I stumbled backwards onto the bed. With brutal efficiency, he sliced through my gown, stays and chemise with his lethal claws, baring my naked body to the cool night air and his scorching gaze. The heat of desire that had cooled to a slow simmer came blazing back.

"How does this all stop?" he rasped, divesting himself of his jacket, waistcoat, breeches and shirt in frenzied haste.

"Almond cake," I replied obediently.

"Good girl," he said with a nod.

Pushing me onto my back, he crawled forward, covering my body with his. With a snap of his fingers and an unfamiliar word, the door and the window slammed shut, extinguishing all but one of the candles. In its guttering light, shadows danced across Rafael's handsome face, making his beauty all the more sinister. Reaching beneath the mountain of pillows, he extracted several lengths of black silk cord.

"I've always fantasized about tying you up, my Mina," he said, the hitch in his voice the only sign he was at the precipice of control. "When we were apart all those years, I stroked myself often over the same visions—binding your glorious body to my bed and visiting unending pleasures upon you until you agreed to be mine—until you relented and realized how perfect and horrifying my devotion is."

His hands shook as he tied my wrists to the headboard, and then with a wicked grin, tied my ankles to the bedposts, splaying my body shamelessly wide for his roving attentions. Once he was satisfied with the gentle but firm bindings, he sat back on his heels. His erection bobbed between us and he ran one hand along it, leisurely stroking as his eyes bored into mine. Liquid desire pooled between my legs and I swore.

For the first time, I began to worry that I'd bitten off more than I could chew.

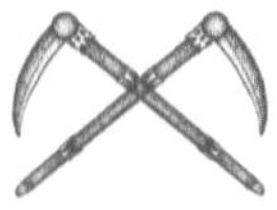

RAFAEL

Mina. Mine. Mine. Mine. Mine. Mine. Mine. Mine. Mine. Mine. Mine. Mine. Mine. Mine. Mine. Mina.

MINA

"Rafael," I pleaded.

"That doesn't sound like a scream to me," he snarled.

With a growl, he lunged forward, capturing one peaked nipple in his mouth and running the smooth backs of his claws over the other, sending lightning bolts of pleasure across my nerves. As he laved my breasts with his tongue and pricked the sensitive points with his claws, I couldn't fight the reflexive need to grind my hips upward, seeking his hard cock.

"Poor little Mina," he drawled, lowering a hand to cup my heated sex. "We've only just begun and already this sweet cunt is dripping for me." One fingertip slipped through the slick seam and mercilessly circled the tight bud of my pleasure. I bucked against his hand, seeking more—more, until he relented and slipped one, then two fingers inside me. His deep groans melted into growls as he worked me to a fevered pitch.

"Yes, yes, my love—oh, Rafael, I'm going to come. I'm so close!" I keened.

Mina. The word echoed through my head. *Mina. You will not. You have not yet screamed prettily enough for me.*

I grunted a curse and bucked harder, determined to seize the pleasure that dangled from my husband's tantalizing fingers.

As I felt the sharp edge of bliss near, I started to cry out— only to be silenced by Rafael's voracious mouth on mine.

That is not the scream I want, he said in my head.

I'm going to come—you cannot stop me, I shot back, shuddering against him, sucking at his tongue and lips in a wild frenzy.

Just as the orgasm started to crest, cold enveloped me, as though I'd been dunked in a glacial sea. My pleasure faded away and I stared up at Rafael—shocked.

The devilish glint in his eyes told me what I needed to know. Suddenly, I remembered his threats to me once in Charlotte's home:

"I could have you bouncing naked on my lap, your breasts in my hands and your perfect little clit stroking my shaft and even then, I could invade your mind and keep your release at bay. Could you imagine that, my Persephone? Endless days and nights of sex without an orgasm, all because I might have a torturous whim."

Understanding dawned and I beheld satisfaction on Rafael's face as he realized I'd connected the dots. I opened my mouth to rage at him, my lust warring with my anger, but then I remembered he'd given me the key to this all at the very beginning. *Almond cake.* I could say it—give in to his torment and beg him to release my pleasure. He would, I knew. He would make me come a thousand times if I asked—if I ended our game. A perverse delight sparked in my chest, my stubbornness and pride winning out for the moment.

"Do you have something to say, my beloved?" he asked softly, circling my nipple with one claw.

"Yes," I replied on a gasp. His eyes met mine expectantly. "Is that all?"

With a wicked chuckle and no other preamble, he dove between my legs, covering my sex with his mouth and sucking my clit with fierce abandon. Bright pleasure sheared through my thoughts again—a symphony of sensation. Fangs grazing my slick lips, he plunged two fingers inside my heated channel, curling them against the hidden spot where pleasure lay. A denied orgasm started to rise from the ashes of the previous one, closing in on me in haste.

"Yes, my love. *More.* I need more," I begged.

I know what you need, he said in my head, not pausing in his onslaught of sexual worship. The thought came with graphic visions of what was to come, along with phantom sensations of being filled—stretched—to the point of devastating rapture. This time, the combination of his mesmeric powers and his expert tongue and fingers brought me screaming to the start of another orgasm and suddenly...

Cold.

A void where ecstasy should have been.

Rafael sat back once more, licking my wetness from his claws and glaring at me in challenge. Precum dripped from his hard cock and a muscle ticked in his jaw—the only signs that gave me the sense that he was just as desperate as I was.

I considered ripping through the bonds and attacking him out of pulsing fury and lust, or sobbing out my safety words to end my aching torment. Both felt like defeat to me, and I would not be so easily defeated.

I would beat him at this game.

Closing my eyes against the silver tears that threatened, I centered myself and reached for the darkness that knelt in me, always at the ready.

Rafael, I called to him through our mental connection. *Do you not wish to claim my body? To sink into me? To fill me utterly with your very essence? Do you not long to sear my needy cunt with your heat? I need you, my love. I am yours.*

The words were my siren song to him, accompanied by my own phantom touches along his ears, neck, abdomen, and straining erection. An unwilling groan rumbled from his chest and his mouth dropped open, on the cusp of uttering our safety words. His breathing stuttered as he watched me writhe against my silken bonds.

"Mina," he rasped, running his fingers through his hair. "I fear I started a game I no longer have the strength to finish."

He quickly reached down to untie the ropes on my ankles and wrists, sowing fevered kisses up my skin.

"Forgive me for indulging my demons too much," he

begged, notching the slick head of his cock at my quivering entrance.

"Perhaps I enjoy your demons," I laughed, shifting into my massive demon form. Curling horns, broad bat wings, and a long, pointed tail erupted from my blue-grey body as I changed into my favorite she-devil shape—the stuff of nightmares. Startled, Rafael rolled to the side as I burst through the door of the cabin and shot into the sky. A cry of anguish rose from the deck of the gondola, followed by the sound of splintering wood. I hoped he hadn't destroyed our lovely boat in his frustration.

It wasn't long before he'd caught up to me, his expansive wings powering him through the night sky toward me.

Torturous minx, he laughed. *Once again, you run from me! I should've kept you tied to my bed.*

Grinning back at the bat-like monster pursuing me, I dipped low over the lagoon and skimmed my claws through the black water. I loved Rafael's demon form— glossy black wings, a thick, barbed tail, claws twice the length of his vampiric fingers. If I'd become the stuff of nightmares, he was something out of my darkest dreams. He gained on me inch by inch, until he was close enough to seize me by my tail. The move pulled us both off balance and we tumbled out of the sky, rolling together onto a beach of silty gray sand along the small island nearby.

When we stilled, Rafael pinned me beneath him and inhaled deeply at the crook of my neck. His long, forked tongue snaked out, tracing the outer shell of my ear. I shivered against him as it caressed a path south, swirling over my breasts and dipping low between my legs. He rumbled with pleasure at my whimper when his tongue speared me and rolled through my pussy in a torturously slow twist. When he had me squirming beneath him, he pulled his tongue back into his fanged maw with an obscenely wet *pop*.

Do you want to continue this game, wife? Rafael asked, his thick length a heated brand between us. In this demon form, his cock was red veined with black, and I was desperate to see it sliding between my blue-gray lips.

Have your demons had enough, husband? I responded, hooking one clawed foot behind his ass and positioning him at my entrance, still slick with arousal. His tail snaked up to my breasts, rubbing at the sensitive peaked points.

He nodded, bending down to kiss me with tenderness unbecoming of his monstrous form.

Sometimes, my demons forget I have the keys to Heaven right here, he purred, sliding into me on a growl from us both. The drawn-out foreplay had us both in a frenzy, sensations heightened to the apex of pleasure. Every slow stroke of his cock, every pricking of his claws, every shuddering grunt of desperation stoked the fires hotter and hotter, until his movements stuttered, and his rhythm began to falter.

I don't think I can hold back much longer, my love, Rafael groaned, his thoughts coming through in a rough crackle of oncoming need. Reaching between us, he pressed the flat of his thumb against my over-sensitive clit, and pleasure arced from the touch like lightning finding metal.

Nor I, I moaned, bearing down on his pistoning hips. As the orgasm wound its tendrils through my nerves, I clutched at Rafael, sinking my claws into his back and wrapping my tail around his thigh.

Come with me, my beautiful doctor. My wife. My Mina, he gasped, sinking his teeth into my neck as pleasure rocked through him. His bliss gave way to my own, and I followed him over the edge—my monstrous screams fracturing the night like an orgy of demons.

Collapsing on top of me, I felt Rafael smile against my shoulder.

"How beautifully you screamed for me," he huffed, as we shifted back to our human forms. "It will live in my memories for years to come."

I sighed in satisfaction, staring up into star-studded sky. Soft silver clouds scraped across the fat, round moon, casting our naked forms in a pale gold-tinged glow. My hands drifted over Rafael's smooth, cool skin in reverence. As beautiful as my dark prince was, I found his primal demon form equally compelling.

"Let's head back to the gondola. I could use some refreshment and a bite of something sweet before we continue our... diversions," I said, placing a chaste kiss on his nose.

"Anything you desire," he replied, lifting me into his arms. "What sort of refreshment did you have in mind?"

Almond cake.

ACKNOWLEDGMENTS

Before I get into the acknowledgements from the original version of this book, thank you to my Discordant Owls: my flock, my readers, my cheerleaders. This edition would not exist without your continued support and I love you all so much. A huge, extra special thanks to Brian for being my copy-editing champion.

I also want to say thanks to all the talented artists I've had the pleasure of working with on book covers, character art, and graphics. Sometimes the only thing that keeps me coming back to my draft is the thought of an art commission I'm waiting for.

This book was absolutely a labor of love and I'm not exaggerating when I say it wouldn't have made it to the page without the support of my family and friends. Big thanks to Finn, Zoe, Michelle, Dad, Mary, Cassie, Alisa, Heather, and everyone else who helped me get from book two to book three. Susan, you sweet soul and stunning talent, I'm so grateful to have you as a critique partner and author bestie. Megan, you helped me get this baby across the finish line and into the hands of readers and I'm so grateful for your generosity. Thank you.

ABOUT THE AUTHOR

Photo by Kara Brodgesell

Lily Riley is a romance novelist currently focused on books that feature a little bit of cheek and a lot of steam.

Her *Vampires in Versailles* series begins with *The Assassin and the Libertine,* continues with *The Agent and the Outlaw,* and ends with *The Doctor and the Devil.*

When Lily isn't writing about dreamy, supernatural beings in 18th century France, she enjoys sipping champagne, eating cake, and dancing naked by the light of the full moon.

To sign up for her newsletter or read more about her upcoming projects, visit: www.authorlilyriley.com

OTHER BOOKS BY LILY RILEY

Vampires in Versailles series:

The Assassin and the Libertine

The Agent and the Outlaw

The Doctor and the Devil